ACCLAIM FOR COLLEEN COBLE

"I loved returning to Rock Harbor and you will too. *Beneath Copper Falls* is Colleen at her best!"
>—Dani Pettrey, bestselling author of the Alaskan
>Courage and Chesapeake Valor series

"Return to Rock Harbor for Colleen Coble's best story to date. *Beneath Copper Falls* is a twisting, turning, thrill ride from page one that drops you head first into danger that will leave you breathless, sleep deprived, and eager for more! I couldn't turn the pages fast enough!"
>—Lynette Eason, award-winning, bestselling
>author of the Elite Guardians series

"The tension, both suspenseful and romantic, is gripping, reflecting Coble's prowess with the genre."
>—*Publishers Weekly*, starred review for *Twilight at Blueberry Barrens*

"Incredible storytelling and intricately drawn characters. You won't want to miss *Twilight at Blueberry Barrens!*"
>—Brenda Novak, *New York Times* and *USA TODAY* bestselling author

"Coble has a gift for making a setting come to life. After reading *Twilight at Blueberry Barrens*, I feel like I've lived in Maine all my life. This plot kept me guessing until the end, and her characters seem like my friends. I don't want to let them go!"
>—Terri Blackstock, *USA TODAY* bestselling author of *If I Run*

"I'm a long-time fan of Colleen Coble, and *Twilight at Blueberry Barrens* is the perfect example of why. Coble delivers riveting suspense, delicious romance, and carefully crafted characters, all with the deft hand of a veteran writer. If you love romantic suspense, pick this one up. You won't be disappointed!"
>—Denise Hunter, author of *The Goodbye Bride*

"Colleen Coble, the queen of Christian romantic mysteries, is back with her best book yet. Filled with familiar characters, plot twists, and a confusion of antagonists, I couldn't keep the pages of this novel set in Maine turning fast enough. I reconnected with characters I love while taking a journey filled with murder, suspense, and the prospect of love. This truly is her best book to date, and perfect for readers who adore a page-turner laced with romance."

—Cara Putman, award-winning author of *Shadowed by Grace* and *Where Treetops Glisten*, on *Twilight at Blueberry Barrens*

"Gripping! Colleen Coble has again written a page-turning romantic suspense with *Twilight at Blueberry Barrens*! Not only did she keep me up nights racing through the pages to see what would happen next, I genuinely cared for her characters. Colleen sets the bar high for romantic suspense!"

—Carrie Stuart Parks, author of *A Cry from the Dust* and *When Death Draws Near*

"Colleen Coble thrills readers again with her newest novel, an addictive suspense trenched in family, betrayal, and . . . murder."

—DiAnn Mills, author of *Deadly Encounter*, on *Twilight at Blueberry Barrens*

"Coble's latest, *Twilight at Blueberry Barrens*, is one of her best yet! With characters you want to know in person, a perfect setting, and a plot that had me holding my breath, laughing, and crying, this story will stay with the reader long after the book is closed. My highest recommendation."

—Robin Caroll, bestselling novelist

"Colleen's *Twilight at Blueberry Barrens* is filled with a bevy of twists and surprises, a wonderful romance, and the warmth of family love. I couldn't have asked for more. This author has always been a five-star novelist, but I think it's time to up the ante with this book. It's on my keeping shelf!"

—Hannah Alexander, author of the Hallowed Halls Series

"Second chances, old flames, and startling new revelations combine to form a story filled with faith, trial, forgiveness, and redemption. Crack the cover and step in, but beware—Mermaid Point is harboring secrets that will keep you guessing."

—Lisa Wingate, national bestselling author of
The Sea Keeper's Daughters, on *Mermaid Moon*

"I burned through *The Inn at Ocean's Edge* in one sitting. An intricate plot by a master storyteller. Colleen Coble has done it again with this gripping opening to a new series. I can't wait to spend more time at Sunset Cove."

—Heather Burch, bestselling author of *One Lavender Ribbon*

"Coble doesn't disappoint with her custom blend of suspense and romance."

—*Publishers Weekly* on *The Inn at Ocean's Edge*

"Veteran author Coble has penned another winner. Filled with mystery and romance that are unpredictable until the last page, this novel will grip readers long past when they should put their books down. Recommended to readers of contemporary mysteries."

—*CBA Retailers + Resources* review of *The Inn at Ocean's Edge*

"Coble truly shines when she's penning a mystery, and this tale will really keep the reader guessing . . . Mystery lovers will definitely want to put this book on their purchase list."

—*Romantic Times* review of *The Inn at Ocean's Edge*

"Master storyteller Colleen Coble has done it again. *The Inn at Ocean's Edge* is an intricately woven, well-crafted story of romance, suspense, family secrets, and a decades-old mystery. Needless to say, it had me hooked from page one. I simply couldn't stop turning the pages. This one's going on my keeper shelf."

—Lynette Eason, award-winning, bestselling
author of the Hidden Identity series

"Evocative and gripping, *The Inn at Ocean's Edge* will keep you flipping pages long into the night."

—Dani Pettrey, bestselling author of the Alaskan Courage series

"Coble's atmospheric and suspenseful series launch should appeal to fans of Tracie Peterson and other authors of Christian romantic suspense."

—*Library Journal* review of *Tidewater Inn*

"Romantically tense, but with just the right touch of danger, this cowboy love story is surprisingly clever—and pleasingly sweet."

—USAToday.com review of *Blue Moon Promise*

"[An] outstanding, completely engaging tale that will have you on the edge of your seat . . . A must-have for all fans of romantic suspense!"

—TheRomanceReadersConnection.com review of *Anathema*

"Colleen Coble lays an intricate trail in *Without a Trace* and draws the reader on like a hound with a scent."

—*Romantic Times*, 4½ stars

"Coble's historical series just keeps getting better with each entry."

—*Library Journal* starred review of *The Lightkeeper's Ball*

"Don't ever mistake [Coble's] for the fluffy romances with a little bit of suspense. She writes solid suspense, and she ties it all together beautifully with a wonderful message."

—LifeinReviewBlog.com review of *Lonestar Angel*

"Colleen is a master storyteller."

—Karen Kingsbury, bestselling author of *Unlocked* and *Learning*

BENEATH COPPER FALLS

ALSO BY COLLEEN COBLE

BENEATH COPPER FALLS

COLLEEN COBLE

THOMAS NELSON
Since 1798

Beneath Copper Falls

© 2017 by Colleen Coble.

Published in Nashville, Tennessee, by Thomas Nelson. Thomas Nelson is a registered trademark of HarperCollins Christian Publishing, Inc.

Thomas Nelson titles may be purchased in bulk for educational, business, fund-raising, or sales promotional use. For information, please e-mail SpecialMarkets@ThomasNelson.com.

Scripture quotations taken from the ESV® Bible (The Holy Bible, English Standard Version®). Copyright © 2001 by Crossway, a publishing ministry of Good News Publishers. Used by permission. All rights reserved.

ISBN: 978-0-7180-9071-5 (HC)

Library of Congress Cataloging-in-Publication Data

Names: Coble, Colleen, author.
Title: Beneath copper falls / Colleen Coble
Description: Nashville, Tennessee : Thomas Nelson, [2017] | Series: Rock Harbor series ; 7
Identifiers: LCCN 2017004729 | ISBN 9781401690328 (paperback)
Subjects: | GSAFD: Christian fiction. | Romantic suspense fiction.
Classification: LCC PS3553.O2285 B46 2017 | DDC 813/.54--dc23 LC record available at https://lccn.loc.gov/2017004729

Printed in the United States of America
17 18 19 20 21 LSC 5 4 3 2 1

For my many loyal Rock Harbor readers
who have asked for more Rock Harbor books nearly
every day since Without a Trace came out in 2003.
Thank you for your encouragement and loyalty!

PROLOGUE

Two Years Earlier

Renee huddled in the garden shed in her pajamas and tried to hear him over the pounding of her heart in her ears. Dust motes crowded close in the dim illumination from the full moon glaring through the windows, and she suppressed a sneeze. The stench of gasoline from the mower hung in the air along with the odor of decaying grass. The smell should have comforted her with its familiarity to what she loved most, but it only added to her terror. The last time she'd worked in the garden had been with *him*.

Surely he wouldn't search for her here and would think she'd already started for town. The straps of the backpack bit into her shoulders, and she longed to take it off and hide it, but it was the only evidence she possessed.

Evidence of what a monster she had loved.

She might need a weapon. Now that her eyes adjusted to the gloom, she darted her gaze around the shed. About eight by eight, it overflowed with gardening tools and old pots. The hoe. It might work. Or maybe she could wield the hedge clippers like a sword, though the thought of plunging those steel blades into the chest of a man who'd once whispered sweet words in her ears nearly paralyzed her.

The clippers would be less cumbersome than the hoe. As she lifted the shears something fell from the workbench. The clatter sounded as loud as a crack of lightning overhead.

She froze and listened for footsteps heading her way. Nothing.

The breath eased out of her chest, and she moved in a half-crouched position toward the door in her bare feet. She twisted the knob and the latch released a soft click.

Renee waited a moment before she pushed the door open a few inches to peer out.

The moonlight shone on her sweet home, a home she thought she'd be sharing with the perfect husband. Her vision blurred, and she swiped the tears away. He was a psychopath. And she'd fallen for his act. Hard.

Her warm breath fogged in the cool Washington air. Spring came in fits and starts in this northwest corner of the state, and today's warm sixty degrees had plunged to forty after the sun set. Nothing moved across the lawn to the wide front porch. Her car, an older Miata, beckoned her from the driveway. If only she'd had time to grab the keys.

She opened the door wider and stepped out. The ground was nearly frozen, but maybe the soles of her feet would go numb soon and she wouldn't notice. If she could cut through the woods lining the edge of her property, she'd reach the road leading to town. Maybe a third-shift worker at one of the factories would be getting off or heading into work. Her feet carried her over the frosty grass toward the birch trees.

A shadow moved to her right, and she whirled around, then

relaxed. One of her goats was moving to the water trough. But even as the tension edged from her shoulders, a hard hand fell on her left arm.

He whipped her around toward him. His handsome face contorted to match the monster she realized he truly was. He ripped the backpack from her. "I thought you were different from the rest, Renee."

She tipped her chin up though she shuddered inside at the remorseless glare in his eyes. "The rest of the women you killed, you mean?"

"I was really going to marry you. The others failed me, but you were perfect." His long fingers caressed her cheek, and his eyes darkened when she flinched. "Why did you have to go snooping? I didn't want to hurt you. You brought this on yourself."

His gaze shifted down as his hand dropped away to fish for something in his pocket. Now was her chance. She spun around to run, but he grabbed her arm again, then marched her a few feet to her right.

Renee had no idea what he planned to do with her until his hand went to the back of her neck and he shoved her head forward. Cold water closed around her face and head, and her hands gripped the metal edge of the goats' water trough. Using the trough as leverage, she fought to lift her face out of the water, but her puny strength was nothing compared to those muscles he worked out every day.

Her vision began to darken. *Boone . . .*

CHAPTER 1

A military ball was the last place she expected to be tonight. Dana Newell craned her neck and looked around the ballroom filled with dress uniforms and women in formal gowns. She'd barely managed to remember her name as her unsmiling brother steered her through the receiving line, but she had to pull herself together. She had to do Chris proud. She forced herself to smile and act the part of an elegant companion.

They stopped in front of his superior, Major White. Though middle aged, he held his trim body erect, and his brown eyes were sharp below his short salt-and-pepper hair.

The major took her hand and pressed it firmly with strong fingers. "Ah, this must be your sister, Lieutenant. Thanks for bringing her. Ms. Newell, I wanted to thank you personally for talking my wife through the Heimlich when our grandson choked on that cracker. It saved his life. We're most appreciative. She wanted to thank you as well, but she fell ill with the flu today."

Heat washed up Dana's face. "I'm glad I was able to help, sir." The terrifying dispatch call had lingered with her because she'd heard the little guy choking on the other end of the phone. It was outcomes like this that drove her to stick with the difficult job of emergency dispatch.

They chatted a few more minutes, then Chris guided her on down the receiving line. Her face hurt from keeping the smile pinned in place. She couldn't let her brother down by gawking or acting ill at ease. He hadn't wanted to bring her, but his protective streak often chafed. She found herself relaxing just a tiny bit as they finished the receiving line, then found chairs.

"I'll get us something to drink," Chris said.

She watched him stop and flirt with a pretty blonde on the way to the food table. Few women could resist her brother's blond good looks and genial manner. Dana studied the room while he was gone. Thank goodness Chris had helped her pick out her dress, a demure tea-length number in royal blue that didn't show too much skin. All the women were adorned like they were attending a Hollywood premiere, though in modest necklines. Left to herself, she would have picked her best church dress and called it good enough.

She tapped her toe a bit to "God Bless the USA" playing in the background. The back of her neck prickled, and she glanced around before her gaze collided with the most handsome man she'd ever met. Four women clustered around him, and snippets of their conversation floated above the sound of Lee Greenwood's voice.

"Garret, I heard you won the marksmanship medal. I'm not surprised. You can do anything."

"Garret, would you get me something to drink? I'm parched."

He didn't seem to hear the women vying for his attention. His blue eyes never left Dana's, and he wove his way toward her through the women as they plucked at his uniform sleeves and demanded he stay to talk with them.

Dana couldn't have moved if a tornado was sweeping through

the place—not with those eyes burning into hers with a question her heart responded to immediately.

It was as if she'd been waiting for him all her life. Her lips parted when he reached her, but she couldn't speak. He stopped only six inches away, well within her personal space, but she didn't step back.

"I haven't seen you before."

"I–I came with Chris." She forced the bright smile again.

He reached out and brushed a curl off her cheek. "You're Dana? He didn't mention how beautiful you are."

Beautiful, her? Dana's light-brown hair was neither blonde nor lustrously dark brown, and she was average in every way. But he could believe what he wanted about her as long as he looked at her that way.

"I love your eyes. They're like the sea, full of mystery and promise." His fingers lingered on her face.

Heat spread across her skin in a slow, delicious wave. "Y-You know my brother?"

He nodded. "I'm Garret. Garret Waterman. We're buds, well, at least we were. I'm not so sure now that I know he's been holding out on me." He took her hand. "Let's step outside for some air. It's too hot in here."

Her lonely heart soaked up the admiration in his eyes. And just like that she was his.

———

"You know I hate pot roast." Garret lifted the tray of food and glared at her over the top of it. "This was supposed to be a special night. I've been gone for two weeks, and this is how you show me you've missed me?"

Her fingers went to the tiny scar by her right eye, and she bit her lip. Where had the charming man she'd fallen in love with nine months ago gone? She swallowed hard. "You never said you didn't like pot roast. Besides, you might like mine. Everyone loves it. It's my grandmother's recipe."

What was she thinking? She shouldn't have argued with him, not when he was in this state. She'd seen what happened when he got mad.

His mouth tight, he carried the entire tray of roast over to the trash and dumped everything into it.

All thought of placating him vanished, and she leaped up from her chair. "How dare you! I bought an expensive cut of grass-fed beef and worked all day on this meal."

She snatched the empty plate from his hand and walked to the oversized stainless-steel sink already filled with soapy water. She plunged the tray into the water, but before she could wash it, his hard fingers clamped onto the back of her neck. "Let go of me!"

She wasn't afraid, not while the adrenaline from her righteous anger raged through her. She tried to twist out of his grip, but he still worked out even though he'd gotten out of the military. "I said let go of me or I'll call the police!"

"You're not calling anyone." His voice pitched low to a calm and deadly timbre. He pushed her head down into the sink.

Warm water filled her nose and mouth and the suds stung her eyes. She gripped the counter with both hands and tried to pull out of the water to breathe, but he held her neck relentlessly in place until her chest burned and spots danced in front of her eyes.

He's going to kill me.

Panic gave her a new surge of energy, and she fought with all her strength, though her efforts were useless.

Then his fingers moved to her hair, and he yanked her head out of the water. She drew a sweet lungful of air and sank to the floor where she gulped in oxygen as fast as she could until her vision began to clear. By the time she found the strength to stand he'd gone.

She staggered to the bathroom in time to vomit.

Surely he hadn't really meant to hurt her, had he? She hugged the cold porcelain of the toilet and let the tears fall for the ruin of a dream that she should have seen was too good to be true.

Three Months Later

"Nine-one-one, what is your emergency?" Dana rested her fingers on the keyboard to enter the last call of her night shift.

The familiar background noise of talking and keyboards in the dispatch room enfolded her. A room she would say good-bye to today. Her departure couldn't come too soon for her.

"My husband's had a heart attack! Please, I need help." The woman's desperate voice quivered.

Dana inputted the nature of the emergency and checked the address on the computer. "What is your address?" The woman rattled off the same address on the screen. "Stay on the line with me while I send paramedics on the way." Dana put reassurance into her voice and keyed in the request for an ambulance.

"He's not breathing!"

"The ambulance is on the way. Do you know CPR?"

"No, I never took any training. I should have learned! I knew he had a heart issue."

"Take a deep breath, ma'am. This is not your fault, okay?" Dana badly wanted to pray with her, but after glancing sideways at her coworker, she opted to shoot up a silent prayer. Even though this was her last shift, she'd gotten into trouble so many times that it had become impossible to speak up any longer.

Dana stayed on the line and tried to keep the woman calm until the siren's wail came over the phone.

"The ambulance is here! I have to get the door. Thank you for being here with me." The line clicked and went dead.

Dana rubbed her tight right shoulder. Clear emergencies always left her tense and upset. Another call rang through. "Nine-one-one, what is your emergency?"

"Miss me, baby?" Garret's deep voice impaled her.

Her fingers went to her throat. "How dare you call me here, especially after what you did."

His voice always got to her. Was she wrong to run away? Maybe he could change. She gave a slight shake of her head. Not this time. She wouldn't let him talk her into going back again. She absently rubbed at the tiny scar by her eye.

"Look, I just lost my temper, okay? I've got a lot of stress right now."

The lump in her throat kept her words locked down for a long moment. A year ago life had seemed so different. The first time Garret had looked her way she'd been shocked. With his sun-streaked blond hair and blue eyes, he looked like a gorgeous surfer instead of a crack sniper for the Marines. Once upon a time she'd thought his expertise was fascinating. Now it terrified her. Friends kept telling her to be patient, that he probably had PTSD, but she didn't want to end up dead.

And really, why had she even thought true happiness could find her? From the age of eight, she'd learned life could change in an instant into something twisted and unrecognizable.

She blew out a shaky breath. "I'm hanging up now, Garret. Don't contact me again." She disconnected the call on her keyboard and leaned back in her chair.

Sandy Corson, a coworker in her fifties, swiveled in her chair to look over at Dana. "Garret again?"

"Yeah." Dana tucked a strand of hair behind her ear. "But he won't be able to contact me for long."

"I hate that you're leaving!"

"I'm tired of looking over my shoulder, and I want a fresh start where other people aren't always telling me to give him another chance. Once I'm sure he's off my trail, I'll give you a call and check in."

A month ago an old friend, Bree Matthews, had held a training seminar for search-and-rescue dogs up in Michigan's Upper Peninsula, and Dana had taken her six-month-old puppy, Phantom, to start learning SAR. A dispatcher job had just fallen into her lap while in Rock Harbor, and the timing couldn't be more perfect. God had opened a door, and she intended to slam it shut behind her as she entered a new phase of life.

Going home seemed the right thing to do, even if Garret knew where she went. Family and friends would support her if he showed up. While she had friends here in Washington, they were the superficial kind, not the heart-to-heart sort who would put themselves in the way of danger for her.

She punched out for the last time at 5:00 a.m. and hugged her coworkers good-bye before she hurried to the exit. All her belongings were on their way in a moving truck, and she intended to drive until she got sleepy today.

The parking garage lights flickered and hummed as she exited the staircase on her level, and the place smelled of tires and oil. The sun wasn't up yet, and the dimly lit space held too many shadows to count.

She fished her car keys out of her purse, then frowned when her gaze lit on her blue Toyota Prius leaning to one side. Both tires on the driver's side were flat, and her pulse kicked as she knelt to examine the front one. There was no mistaking the slash at the rim. The back tire was in the same shape.

Her heart drummed against her ribs as she rose and looked around. "Garret?" She thrust her hand into her purse and wrapped her fingers around her cell phone. "I know you did this."

His mocking laugh echoed against the concrete walls of the nearly empty parking garage, then fell silent. Where was he? The shadows made it difficult to see. She swallowed hard and eyed the staircase to her left. Could she escape before he tried to grab her? No, he was too fast.

She hit the unlock button on her keys, then threw herself under the steering wheel and locked the car. She punched 911 on her phone as a shadow to her left came at her. She ducked as a crowbar smashed into the window beside her. The window shattered but held together.

She screamed and cowered in her seat. His blue eyes narrowed in a hard glare as he lifted the crowbar again. This blow would break the glass and bash her head. Shaking and crying, she brought up the bear spray and aimed it at the largest crack in the window. But before she could press the button, shouts rang out. Garret whirled and ran for the exit.

She exhaled and, with a trembling hand, reached for the door handle. She wouldn't be leaving for Rock Harbor today.

CHAPTER 2

He couldn't see the last of these folks any too soon. Boone Carter shook hands and thanked the family as they piled into their Mercedes SUV. The parents had been more interested in squabbling with their teenage daughters than with hauling in the salmon along the Ontonagon River. He'd taken them out for the day, and by the time they'd been out for half an hour, he realized it was an exercise in futility.

His cabins squatted in woods along the shore of Lake Superior in Michigan's Upper Peninsula. He'd bought the land from his uncle, then built every one of the ten cabins himself. Carter's Cabins had become known as one of the best places to stay for the adventure seeker, a reputation he'd fought hard to gain.

He gave a final wave to his departing guests, then went toward the large red barn housing his outfitter business. His cousin's small red convertible had pulled into the gravel parking lot a few minutes ago. She got out of her car and hurried to join him as he neared the front door.

Allyson was a beautiful young woman. She and his sister, Renee, had worked at a small newspaper in Washington. Allyson had been a bulldog about finding out who had killed Renee. She'd arrived a couple days ago to talk to him about what they'd turned up so far. All their efforts had come to a big fat zero. He'd talked to the lead detective just two weeks ago, and the police were stymied too.

A familiar wave of grief swamped him, and he tamped it down and smiled at her. "Coffee? I need some after dealing with that family."

She put her hand on his arm. "There's been another murder, Boone. It's eerily like Renee's."

Some other family was going through the trauma they'd endured. He shoved open the door and wished he could push away the memories that easily.

He led her past the rough wooden counter where one of his employees explained the various backpacking options to two men. In his office Boone closed the door behind them and went to the coffeepot. The stuff had been sitting there for hours, and he grimaced at the bitter taste.

He handed her a cup of the atrocious brew. "You should be finding a good man instead of pursuing an impossible quest like this. It's been three years since Renee's death. If the police can't pin down a lead, what hope do we have?"

Allyson dreamed of being a bonafide investigative reporter, but she was grasping at the wind with this case. His smack down didn't dim the light in her hazel eyes as she pushed away the coffee, then waved a blue folder his way.

"Faith Rogerson, an elementary school teacher in Portland, Oregon. Twenty-six, light-brown hair and blue eyes. She was supposed to get married the next day, just like Renee. Her engagement ring is missing too, just like Renee's." Allyson's mouth flattened to a grim line. "This is his second murder, and I'm going to nail him. I thought of a name for him in the exposé. The Groom Reaper."

The media would eat up that title. "What makes you think this murder is connected to Renee's?"

Allyson perched on a ledge at the window. "Both deaths were the night before the wedding. Not a week, not three days, the night before. And the murder method in both cases was drowning. You have to admit that's not the usual way a bride might die on the eve of her nuptials."

She had a point. "Who was she engaged to?"

"Justin Leyland. He sells pharmaceuticals. He got back in town just in time for the bachelor party that night and had tried calling her several times. When she didn't answer, he went over around midnight and used his key to get into the house. He found her in the kitchen. The sink was still full of water."

"How'd you find all that out?"

"I went to school with the lead reporter at the paper and weaseled it out of him."

Renee had been drowned in a stock tank outside. While not the same location as this one, it did hold similarities. And both fiancés had been at a bachelor party. "Did you call Leyland?"

"I tried but his voice mail was full. The local media is probably all over it. I'm sure no one has connected the two cases yet."

"*If* they're connected."

Allyson flipped open the folder. "Look at Faith's picture."

The woman in the picture held a vague resemblance to his sister. His interest stirred. "Anything else?"

"Yep." She flipped a couple of pages in the folder. "They planned to honeymoon in Jamaica just like Renee."

"That's a popular honeymoon destination. Any pictures of

this Leyland fellow?" It was the one thing that rankled—he'd never met Renee's fiancé. He'd planned to be at the wedding until an accident landed him in the hospital the day before he was supposed to fly to Washington.

After the police had cleared Tyler, Boone had tried to call his cell number and found the account had been closed. It didn't necessarily mean anything since Dixon could have moved and started a new job. But the killer might also have eliminated him. And left clues this time.

"No pictures that I could find. There wasn't an engagement picture, and there were no photos on her cell phone of the two of them, which seemed odd. Another similarity."

He stared at Allyson, then reached for his phone. "I think I'd better mention this to Detective Morgan. I have a call in to him."

His cell phone dinged, and he looked at the time. "I need to run an errand. I'll let you know what Morgan says."

Though her eyes burned with fatigue from the three-day drive, passing the Rock Harbor welcome sign filled Dana with new vigor. The familiar streets and storefronts enveloped her with a sense of homecoming. Her family had lived in the country, but she'd gone to Rock Harbor at least once a week for shopping.

Driving down Houghton Street was like stepping into a Norman Rockwell painting. She spotted Bree's familiar green Jeep Cherokee parked by the Suomi Café on Kitchigami Street, just off Houghton, and Dana's stomach growled. She hadn't eaten breakfast, and it was already past five and getting dark.

She made her way back to Kitchigami, then pulled her Prius

behind the Jeep and got out with Phantom. She left her vehicle unlocked in a sudden burst of defiance. This was Rock Harbor where no one locked their houses or cars. She was safe here.

The bell on the café's door jingled as she opened it, and Dana stood for a moment inhaling the familiar scents: *pannukakku*, beef pasties, and *pulla*. Snippets of conversation floated to her, familiar topics like the upcoming winter festival and the fish that got away.

A smile stretched her lips when she saw Bree sitting at a booth with Samson at her feet. Her friend's short red curls were tousled, and a smile lit her heart-shaped face as she talked with animation to another woman, whose back was to the door. Bree looked twenty-five instead of thirty-nine.

Dana threaded her way through the café to the booth. "Care if I join you?" Samson leaped up to touch noses with Phantom.

"Dana!" Bree jumped to her feet and enveloped her in a hug. Her hair was scented with the raspberry *pannukakku* on her plate. "I thought you'd be here several days ago. I tried to call your cell phone, but I got a recording saying the number wasn't in service."

Dana returned the hug. "I should have called to let you know I'd be late. I disconnected the phone until I got here to buy a new one. I–I had a delay."

She and Bree had become friends when Bree moved to town with her first husband, Rob Nicholls. Dana had babysat for her tiny son, Davy, quite often. Rob had died, and Bree remarried a park ranger. They had four-year-old twins now, Hannah and Hunter.

Dana glanced at the booth's other occupant who had stood as well. "Ally Cat! I didn't know you were living back here." She hugged Allyson Hegney in a tight squeeze. "I haven't seen you, gosh, it's been at least five years. The last class reunion, I think."

"I haven't heard that old nickname in forever." The leggy woman returned the hug, her light-brown hair cascading down her back in a straight, shiny curtain. "I took a leave of absence for a month. Have a seat. I want to get caught up." She sat and scooted over on the booth seat.

Dana slid her purse from her shoulder and ordered Phantom to lie down by Samson. "You won't believe what's been happening."

Reliving the past year of being on the mountaintop in love, only to come crashing to reality the first time Garret hurt her made her voice go rough. "The first couple of times I just thought it was my fault—that I'd been a nag or something. Then I realized he had a violent, possessive streak. When I told him we were through, that's when the trouble really started. He began following me and having friends call to tell me I was wrong. That he had PTSD from the military and I needed to be more understanding. I even took back him a few times, but h-he got rough again. I knew if I stayed, he'd eventually really hurt me."

"Or kill you," Bree said softly.

Dana nodded. "Or kill me." She launched into the attack that had delayed her arrival. "It took two days to get Dolly repaired, then another three days to get here."

"Dolly's your car?" Bree smiled and signaled for Molly, the café's longtime waitress. She brought over coffee and a plate holding a pasty. "I knew you'd want your favorite, Dana. Welcome home." She still wore her graying hair in a low ponytail, and her smile enveloped Dana.

"Thanks, Molly. You know me too well." The beef gravy in the pasty hit her tongue, and the explosion of flavor made her just plain giddy. How good it was to be home.

Allyson lifted her coffee cup and stared at Dana with troubled hazel eyes. "That guy sounds just too creepy. I hope he doesn't figure out where you've gone and come here."

"I'm sure he'll assume I came home, but I have lots of friends here. And for now I'm going to live with Chris for a while." Her brother had bought a house on Quincy Hill nearly a year and a half ago when he decided to get out of the Marines and settle in their hometown. "He's already restored the downstairs for himself, and he says I can have the other floors until I want to get my own place."

Bree frowned and tucked a red curl behind her ear. "But he's gone a lot with his job. I don't think he'll be much protection."

"True, but his house is right here in town, within hailing distance of the sheriff's office. And I'll have Phantom." She reached down to rub her dog's ears. She'd given him the name the moment she picked him out from the litter, the only black Lab in a sea of yellow. "I'm done letting Garret terrorize me. And quite honestly, if he comes here, he'll know I have plenty of support. I think it's over."

Bree's green eyes still held skepticism. "I hope you're right. Is he in jail for attacking you?"

She looked away. "Well, no. I didn't press charges because I didn't want to have to go back for a trial or anything. I just want to get away from him."

"So he could be on his way even now."

Dana bit her lip and stared across the table at Bree. "I suppose so."

"I don't want to scare you, but you need to be on guard. Always lock your car. Keep bear spray at the ready anytime you're by yourself. Get a security system installed at the house."

Dana sank against the booth back. "I have bear spray, but this is Rock Harbor. No one locks up."

Bree's eyes narrowed. "You've got to start. A stalker isn't like any other danger. He's not rational and is only focused on revenge.

Your ex proved that by attacking you in the parking garage. He had to know the police were just steps away. That's brazen."

Bree was right. Dana had seen it a hundred times in her job. She just hadn't wanted to believe it could apply to her.

She blew out a shaky breath. "Let's talk about something else for a while. I want to forget all about Garret." She turned a smile toward Allyson. "So you're here on leave seeing your family?"

Allyson ran her finger around the cup's rim. "Well, it's more than that. My cousin was murdered three years ago. I don't think you ever met Renee. I came to town to go over the latest details with her brother. He lives here."

Dana's chest squeezed. "I'm so sorry. Did they find her killer?"

Allyson shook her head. "I took some investigative psychology classes in school before I changed my major from criminal justice. I felt the killing was the work of a budding serial killer. His MO was too odd. And there's been another similar murder this week."

"How did he murder them?"

"Drowning. My cousin was drowned in a water tank for her goats, and the second woman was drowned in the kitchen sink."

Dana clenched her hands together in her lap, and her skin prickled. She glanced out the café's windows. This sounded way too familiar.

CHAPTER 3

D ana parked on Quincy Street and craned her neck to take in the three-story brick building in front of her in the fading light. Once upon a time, copper miners trudged the steps to their rooms here at the Copper Junction Hotel. The sign was long gone now, and her brother had replaced the aging stoop with an elegant porch with beautiful posts and a new front door in dark red. She'd fallen in love with it the second she'd seen it a month ago.

The thick clouds overhead promised snow and cast a gloom over the landscape. The cold November wind cut through her thin jacket, and she quickly ascended the brick steps to the welcoming front door. Phantom bounded after her and sniffed at the door. The lock opened with a click, and she turned the doorknob to open it.

"Chris isn't home."

She turned at the deep male voice behind her. The man on the sidewalk looked like he'd be more at home in Wyoming or Arizona with his boots and cowboy hat. If she wasn't mistaken, those boots were snakeskin. His hat shadowed his face, but she got an impression of a strong jaw as he took a step closer. He wore a black-and-red Arizona Cardinals jacket and jeans.

She squared her shoulders and stared him down. "And you are?"

He snapped his fingers. "You're Dana, aren't you? I've seen pictures." He retreated toward a black pickup that was parked behind her. "I have some stuff for you."

He was probably six-two or so, and his long stride had him at the truck in seconds. The man opened the passenger door and reached inside. A dog that looked more wolf than anything leaped down to follow as he turned toward her with a box full of groceries. "I was going to leave the food for you. Chris has been gone for a month, and anything left in the fridge is likely to be growing something green."

She glanced at the box and spied bread, peanut butter, cereal, coffee, milk, cream, and butter. "And you are?"

Close up he was even more handsome than her first vague impression. Dark hair fell over his forehead from under his hat. The cologne he wore was pleasant, something spicy with sandalwood.

"Boone Carter. This is Spirit." His hand rested atop the dog's head. Spirit took a step forward to sniff Phantom.

"I've heard the name." Chris had started ice sailing when he came back to town two years ago, and Boone had taken her brother under his wing. According to Chris, Boone was the best outfitter around. Even though he was Chris's friend, her hackles stayed up. Something about him put her on edge.

He tipped his head toward the door. "If you'll open it, I'll carry this to the kitchen."

Heat flooded her cheeks. "Of course." The door swung open without a sound, and she stepped into the entry. The walnut floors and wide trim contrasted with the pale gray-green walls, a color she'd helped Chris pick out when he was redoing the place. She flipped on the overhead chandelier and blinked when light flooded the space.

He strode past her. "This way." The dogs on his heels, he

passed the huge curving staircase and disappeared through a door on the other side of the foyer.

The living room to the right of the entry was large with floor-to-ceiling windows along two walls. She took in the space with the new white tables and blue-and-white furniture. The nautical touches made her smile. Chris loved the water.

She hurried after Boone across gleaming hardwood floors. She went through the dining space with its white distressed table and chairs that opened to a large kitchen with gray cabinets. She'd had to talk Chris into the color, but it was perfect. Boone was unpacking the box at a large marble island.

She walked around the side of the island to face him. Now that she saw him square on in the full light, she barely bit back a gasp. Scars ridged the right side of his face from jaw to temple.

He paused and his lips twisted in a grimace. "Seen enough?" He grabbed the milk and yogurt, then turned to the refrigerator.

She reached toward his retreating back, then dropped her hand. "I'm sorry. You were burned?" Burn scars were hard to miss.

"Forest fire. I was a smoke jumper." After depositing the milk and yogurt, he faced her again.

If not for the smoldering heat in his eyes, she would have guessed he was used to comments about his face. "The scars look old. When did it happen?"

"About five years ago. Look, I'm sure you're tired. You have luggage?"

She nodded. "I can get it though. The groceries are more than enough. I really appreciate it."

He held out a tanned, muscular hand, and she stared at it blankly for a long moment. "Your car keys."

His tone told her he wouldn't take no for an answer, so she

pulled them from her coat pocket and dropped them into his palm. Her warm feelings vanished in an instant as she watched him leave.

"Stay," he told Spirit.

Noticing an injury was a normal part of her job, but he'd made her feel small and mean. Had that been his intention?

She could give him the benefit of the doubt. Chris might have more information about the injury and why the man was so touchy. Or maybe Allyson or Bree would know. Dana draped her coat on the back of a chair and went to hold open the door while he hauled in her suitcases. Spirit and Phantom padded along behind her. Spirit's vivid blue eyes made her feel as if he was watching her every move for his master.

"This all you got?" He set down the two medium suitcases.

"The rest is on the moving truck. It will be here in a couple of days. I just needed some clothing and essentials in the meantime."

He jerked his head to the left. "Tell me which one you want, and I'll haul the suitcases there."

"I can handle it from here. Thanks so much."

Was it too much to ask him to get out of here? After the stress of the last week, she wanted some peace and quiet. He could lug that chip on his shoulder right out of her life and let her be.

He picked up the suitcases and looked at her. "Well?"

"Upstairs. The biggest room, the one on the left."

He nodded and headed up the curving staircase with both dogs loping along behind him. Gritting her teeth, she followed him to the top of the stairs where it opened onto a wide hallway. The paint was a fading dull green. She planned to paint it pronto. Three doorways opened off the hall, and he carried her luggage to the large bedroom on her left, then set the cases down on the polished wood floors.

It held an old iron bed with a sagging queen mattress. But it was clean, and she had plans for how to make it hers.

"This is nice." He folded his arms across his chest and gazed down at her. "I get a little testy when someone stares. I'm sure you're going to plunge into the rumor cesspool, so I'll just tell you straight up. I was caught in a firestorm and the gear didn't protect me. Yes, plastic surgery would make it less noticeable, but the scars remind me that love is fickle and most women wouldn't want to look across the breakfast table at this every morning," he touched the right side of his face, "as my fiancée was quick to tell me."

She was still gaping after him when the front door slammed behind Boone and his dog.

———

Bree's training center was a pole building on a tract of land surrounded by woods. The lake behind the building was perfect for water-search training. Kitchigami Search-and-Rescue Training Center's reputation had grown exponentially. Today she had ten new students who needed her attention, but her thoughts kept heading back to Dana's predicament. Most graduates went on to volunteer for area searches, and a few diehard handlers like her made a career of it.

Bree glanced at her watch. Nearly five. She was meeting Allyson at six to take Dana dinner so she needed to wrap up class.

She forced herself to focus. "Take your dogs around back where they can't see. Lauri, you stay here. You can be the victim today." Kade's younger sister had been living with them since August when she finally graduated from college. Jobs here in the U.P. had been scarce, but Bree hoped something would turn up soon for Lauri.

The rest of the students took the dogs around the building.

Lauri got into the scratch box, and Bree dropped the guillotine-type door into position. Carrying a bag with the scent article, she went around the corner.

The dogs were smelling the scent article, and the students would release each dog individually and see how long it took them to find Lauri in the rough wooden box. Zorro, Lauri's border collie mix, barked and raced around the corner. He drove straight for the scratch box, jumped up on it, and barked. He grabbed a stick on the ground, then carried it to Bree with his tail held high in triumph.

Each of the dogs got their chance, and most found Lauri in less than five minutes. They were all improving, and Bree ended the training session with praise and treats for the dogs.

Lauri followed her and the dogs inside the building. "I have something I want to talk to you about."

Uh-oh. When Lauri adopted that serious tone, Bree braced for impact. "Okay." She snapped her fingers to Samson, and he limped over to press against her leg.

He'd suffered a minor cut on a paw during the exercises today so she tended to it. She'd fed him a raw-food diet all these years, and he still had very little gray in his rough, curly coat. Most people quickly guessed the German shepherd part of him from the black and tan of his fur, but the curls were pure Chow. He slurped up the water she had poured into his bowl, and Zorro did the same. Then both dogs curled together on the floor to rest by her feet.

Lauri had recently cut her long brown hair into a becoming shoulder-length style that flipped up on the ends and accentuated her bone structure. Her blue eyes held a trace of worry as she propped one booted foot on her chair's bottom rung. "I got a job." Lauri's eyes gleamed.

"That's great! Where will you be working?"

"I'll have to travel all over the place. I'll only be home once in a while." Lauri motioned around the space. "I won't be able to help you here any longer. I hope that's okay."

"I'll manage. You hate being stuck in a one-horse town like Rock Harbor. What will you be doing?"

Lauri stared at Bree as if to make sure she was really okay with the news. "I'll be an auditor. I always said that was the one accounting job I'd never do." She made a face. "Going in and looking for all the mistakes the employees have made is like standing on a shooting range with a bull's-eye on my back. It will be uncomfortable all the time. But it'll be a great experience!"

Bree rose and hugged her. Lauri went tense for a long moment, then hugged her back. Bree pulled away and gave her a little shake. "And you never know where it might lead. You'll get to see some new places."

Lauri shrugged off Bree's grip and tucked a strand of brown hair behind her ear. "I won't get to see Zoe much. When I gave her up for adoption, I never wanted her to know who I was. Now that she does, it seems cruel to leave her."

Bree's heart swelled at Lauri's admission. The girl had matured in the past year. She thought of other people instead of only herself. Bree had always loved Lauri, even though she wanted to shake her at times. At sixteen Lauri had a daughter out of wedlock who Mason and Hilary Kaleva had adopted. Hilary was Bree's first husband's sister and the town mayor. Mason had been Rock Harbor's sheriff forever. Zoe adored them both so Bree was sure she'd be fine.

"Zoe's got a good mom and dad, and you can see her at least a few times a year."

"I guess." Lauri patted her leg, and Zorro came to her. "I've got to go home and pack. Zorro won't be able to come with me. Will that be a problem?"

"Of course not. When do you start?"

"I fly to Lihue, Hawaii, on Sunday. I'll be there for a week, then to Oregon for a week."

"Where will you stay when you're gone? Hotels?" Bree didn't like the sound of that. Without stability Lauri could fall back into her old partying ways.

"Don't look so worried, *Mom*." Lauri grabbed her coat and shrugged it on. "The company has several condos, and I'll have my own place when I'm there. I'll be able to cook and invite friends over." She wrinkled her nose. "If I make any friends with a schedule like that."

"You will. People gravitate to you naturally." Bree walked with her to the door. "Have you told Kade yet?"

"Yeah, I called him this morning and endured the lecture about being on my guard and making sure the doors are locked at night."

Kade, ever the protector. Bree opened the door and smiled. "He loves you."

"I know, but sheesh, give me a break. I'm twenty-three."

Bree pressed her lips together and looked away. Lauri didn't need a reminder of her past poor choices. They'd pray this job was the right thing.

She shut the door behind her sister-in-law as Samson came to press against her leg. "That leaves me without help, boy. Now what?"

Samson's soft brown eyes seemed to say he'd do all he could.

CHAPTER 4

Spirit leaped onto the backseat of Boone's big truck and settled onto the seat. Boone slid under the wheel and drummed his fingers against it. Until today, he would have said no stares on earth could unsettle him. Why had he acted like such a jerk with Dana? Now that he'd cooled off, he could admit to himself that her behavior had been courteous and professional. She was a 911 call dispatcher and had likely seen and heard it all. She'd almost acted like a doctor or nurse with the clinical questions.

Something about her had gotten under his skin. Maybe it was the fear and vulnerability in those big blue eyes. Chris had told him about the ex-fiancé and his threats. Boone had promised to keep an eye on Dana and make sure she was all right, but if he turned into a porcupine every time he was around her, it would be a difficult assignment. She seemed nice enough, but he'd been taken in by beauties like her before. Never again.

He glanced at the time. Six in the evening in Washington wasn't the greatest time to be calling Morgan again, but Boone had already tried twice, and the detective hadn't returned his calls. He pulled out his cell phone and called the familiar number.

Detective Morgan answered on the first ring. His voice always reminded Boone of molasses: smooth and southern. Harry Morgan sounded like a transplant from Alabama.

"Detective, it's Boone Carter."

"I was just about to call you. I've been out all day and just got back to my office. I assume you're calling for an update on your sister, but I'm sorry to say we have no new leads."

Boone slid down in the seat and a picture of Renee on the tree swing behind their house slammed into his head. She'd been four to his eight, and she shrieked, "Higher, Boone, higher," with every pump of her short tanned legs. Had she cried out for him at the end? He'd always been the one she turned to when she needed a hundred dollars for the rent or a shoulder to cry on after the last dirtbag had dumped her.

Moisture flooded his eyes, and he blinked it back. "I wondered if you caught wind of the Faith Rogerson murder."

"Hmm, can't say as I have." The detective's drawl grew more syrupy, a sure sign of interest.

"She was killed the night before she was to be married, just like Renee." Boone laid out everything Allyson uncovered. "It sounds like it could be the same killer."

"Where was this?"

"Portland, Oregon."

"I'll check into it."

"One more thing. Have you had any contact with Tyler Dixon lately?"

"No, sir. We cleared him, remember?"

"And he hasn't called to check on the investigation?"

"Nope."

"I tried to call his cell phone, but it was disconnected."

"No crime in that. He might have moved and gotten a new one."

Boone couldn't argue that. "What if the killer got to him too?"

Spirit must have sensed his mood because he pressed his head into the crook of Boone's neck and huffed warm breath against his skin. He rubbed the dog's nose, and Spirit finally retreated to the backseat and lay down.

"I will say it's a little odd Dixon hasn't checked in. I was just looking at my notes, and the last time I spoke with him was eighteen months ago. Usually people call on occasion to check the status. You call every couple of weeks."

His tone was mild as though Boone's frequent calls hadn't been the nuisance Boone had expected. "Is there a way to check on his status?"

"I could call his employer. I think there's a number in my records."

"Could you let me know what you find out?"

Detective Morgan didn't answer for a moment. He cleared his throat. "What is it you're suggesting, Mr. Carter? I think it's more than your fear for Dixon's safety."

"I'm still not convinced he didn't kill Renee."

"He had an ironclad alibi. Three people placed him at the bachelor party until he left to go check on why your sister wasn't answering her phone."

"I've heard all that, but the party was being held five miles down the road. What if he slipped out for a few minutes, killed her, then went back to the party? The thing turned into a drunken binge as they watched the football game. It wouldn't be hard for exact times to be a little iffy for the men who were there."

Morgan heaved a sigh. "Listen to yourself, Mr. Carter. What

you're saying doesn't really make sense. Renee put up quite the struggle. Water was sloshed all over the ground around the watering tank. Whoever did this would have been soaked and chilled to the bone. I know the lack of progress in the case is frustrating, but we want to find the killer, not just book a suspect."

A wind gust rattled the truck, and Boone leaned his forehead against the cold window glass. His warm breath puffed white in the November chill. He wanted to reject the thought that the sheriff might be right, but the truth was he missed his sister with an ache that only grew sharper with each passing day.

He'd hoped finding justice for Renee would be a balm on his pain, but it looked like that might never happen. It had been three years, and an arrest wasn't any closer than the night he'd gotten the call. No DNA match to the skin under her fingernails, no clues, and no real leads.

If only he'd been there for the wedding.

He lifted his head and started the engine. "Thanks for your honesty, Detective. Please let me know what you hear about Dixon. I'll try to keep my suspicions in line."

———

Dana loved her room on the second floor with its gray-green walls and fresh white linens. Even though the attached bathroom had an aging marble tile shower and floor, it had a timeless elegance. On his last trip home, Chris must have bought the fluffy towels and expensive toiletries to welcome her.

She had barely unpacked her suitcases when the doorbell rang. Her stomach rumbled as she hurried downstairs to answer the door, and she glanced at her watch. A little after six.

She doubted Boone had returned, but she hoped she'd get the chance to apologize to him. His parting words kept ringing in her head, but he wouldn't want her compassion. He struck her as the type who wasn't afraid to take on a battalion by himself, much like Garret. That type of he-man was best avoided.

She spotted two figures through the glass and opened the door with a fresh surge of excitement at the sight of her friends. Hoods up over their heads to combat the wind, Bree and Allyson stood on the porch. Bree's nose was pink, and Allyson shivered a little as the wind howled with joy to chase leaves along the yard.

Bree held up the Crock-Pot in her hands. "I thought we'd share some chili with you for dinner tonight." Phantom pushed past Dana and leaped on Bree's leg. She petted him a moment, then made him get down. "Sorry, I didn't bring Samson, Phantom."

"I was just feeling lonely." Dana stepped out of the way to allow them in. She spied the pie in Allyson's hand. "That wouldn't be your mom's peanut butter pie, would it?"

"She made it just for you and guarded it with her life from Dad." Allyson paused on the rug as Dana shut the door and kicked off her boots. "Which way is the kitchen?"

"I'll show you. How'd you both get away for the evening? No kids, not even Samson."

Bree kicked off her boots too and followed Dana. "Kade decided to take them all to see the new Disney movie and told me to get a pedicure or something. This sounded a lot more fun since I haven't seen you in ages. Samson cut his paw in training this afternoon so I left him on the bed resting." She stopped in the kitchen doorway. "Wow, this is gorgeous. I love the gray cabinets. Is that a marble countertop?"

"Yes." Dana took the slow cooker from Bree and set it on the large island, then removed some bowls from the cabinet. "I'm not sure if there are any crackers."

Allyson held up a plastic bag. "We came prepared."

Dana's mouth watered at the rich aroma of tomatoes and onion as she ladled up the soup. The women carried their steaming bowls to the seating area at the island. She grabbed her purse and took out her sea salt tin in case she needed it.

Dana perched on a stool beside Allyson. "I bet Chris has never even eaten in here. He's probably thrown something in the microwave, then eaten it in front of the TV in the living room." She tasted the chili and nearly moaned as the chilies and tomato sauce hit her tongue. "This is so good. I've only had fast food for the past three days. Anyone want something to drink? Chris asked your cousin, Boone Carter, to bring over some things." She snapped her fingers and made Phantom lay down at her feet.

Allyson had been smiling, but at the mention of Boone's name, she went somber. "Poor guy has been through so much."

Dana clamped her mouth shut. She wasn't about to join the rumor mill Boone had mentioned. She took a big spoonful of chili to mask her silence.

Bree crushed crackers into her chili. "His sister's death really hit him hard."

Dana choked on her mouthful. "He didn't mention his sister. Car accident?"

"No." Allyson's voice softened. "He's my cousin so she's talking about Renee."

"Your cousin who was drowned the night before her wedding?" Dana's fears came surging back. Maybe it was all in her head, but she wanted reassurance that Garret couldn't possibly be a killer. "I—I thought of Garret when you mentioned the drowning."

Bree put down her spoon. "You want to talk about it?"

Dana's eyes filled with tears and she nodded. She hadn't told anyone about this except the police. "It all started so innocently. I fixed a pot roast for dinner, and I had no idea he didn't like roast. He'd never said."

"Stop it." Allyson reached across the table to grab her arm. "Stop blaming yourself right now. Whatever happened, it wasn't your fault for fixing something he didn't like."

Dana's throat spasmed. "You're right. I know you're right." She took a deep, calming breath. "His mouth got all tight and pinched when he entered the kitchen and saw the food on the table. I could tell something was wrong, but I never dreamed he'd get so upset."

She didn't want to relive the terror of that moment, but it washed over her, tightening her chest and constricting her breath. She was gasping by the time she finished telling them about Garret submerging her head in the sink's water.

Bree and Allyson both looked shaken. "You're lucky he didn't kill you," Bree said.

"Seeing you again last month was my opportunity to get away from him. You were a life saver."

Allyson's eyes narrowed. "You said he'd been gone for two weeks. Does he travel a lot? Ever go to Washington or Oregon?"

Dana nodded. "He's a Glock salesman and is gone all the time, usually two to four weeks at a time. Seattle and several cities in Oregon are his usual stops."

Allyson reached for the notebook in her purse. "I'd like to hear more about Garret."

CHAPTER 5

He couldn't get Allyson's theory out of his head. Boone rubbed his scar and stared at the flames flickering in the stone fireplace. The kitchen still held the aroma of his microwaved lasagna. Spirit eyed him mournfully from his rug by the kitchen door. He'd danced around begging for a walk until Boone gave him an emphatic no.

He looked up at a knock at the front door. Who was out in this fifty-mile-an-hour wind? He went to the door and opened it. Allyson stood on the step huddled in her peacoat.

"You look frozen." He let her in and shut the door behind her. A whisper of her car's pine air freshener followed in her wake.

"I need to talk to you." Shivering, she walked toward the fireplace and held out her hands toward the warmth.

He took her coat and grabbed a throw from the back of the sofa for her.

She pulled the armchair closer to the fire and snuggled under the throw. "Thanks."

"Want some coffee or hot tea?"

"Not just yet. Maybe in a little while." She stared into the fire with a pensive expression. "Bree and I talked to Dana tonight. She said you brought over some food."

"Yeah, that was the errand I left to do when you were here earlier. I'd promised Chris." And he could just imagine the conversation they had. He touched the ridges on his cheek. Dana had likely grilled Allyson about his scar.

"She mentioned something that made me go digging. That ex-boyfriend of hers, Garret Waterman, plunged her head underwater in the kitchen sink once. Scared her to death."

He went rigid as a horrific mental image flashed. "He sounds like a real winner."

"Faith Rogerson was drowned in her kitchen sink."

"Yeah, in *Portland*. Waterman lives in Washington. At least I assume so since that's where Dana lived. What's your point?"

She tightened her grip on the blanket at her neck and stared at him. "Garret is a salesman. He travels all the time selling Glocks. Portland is in his territory. He goes there every few weeks."

He frowned. "You're saying you think Waterman might have been calling himself Justin Leyland and masquerading as a pharmaceutical rep? That's a stretch, even for you, Allyson."

Color rushed to her cheeks. "Just hear me out, okay? Waterman was in Portland when Faith died. It's part of his territory. What if he travels around and woos women in different areas under an assumed name?"

Couldn't she see the obvious problem with her theory? "Wouldn't the groom worry his picture would get out and his real identity would be exposed?"

She wrinkled her nose. "I don't know. You hear about bigamists all the time. Maybe our guy is that type with a woman in every port. He couldn't run the risk of using his real name."

"I don't buy it. For one thing, would the killer say he was a pharmaceutical rep if he really wasn't one? You'd think he'd have to know something about the job."

"Both fiancés had claimed to be in the same profession. What are the chances of that? And of their future brides being murdered the same way? I think there's some kind of connection, and I'm going to prove it."

The determination on her face sent a shock of alarm down his spine. "This Waterman guy sounds dangerous, Allyson. Don't poke a stick at a rattlesnake."

Throw still clutched around her, she rose and stalked back and forth in front of the fire. "Detective Morgan isn't getting anywhere, is he?"

"Nope. I called him today and told him about the Rogerson murder though. He hadn't sniffed it out yet, but he was going to check on it."

"Check on it," she scoffed. "That's all he ever does is *check on it*. How about getting off his duff and finding Renee's killer?"

"You think I don't know that? Look, I'm as frustrated as you are, but we need clues, real facts, to get anywhere. This killer is smart. We can't manufacture evidence out of thin air."

"I'm going to find the evidence." She tossed the throw onto the chair and went to the closet where she jerked her coat from a hanger and shrugged into it.

He followed her. "Don't do anything stupid. I don't want Waterman to make you a target of his anger when there's likely no connection at all."

Tears hung on her lashes, and she kept yanking on the door before she paused long enough to unlock it. "I can't stand by and do nothing."

Grasping her shoulders, he pulled her around to face him. "I haven't been doing nothing. I asked the detective to find out what's going on with Dixon. Morgan seemed intrigued when he realized Dixon hadn't called in quite a while. He'll let me know in a couple of days. And he's checking to see if there's any connection to the Rogerson murder."

She leaned her forehead against his chest. "Ignore me. I'm just tired tonight. And I'm running out of savings and will have to go back to work soon. I was sure I'd be able to track down Renee's killer myself, and I'm worried this psycho will strike again."

If it was the same guy. He hugged her before she pulled away. "I'll call you when I hear from Detective Morgan."

She nodded and slipped out into the howling wind. He stood in the doorway and watched her slide into her red car. The taillights blinked twice, then disappeared in the blowing leaves and dust.

Spirit pushed his head against Boone's knee, and he rubbed the dog's head. His own determination about not finding Renee's killer was just as deep as his cousin's.

Garret drove the old pickup slowly through the streets. He curled his lip at the sight of the picturesque town. If he didn't know better, he'd guess he'd entered a time warp and been transported back to the fifties. The storefronts had clearly been built in the 1800s, and most were painted multiple colors.

Snow clung to the trees' branches and contrasted with the brightly colored leaves still clinging to them. Pedestrians hurried to their destinations under glowering skies that threatened more snow. A few flakes already drifted in the glare of the streetlamps.

He kept a look out for Dana, but there was no sign of her. Where else would she go? The minute she'd left Washington, he knew she'd run back to Chris for help.

An empty parallel parking spot was ahead, right in front of a neon *Open* sign in the Copper Club Tavern's window. He was parched and hungry, and this place would do.

The bar was nearly empty when he went inside, and Garret's mouth watered at the yeasty smell of the beer on tap. The bartender glanced up as Garret slung himself into a corner table. He sat and watched out the window at the town. It would be hard to escape notice here. What did Dana see in this place? Sure, she was born here, but what a little backwater. They could be sitting along the wharf and watching whales right now instead of gearing up for a snowstorm.

Women. There was no understanding them.

A young woman stopped at his table. With her raven hair, dark-brown eyes, and pale skin, she was quite the looker. She wore a short black skirt and knee-high boots. Her red top didn't leave much to the imagination.

She smiled down at him. "Hi, honey, what will it be? The cook has his special pasties coming out of the oven."

"What's a pasty?" He had a vague idea what they were because Dana had tried to make them a time or two, but he wanted to keep this pretty young thing around a bit. There was no mistaking the admiration in her glance as she took in his bulging biceps.

White teeth flashed in a seductive smile. "Honey, you're not from around here, eh? It's a meat pie usually stuffed with beef, onion, potatoes, and rutabaga. It's a dish you won't find much of anywhere in the States except up here in the U.P. It will put hair on your chest." She leaned close enough for him to catch a whiff of the mint on her breath. "Not that you'd need that. Give it a try."

Since Dana was being so skittish, he might relieve his stress with this bit of fluff. He gave her a smile. "You talked me into it. What time you get off, beautiful?"

"Midnight, but if the storm comes in, we might close early." Her full lips curved up. "Where you staying?"

"Nowhere yet. Any hotels around?"

"You passed the only one on the way in, out where Houghton Street starts."

He nodded. "I saw a *No Vacancy* sign. Any other towns close by?"

"Ontonagon is about twenty minutes south, and Houghton is on up north about half an hour." She chewed her lip a moment. "I got room though if you don't mind the sofa."

"I don't mind." He added another lazy smile to his comment. No way would he be sleeping on the sofa. She was ripe for the picking.

"Let me get you fed, and I'll see how the evening goes. Smitty might let me off early. I think the weather is going to kill any business."

"Sounds good."

He settled in for a leisurely evening of flirting with the server, whose name he still didn't know, and figuring out this little town. A few customers came in, and their broad Yooper accent made him smirk. Dana had an accent like that once, but she lost it. He planned to make sure she was gone long before it came back. He'd even tried calling Chris, but the jerk hung up on him.

Garret drummed his fingers on the table, then decided to call his grandpa. The old man got lonely in the nursing home, and Garret tried to call a couple times a week. "Hey, Gramps, how's it going?"

"I thought you'd call today. Wish you were here, boy. I won

the chess championship. Got a trophy and everything." His grand-pa's quavery voice strengthened as he talked.

"Great going, Gramps! I'll be in Washington in a few weeks so I'll stop by. See if someone will text me a picture of you with the trophy."

"Already thought of it."

Garret's text-message alert dinged, and he glanced at the picture. His grandpa wore a chambray shirt and baggy jeans. The trophy was a small, cheap one, but there was no missing the old man's pride as he held it up. "I just got it. Congratulations! Has Mom been by to see you?"

"She was here over the weekend."

"That's good." Garret wasn't on speaking terms with his mother, but at least she put the booze down long enough to check on her dad once in a while. He chatted a few more minutes with his grandfather who'd helped raise him until he heard the fatigue in his voice. "Love you, Gramps. Gotta go." The warm feelings ebbed as he sat in the bar by himself. He shouldn't be alone. Dana should be here.

Its lights still on, the library sat across the street and he watched a few hardy folks enter and exit before the lights finally winked out at nine. A streetlight illuminated a familiar face, and he bit back an expletive. He'd seen dozens of pictures of her and Dana. Bree Matthews, a kid on each side of her and one trailing behind, walked toward a Jeep parked almost directly across from his truck.

His gaze swept back to the library entry. No sign of Dana. Maybe she was waiting in Bree's vehicle. He waited until Bree opened the driver's door and the interior light switched on. It was empty.

Would she recognize him if he walked out and confronted her? This was all Bree's fault. If she hadn't coaxed Dana away, life would be perfect. Through slitted eyes, he watched her buckle in the younger kids, then climb under the wheel. She took out her cell phone and made a call while the engine idled. Her husband maybe or was she calling Dana? Had she recognized him?

He turned his face away from the plate-glass window and took a sip of his beer. Maybe he should get out of here. For all he knew, she'd called the sheriff who was already on the way to arrest him. He rose and tossed some bills on the table. The server rushed to intercept him.

"I just got the okay to leave." Her voice was breathless. "I'm parked around back. That's your truck out front?"

"Sure is."

"I'm in a blue Chevy Blazer. I'll pull around and flash the lights. You can follow me home."

"Honey, I'd follow you anywhere." He grabbed his coat and slipped it on.

"The name's Tracie. Tracie Pitt. Just in case you want to know."

He grinned. "Jarret. Jarret Mannon." No sense in giving her his real name. He had to go to his job for a few days, but she would be a nice diversion while he figured out what to do about Dana.

She sent a smile up his way, then rushed for the kitchen. When he checked before stepping outside, Bree's Jeep was gone. He darted to his truck and hopped inside. The snow was light and dry, easily removed by the wipers. In a few minutes, Tracie's car paused beside his truck, and she waved at him. He waved back and followed her down the street toward a light winking in the distance.

He reached under his seat to make sure his gun was still there. Its cold surface reassured him.

CHAPTER 6

A dirty bulb pushed away the shadows from the third floor. Dana stood at the top of the stairs with her hands on her hips and surveyed the space. The ceiling rose ten feet, then angled down, giving it a cozy feel in spite of the dirty beige walls and dusty wooden floors. She'd expected to find the top floor crammed with old furniture and boxes, but the few items here had been pushed against the walls. Light filtered through the dirty windows from cars and streetlamps, but there wasn't enough illumination to clearly make out much beyond the size.

Phantom left her side and went to nose around the room's perimeter. Dana felt along the wall for a switch. When she flipped it on, one lightbulb from a bank of three in the ceiling came on.

"With a little paint this would make an awesome living room area for me," she told Phantom, who didn't look up from his sniffing of a cedar chest under one window. "What do you have there, boy?"

She'd seen the chest before in her parents' room. It had been her grandmother's and her mom often waxed it lovingly. "I thought this old chest burned up in the fire."

Kneeling beside her dog, she ran her fingers over the wood. Her pulse sped up as memories flooded over her, visions of her life before everything turned upside down when she was eight. Mom used to keep mementos in this—things like old report cards, picture albums, and the family Bible. A padlock prevented her from lifting the lid, and she made a mental note to ask Chris for a key. What if the many things she thought were lost in the fire still existed? Chris should have told her.

He'd always been protective of her though. Maybe because he tried to live up to the role of a big brother even though they weren't blood relatives. After her real parents and brother had died in the boating accident, her aunt and uncle adopted her. Chris was her uncle's stepson, but he had always been there for her. Maybe he'd thought seeing this would hurt, and maybe it would have a few years ago. But the pain of losing her parents had faded enough over the twenty years since they'd died that she could handle it now. She struggled with the lock a bit, then gave up. It wouldn't budge without a key.

As she rose, she heard a squeak as if someone was coming up the steps. Could Garret have found her already? There, it came again. Her chest squeezed and she looked around for her purse, then remembered she'd left it in the kitchen. Without her fingers around the reassuring barrel of a can of bear spray, she felt helpless and exposed.

Phantom trotted toward the door with his tail wagging, and a bit of her trepidation lifted. The dog hated Garret. "Who's there?"

"Hey, Phantom." A familiar male voice echoed up the steps.

Relief nearly made her light-headed. "Chris? What are you doing here? I didn't think you were due back from your trip for another week."

Her brother came into view. His blond hair was in need of a trim, and a swath of it lay on his forehead. He wore a crisp gray suit and white shirt. His blue eyes lit when he saw her. He held out his arms, and she ran to hug him.

She buried her nose in his jacket's rough texture and inhaled the scent of cold and wool. "You scared the fire out of me. I heard your footsteps on the stairs and thought Garret had found me."

Chris released her, and his smile vanished. "Garret called me today. I told him to take a hike. I can't believe how he's treated you. I hate to say I told you so. I never wanted you to leave and go to a big city. It's not safe. But you'll be safe here."

Chris and Garret had been bunk mates when they both joined the Marines right out of high school. Though they'd come from different parts of the country, they became best friends immediately. Chris had gotten out after six years to work as a college recruiter, and Garret had gotten out right after that. Chris had been livid when she moved to Washington to be with Garret a year ago. He'd been right all along.

It was good to see her older brother again. Since their parents died in a house fire five years ago and she left Rock Harbor, they'd spent three Christmases and a week one summer together. It wasn't enough.

She gave him another hug, then released him. "What did he say? Does he know I'm with you?" Her hands shook as she tucked a loose strand of hair back into place on top of her head.

"I didn't tell him if that's what you mean, but yeah, he suspects. I mean, why wouldn't he assume you'd run back to your hometown? It makes sense, and he's not stupid. I told him not to try to find you and if he hurt you again, I'd kill him."

"You don't think he'll come here?"

Chris hesitated before he shook his head.

She studied his expression. "What aren't you telling me?"

He loosened his tie with a blue stripe. "I heard some background noise that sounded like a waitress. She said, 'Here's your beef pasty, love.'"

Dana reached out to touch Phantom's head and took a calming breath. "So he must be in the U.P." Up here in Yooper country was about the only place she knew where pasties were commonly sold.

"Maybe." His smile came back. "But hey, I'm home until Sunday. I'll be on the lookout for him." He glanced around. "What do you think of your room?"

"It's gorgeous, Chris! The touches you had for me on the second floor made me feel right at home. I can't wait to dig in with paint."

"Good. It's your home forever if you want it. I have plenty of room, and I'm not here enough for us to get in each other's way."

She pointed to the cedar chest. "I didn't know that survived the fire. It was my real mom's."

The smile seeped from his eyes. "I didn't want to make you sad."

"I'm okay now. I'd love to see what's left. Could I get the key?"

"I don't have it. I never had the heart to look through it myself. There's a box of stuff in the basement I saved from the fire. It might be in there. We could look." He gave a mighty yawn. "I'm starved. Is there anything in the house to eat?"

"Boone brought some food by, and I got a few groceries." She went toward the stairs. "I'll fix you some dinner."

Her loneliness and fear were gone with her brother here. Chris would make sure everything turned out all right. He always did.

Sitting in the kitchen with Chris was like old times. She watched him as he wolfed down a sandwich. He'd taken off his jacket and rolled up the sleeves of his white shirt. They'd often spent evenings like this together, and she was so blessed to have him to herself again. He was incredibly good looking and such a kind man as well.

He lifted a brow her direction. "Why are you looking at me like that?"

She couldn't hold back a small giggle. "Just wondering how you've managed to escape the clutches of a wife. You're everything a woman would want."

He grinned. "Spoken like a loving sister." Rising, he carried his plate to the sink, rinsed it, then placed it in the dishwasher.

"Way to avoid the question." She stretched and yawned. "My furniture is supposed to get here on Monday. That space on the third floor is fabulous too. I might take that for a living room area if you don't care."

"I told you that you can have both floors. I have everything I need down here. It's really too big a house for me, but Dad always talked about how it would be a great building to restore and turn into a home. I couldn't resist it when it went to auction." He nudged her shoulder and grinned. "I'm just glad to have you here. I've missed you."

"I missed you too. It's good to be home." Things between them had been a bit strained since she'd left to follow Garret to Washington. If only she'd listened to Chris right from the beginning.

He held out his hand to help her up. "Want to look for that key in the basement?"

Though she was feeling a little lazy, his suggestion perked her up. "You bet."

"I'm warning you that there are likely spiders down there. I've never gotten around to cleaning out the place. Things are stored down there from when this was a hotel."

She suppressed a shudder. "My brave knight of a brother can bring the flyswatter. You can go first."

He grinned and went to the pantry for the flyswatter and a broom, then led her to the basement door on the pantry's other side. "Let me sweep the cobwebs out of the way first." Brandishing the broom, he brushed down the ceiling as he descended the stairs. "All clear," he called up to her.

She sneezed at the basement's musty odor and kept an eye out for creepy crawlies as she joined Chris at the bottom of the steps. The single bulb overhead cast a sickly light over the space. One room branched off to the right and another to the left. The limestone walls told her the building was old, and the heavy shelves lining the walls were equally old and filled with ancient items like bent and rusting flatware, old linens thick with mildew, broken Christmas tree ornaments, cans of rusty paint, old shoes, and several old paintings.

She blew the dust off a watercolor of a Paris scene. "This is pretty. I might put it in my room."

"It's all yours." Chris's shoes crunched on grit as he walked off to her right. "I think that stuff I told you about is over here under the stairs." He stopped to click on another light, and the back area grew brighter.

This area looked more likely to contain spiders, so she gingerly followed him. "Keep that flyswatter handy, Sir Chris."

His low chuckle rumbled. "Here it is."

His broad back obscured her view, but the scrape of something on the floor told her he was pulling it out and checking for nasty creatures. She caught a glimpse of a large cardboard box, the kind copier paper came in.

He scooted it around under the light and brushed it off with the broom, then lifted the lid and set it aside on the floor. "Have at it, kiddo."

The scent of smoke still clung to the contents, and she could hardly force herself to dig into them. "Who packed this stuff?"

"Jane Cork. She said she threw in things she thought we might want someday."

Jane was their mother's best friend. She'd lived next door with her husband who owned a marina. The box contained a jumble of things. Dana spied an old Bible, two passports, a Best Teacher trophy with her uncle's name on it, several books that might be journals, and a mishmash of old jewelry in the bottom.

She sorted through the jewelry. "Here's the key." She lifted it in triumph. "I think I might like to take the Bible and journals to my room if that's okay."

"Better off with you than stuck in this old, damp basement."

She tucked the items under her arm. "Let's go check out the chest."

Chris put the lid back on the box and slid it into its hiding space under the stairs. "Lead the way."

It was like a treasure hunt, an exploration into their past. Did he feel the excitement of it the way she did? She shot him a glance, and his blue eyes held an intent expression too. It was like reconnecting with their former selves.

The third floor held a glimmer of light from the moon outside. She flipped on the lights and went straight to the chest. "I hope this fits it." She inserted the key and turned it until it clicked. "It's open!" She struggled to open the lid, so she stepped back and let Chris lift it.

Kneeling in front of it, she removed the contents: old baby pictures of her, her birth certificate, report cards from her early school years, old baby clothes, and several favorite old toys she'd forgotten about long ago.

Chris bent over and picked up a picture of Dana with a little boy and two smiling adults. "This is from when you were little, before you came to us."

A lump formed in her throat as she took the picture and stared at her first family. She wanted to cling to her few memories of that time, but she didn't want Chris to see how much it hurt. It would bother him if he thought he wasn't enough to make up for the loss of her first family. "I sometimes forget you're really my cousin and not my brother."

"Since our parents made it legal, I'm your brother in all the ways that count."

She placed the items back inside the chest, then shut it. "I don't know what I would have done if it hadn't been for you."

"Luckily, you'll never have to find out."

CHAPTER 7

The sun shone out of a crazy blue sky, and the temperature in Lihue was a balmy eighty degrees when Lauri exited the terminal into the open air baggage claim. The sweet scent of flower leis filled the air. Her spirits immediately soared as she retrieved her luggage, then made her way across the drive to a covered area servicing car rental customers. She got in line behind a man with short brownish-blond hair who smiled at her. He reminded her a little of Brad Pitt when he was in his early thirties. The appreciative expression in his intensely blue eyes filled her with warmth.

"Been to Kauai before?" His voice was deep and masculine.

"It's my first time." She shifted her shoulder bag to her other arm. "I'm here on business. You?"

"Here on business too. I come this way every few weeks." He stuck out his hand for her to shake. "Peter Lovett. I sell pharmaceuticals so I hit all the clinics and the Lihue hospital when I'm here."

"Lauri Matthews. I'm auditing the books at a clinic in Poipu. I'll be here for a week. How about you?"

He motioned for her to go ahead of him in the line. "I'll be here for a week. You staying down in the Lihue area?"

She handed her paperwork to the clerk. "I'm in a condo at Prince Kuhio."

"That's on the south shore, just across the road from my place. You like to snorkel?"

"I've never gone, but I'm eager to learn."

"The best snorkeling on the island is right across the street at Lawai Beach."

She answered the clerk's questions and took her paperwork. Did she dare flirt with this guy? He seemed much more sophisticated than she was used to, but the fact that he was a little older and settled appealed to her. She loved the way his eyes never left her face and the way he leaned in slightly when talking to her.

She moved away from the desk to give him space. "I don't suppose you'd like to teach me how to snorkel?"

"I'm all yours." His tone indicated a deeper meaning. "Wait a minute and we can take the shuttle together."

Her smile widened, and she moved a few feet away and waited in the shade. The car rental employee greeted him with a "Back again?" comment. The air felt different on the island, redolent of flowers and the sea. She already loved it.

Peter wore a frown as he joined her. "They don't have a car for me. I can get one tomorrow, but they have nothing today. I don't suppose I could bum a ride with you to South Shore? I'll take you to dinner as a thank-you. I know all the great places to eat in Koloa and Poipu."

She hesitated just a moment, remembering all the warnings her brother had given her over the years. But this was a businessman, and the employee had clearly recognized him. She was being ridiculous. "Of course you can!" She had a hard time keeping her smile from becoming a beacon. "I was dreading my first night alone in a new place."

He motioned for her to go ahead of him in the line to board the shuttle. "I suggest we stop on the way and get a few groceries at Big Save. You'll want food for breakfast at least. Maybe lunch stuff too if you tend to pack your lunch."

"I'm so glad you know your way around. It'll make it so much easier for me."

Fifteen minutes later she took possession of a Chrysler convertible and let him drive. He pointed out interesting attractions along the curving road to Koloa. She took pictures of the tree tunnel into town and felt the stress of the long flight drop away. Had anyone ever made her feel as special as Peter did? She couldn't think of a single person, not even her brother, Kade. Peter had an intensity about him that made her feel she was the most beautiful woman in the world.

They bought a few groceries at a small store in the tiny town of Koloa, then drove out the winding narrow road to the condo complexes. The ocean across the street was impossibly blue, and the salty aroma of the sea blew into her face on the breeze. Prince Kuhio condos were across the road from the ocean beside a small park. Kuhio Shores had balconies right out over the spray of water.

He parked in the Prince Kuhio lot and opened his door. "Here we are. Where are you?"

"Two hundred and twelve." She looked across the street at the surf hitting the rocks. A few snorkelers picked their way down the lava. The sound of the surf carried across the little country road, and she was eager to put her toes in the sand and water.

He opened her door. "I'll carry your bags up, then come back and get mine. We might as well leave the top down since we'll be back down for dinner. Let me see if I can get a reservation at the Beach House so we can watch the sunset. It will be a perfect ending to the best afternoon of my life. I'm glad I met you, Lauri. I think it's going to be life changing."

Warmth circled her like a mother's embrace. Did he really feel like that? She watched him pop the trunk and grab her suitcase. She took her carry-on from the tiny backseat and followed him up the concrete stairs to her condo. They found her door, and she got out her key. How did she attract the attention of such a classy, good-looking guy? It was a miracle.

After she opened the door, Lauri paused on the threshold. "Let's get changed and we can meet in fifteen minutes."

He set her suitcase down inside and grinned at her. "You are so special, Lauri. I saw that right from the start. I can't wait." His voice was low and oh-so-seductive.

Heat ran up her neck, and she couldn't say a word. Smiling, she shut the door and grabbed her suitcase.

———

The bite of the cold air stung Bree's cheeks, and she tightened the scarf around her neck. An early snowstorm had dumped three inches of snow overnight and brought in enough cold air to freeze the falls. The ice all around her crackled a welcome as they stepped on it. Samson romped to the edge of the waterfall through the fresh snow, then turned to look back at her as if to ask what was taking her so long.

Dana and the three others on the search seemed to have no trouble keeping up with the dogs. Dana's blue eyes sparkled with excitement as she paused to wait for Bree with the dogs. "Are you sure about this?" Her gaze seemed locked on to the wall of ice.

The frozen waterfall's glittering surface rose eight feet in the air to Bree's left. The river above them plunged down to a frozen shallow pool before continuing to meander toward Lake Superior. The entire river had frozen over two weeks ago, but there were no tracks in the area, so Bree was sure they would be the first to climb the ice.

"You don't have to go. Ice climbing isn't for everyone. I hid the scent article at the top of the waterfall." Bree nodded toward the dogs who were milling at the foot of the falls. "What I wanted everyone to experience is what to do if your dogs are clearly showing signs of the scent, but it's in a place inaccessible to them. Do you give up?"

Emily, a teenager with soft brown hair, shook her head. She was Naomi's, Bree's best friend, stepdaughter. "You have to at least check it out, right?"

"If I were out looking for a lost person right now and saw the dogs acting this way, I'd assume the target was nearby, maybe at the top of the waterfall because of the direction the dogs are looking. Which is why as a searcher you always have to be in good shape and prepared for anything. How are we going to get up there?"

Dana looked to the top of the frozen waterfall. "Climb the ice?"

"Exactly." Bree slipped the backpack off her shoulders and unzipped it. "I brought ice climbing gear." She dumped out crampons, ice axes, and helmets into the snow. "How many of you are familiar with mountain climbing?" When only Dana hesitantly raised her hand, Bree sent the others a reassuring smile. "The rest of you can stay here while Dana and I demonstrate. If we'd been climbing a higher waterfall, I would have brought belay devices and carabiners, but with this short one, we can easily climb it in a few minutes."

She handed crampons to Dana and watched to make sure

her friend knew how to attach them to her boots. Once they were attached to her satisfaction, Bree put on her own and handed two ice axes to Dana, then took two herself. They both donned helmets, and she led the way to the small waterfall. "We'll use the axes to pull ourselves up, then the crampons will let us stay stable to move up the sheet of ice. You'll notice as the water froze, it left many ledges and ridges that will make it easy to climb."

"I'll watch you climb first," Dana said. "It's been ages since I did any ice climbing. I'm pretty rusty."

"Sure thing." Bree shouldered her ready pack and walked to the base of the falls. She hit her ax into the ice above her head, then drove her crampons into the jagged ice and settled both feet before placing the other ax a foot higher than the first one. She climbed closer to the top ax, then removed the bottom one and continued to replicate her technique.

It took only five minutes to climb the short wall of ice. She looked down to see Dana coming right behind her. The cold wind at the top of the waterfall nearly took her breath away as she watched Dana haul herself up the waterfall. Dana's cheeks were pink from the wind which had teased strands of brown curls out from under the helmet.

"Good job!" Hands on hips, Bree turned to look at the nearby forest of wind-stripped trees. "What should we do now?" she called down to the rest of the searchers. "Our dogs are below and can't lead us directly to whatever they smelled."

Emily cupped her hands around her mouth. "Survey the area yourself. Call out for the missing person."

"Right." Bree raised her voice. "Naomi, where are you?" She'd cajoled Naomi into hiding up here. She waited a few moments. "There's no answer. Do I give up?"

"No," Dana said. "She might be unconscious or unresponsive so we do a sweep of the area on foot." She took off toward a tight cluster of trees protected by a large rock formation. "This would be a natural place to shelter." She stepped around the side of the boulder, then stopped short and put her hand to her mouth. "Bree, come quick! Naomi's been injured. There's real blood and she's unconscious."

Bree felt as though she'd been kicked in the chest. Naomi was like a sister to her. Bree broke into a run across the snow and caught her breath as she rounded the boulder formation. Naomi lay on the ground with a red stain pooling below her head, her thick braid rolled out like a brown rope. A nasty gash gaped on her forehead, and Bree pulled a sterile pad package out of her ready pack and ripped into it.

She pressed the pad against the cut. "Do you have a signal here?"

Dana checked her phone and nodded. "I'll call for help."

"Don't call 9-1-1. Call Mason directly and have him send a helicopter up here ASAP. I don't like the way she's breathing." Naomi's chest barely moved with short breaths. Bree checked her pulse, which was thready and uneven. "Naomi, open your eyes." Through a fog she heard Dana give the sheriff their coordinates.

Dana gasped and Bree looked up. "What is it?"

Dana pointed to a wool scarf caught on an aspen tree branch. "I knitted that for Garret." She sprang to her feet and stared into the shadows. "He must have been here. Maybe he attacked Naomi."

CHAPTER 8

A helicopter? Winded from his hike, Boone exited the trees to see a rescue chopper hovering overhead. A person strapped into a basket dangled from the chopper and slowly rose to the waiting rescue worker.

Boone looked around and saw several people clustered at the top of the waterfall, then recognized Bree and Dana. The puffy coats and snow pants they wore made them look like the Pillsbury Doughboy.

The *whop-whop* of the chopper blades nearly deafened him as he went over to see what was going on. "Who's hurt?" The noise overhead made him lean in close to Dana's ear to be heard.

"It's Naomi O'Reilly. She's still unconscious and has a head wound that's been bleeding quite a lot. I think Bree got the bleeding mostly stopped."

He fell silent as they watched Naomi being loaded into the helicopter. When the sound of the rotors finally faded, he leaned close again. "She fell when climbing?"

Dana shook her head. "She was hiding for us to find, but someone attacked her."

He frowned. "Show me."

"This way." Dana led him toward a stand of boulders. Bree followed slowly.

Multiple boot prints marred the white snow, and a bloodstain emphasized the area as well. Boot tracks led off into the woods to the east. "You didn't come that way?"

"No, we climbed the falls."

When Dana started to follow the prints, he caught her arm. "Mason won't want the scene contaminated any more than it already is."

Dana bit her lip and shifted from foot to foot.

He followed the direction of her gaze to a bright blue-and-black scarf hanging from a tree limb. "That's not yours or Bree's?"

Dana shook her head. "I made it though. It was a birthday present to Garret. Chris got home on Friday night and told me Garret called him. In the background Chris heard a server mention a beef pasty so he thought Garret might be in the area. This makes it clear that he is."

"You think he attacked Naomi? Why?"

"I don't know. Maybe she saw him doing something illegal."

Bree pushed down her hood. "Then why didn't he kill her?"

"Maybe you interrupted him. She didn't say anything?"

Bree shook her head. "She was unconscious the whole time. I've got to call Donovan." She pulled off her gloves, then dug into the pocket of her down jacket and extracted her cell phone.

She walked a few feet away to call Naomi's husband, then turned back to Dana. Her eyes were shadowed. "This isn't your fault."

"You don't know that." Her voice quivered. "He might have been waiting for me."

"How would he know where you were?"

"I texted Chris to let him know I was on a training session this morning. What if Garret figured out my cell phone number and is intercepting my texts? He's a whiz at anything to do with electronics. You should see the toys he has." Dana's voice rose the longer she talked. "He even has some kind of thing that picks up voices from yards and yards away. For all I know he was outside the house when I talked to Bree on the phone and made plans to come out here."

She had a point. Boone looked back toward the woods and wished he could investigate. Once Mason showed up, he'd tag along and see what he could find out. "Did you call Chris to see if he's heard anything more from Garret?"

"He'll just worry. Or say I told you so." Dana sighed and reached into her pack for a bottle of water. "Most days he makes me feel like I'm twelve instead of twenty-eight."

She didn't look a day over eighteen with her pink cheeks and beautiful skin. Boone dragged his gaze away from the intense blue of her eyes. "A big brother is supposed to act that way." His voice trembled a bit, and he cleared his throat.

When she touched his arm, he looked back at her again. "I'm sorry. Your sister was younger than you too, wasn't she? I never met her, but Allyson really loved her."

"They were like sisters. I was two years older, and it was always my job to take care of her. Allyson is taking a look at Garret. You know anything about his travels?"

The softness vanished from her eyes, and she removed her hand. "Not really, just that he has a route, but I'm sure that's the case with most salesmen. I hope Allyson doesn't call him or attract his attention in any way. He's a scary guy, and I'd hate for her to be in his crosshairs."

"You should call Chris and let him know it's likely Garret is here. He's going to hear about it sooner or later."

"True, but I think I'll wait until I get home. He's probably on a recruitment visit." A cell phone played "Phantom of the Opera," and she unzipped her pocket and stuck her hand inside. "It's my brother. He might have already heard." She tugged off her glove with her teeth, then swiped the screen. "Hey, Chris."

Boone didn't consciously try to listen as she turned her back and walked a few feet away, but sound traveled in the cold air. From this end of the conversation, it was clear Chris had heard about the attack on Naomi and thought Garret was in the area.

The sound of voices carried up the slope, and the sheriff and two deputies came their way. With any luck Garret would be in custody soon.

———

The heat vent overhead had finally begun to thaw Dana's icy skin. Perched on a chair in the hospital waiting room, she shrugged off her coat and stared up at the television where a news anchor went over the day's events. She didn't hear a word of it as she waited to hear the squeak of the doctor's shoes.

Surely there would be news of Naomi's condition at any moment. Donovan had arrived, and he'd gone back to Naomi's ER room with Bree. One of the other canine handlers had taken charge of Phantom for her, but Samson had gone with Bree.

Had Garret attacked Naomi? The worry played over and over in Dana's head. If her arrival here had brought danger to her friends, she didn't think she could deal with it. And if he was here, what should she do? Chris assured her Garret couldn't harm her here, but being a dispatcher had shown her how a determined stalker could get past any barrier or protection.

Her stomach gave a hard squeeze. She'd spent so much time

trying to feel safe that she wasn't sure she'd ever truly relax and quit looking over her shoulder. Even if Garret left, she'd worry he'd come back. Was there such a thing as a true haven?

That anticipated squeak of shoes finally came, and she shot to her feet as Bree came through the doorway. A weary line crouched between her green eyes, and she was pale but smiling. Samson pranced behind her with his tail up, another good sign.

The smile gave Dana a bit of hope. "She's okay?"

Bree nodded and tossed her green-and-black down coat onto the chair. She ran a hand through her red curls. "She has a mild concussion, but the hospital is releasing her shortly. Donovan was beside himself until she woke up."

Dana exhaled. "Oh, thank the good Lord! I was so worried."

Bree's smile widened. "And she was more worried about us being upset than about having a concussion."

"D-Did she say what happened?" She steeled herself to hear what Garret had wanted and everything he'd done.

"She thinks she fell and hit her head on the rock, but it's all a little fuzzy, probably because of the concussion."

"What about Garret?"

Bree shrugged. "She claims she didn't see anyone."

Dana frowned and shook her head. "Then what was that scarf doing there?"

"Maybe he was in the woods earlier and lost it."

"Or maybe she's not remembering everything. There were those boot tracks leading off into the woods. Did you hear from Mason at all? Boone was supposed to call me after they were done searching, but I don't have a cell signal in here."

Bree picked up her coat. "Coverage is spotty here, but I had one bar in Naomi's room, and Mason called. The boot tracks ended at the road, and they didn't find any sign of Garret. Boone is an expert tracker, and he thinks the tracks were made earlier. Naomi's tracks were layered on top of the bigger prints."

The blood rushed to Dana's head. "So he didn't try to hurt her. I'm so relieved."

"But Mason found no clues to where he is or what he's doing here."

Heavy footsteps pounded toward them on the vinyl tile floor, and a man's bulky form turned into the room. Dana tensed—had talking about Garret conjured him up?—but she recognized the Arizona Cardinals emblem on the black jacket the man wore.

Boone pulled his gloved hands from his pockets. "I thought you might still be here when my calls went straight to voice mail. How's Naomi?"

"Going to be okay. You didn't find Garret?" Maybe he'd come to let her know Garret was in custody.

Droplets of melted snow clung to his dark hair and glistened in the overhead light when he shook his head. "Sorry. You came with Bree so I thought maybe you needed a ride home."

Dana glanced at Bree who nodded and said, "I'll be here awhile longer, and I thought I'd run past Naomi's house and reassure the kids. Emily is taking care of things, but I know she's worried. I'm going to grab pizza and take the kids over to keep them occupied."

Dana slipped her coat on. "I'll head on home then. Let me know if you hear anything else."

"I will."

Dana walked with Boone through the hospital halls filled with dinner trays spilling out the aroma of roast beef that vied with the smell of antiseptic. Her stomach complained again, and she realized she hadn't eaten since breakfast.

Boone glanced at her as they reached the front doors. "Want to stop and grab something at the Suomi Café? The weekly smorgasbord is being served tonight."

She hadn't had their smoked salmon and Lapland cheese bread in years, and her mouth watered at the thought of the Monday night spread at the café. Chris was working again so no one was home waiting on her.

She zipped her coat tighter against the wind as they stepped outside. "That sounds great. We might as well walk. It's only a block and a half."

"Tough woman, hear you roar? Most people don't want to walk in this wind."

She put on her earmuffs. "It feels good to me after the constant rain in Washington. I'm enjoying the thought of winter, even with all the snow coming. You probably hate winter, don't you?"

He fell into step beside her. "Nope, I like winter sports. Even when I lived in Arizona, I lived up in the Mogollon Rim area, where we get snow."

"Zane Grey country. I've read every one of his books. My favorite was *The U.P. Trail.*"

He stopped and grabbed her arm. "I don't think I've talked to another person who has read that one. It's not one most people think about when they hear his name."

"I think it's the best Western ever written."

He took her hand and guided it into the crook of his elbow. "I think we're going to be friends now."

A warm sensation started in her belly and spread to her chest as she stared up into his hazel eyes. "I thought we already were." She cleared her throat. "How'd you end up here?"

"My aunt and uncle were here. And Allyson. After my injury,

I wanted to get away, do something new." His voice went flat. "I bought some land from my uncle, then built my cabins. It was a good move. I love it."

"What do you love most about it?"

Before he could respond, a horn blared into the cold air. A four-wheel drive truck, blue and rusty, roared by. Garret stuck his hand out the window in a rude gesture before the pickup careened around a corner in a belch of smoke.

Dana gaped after the old truck. *He's found me.* She fumbled for her phone. "I'd better call the sheriff."

CHAPTER 9

The bustle of the café was a warm hubbub of welcome around them with people stopping at their back booth to wish Dana well in her new job and to ask them about Naomi. Boone shielded her as much as he could, answering when she went glassy eyed at the questions.

Molly seemed to understand they needed some quiet, and she began to stand guard a few feet away.

"Here, try some cheese bread. It will calm down those shakes." Boone lifted a still-warm piece of cheese to her lips. Known to Finns as *leipäjuusto*, it was a mild cheese that had been fried or baked in a pie tin and cut into wedges, then topped with lingonberry jam. No true Rock Harbor native could resist it.

She turned her head. "I don't think I can eat." She peered past his shoulder at the dark street illuminated by a lone streetlamp. "How could he get away so completely?"

It had been an hour since they'd seen Garret, and they'd only come inside the café when Mason reported no sign of the old Ford pickup. "He's probably got a hiding place nearby. He'll turn up. Mason and his deputies will keep watch."

"That won't do much good." She stared at the plate of food in front of her, then pushed it away with an expression of distaste.

"You need to eat. Starving yourself will just make you too weak to fight when he comes after you. You need to gain about twenty pounds so you can beat him."

Her jaw dropped, then her lips turned up. "Nice try, but you're terrible at jokes."

He pushed the plate back toward her. "Admit it, it was funny."

"Maybe a little." The smile lifted a bit more, and she speared a piece of smoked salmon with her fork, then ate it. "Mmm. They have the best salmon here." She took a tin of sea salt from her purse and sprinkled a bit on her meal, then picked up a piece of cheese bread and waved it his direction. "The truth is you're right. He's going to come after me, and I'd better be ready."

"Hey, I didn't really mean that. The entire town is on the lookout for him. Mason will get him."

"Do you know how many times I've heard that kind of thing in my line of work? It would take both hands to count the number of women I've talked to on dispatch who were trying to get away from an ex-husband or boyfriend who has broken a restraining order."

She probably had a point. He'd never been a dispatcher, but he'd watched the tragedy play out on the news plenty of times. "You have any weapons?"

"I carry bear spray in my purse."

"Better move it to your coat pocket. It will be easier to grab. What about martial arts?"

She shook her head and finally shrugged off her coat. "Maybe I should take shooting lessons."

"I'll teach you. Jujitsu, I mean. I could teach you to shoot as well, but from what I've heard of Waterman, he's more likely to jump you in the shadows. You wouldn't have time to draw a gun or hit him with bear spray. Close-contact defensive moves could save you."

"And he's a whiz with a gun. He was a sniper in the Marines, and he sells Glocks." Those stunning blue eyes studied him a few moments before she nodded. "Okay. Where do you train?"

"I have a small setup at the cabins. I teach lessons on Monday nights at seven."

She shuddered. "If I showed up, everyone would know why I'm there. I bet half the town knows Garret is here by now."

"That's a good thing. The more people who know, the faster we find him. When do you start work?"

"Next Monday. I've got another week of nesting at the house and unpacking stuff. The moving truck arrived this morning, and boxes are crammed everywhere upstairs."

"What hours do you work?"

She cut another piece of squeaky cheese. "I go in at six and get off at three."

"Let's train in the afternoons then, like at four."

"What about your business? Won't you be taking people out on excursions?"

"I'm usually back by three. We can at least get started with some defensive moves." He watched her nibble on the cheese. Why was he so determined to teach her? She wasn't even his type, if he'd had a type once upon a time.

Esther was tall and blonde with a kittenish manner he'd found attractive when they'd met. She would have crumbled at the thought of learning to defend herself. Dana's determination to save herself from Waterman was much more attractive to him now than some clinging violet who had taken one look at his scarred face and run for the door. Literally.

Careful. He shook off the internal warning. This was a friendly gesture, nothing more. He was immune to beautiful women.

"You look like you just bit into tinfoil," Dana said. "What's wrong?"

He shrugged away the memory of his faithless fiancée. "Just thinking about what I should teach you first." He pushed a plate of *pannukakku* toward her. "Eat up. You'll need your strength."

***

That was a close call.

Garret parked the truck in the lean-to and got out. His face was still wind burned from his run through the woods. He shouldn't have been stalking Dana with people around. Had the woman caught a glimpse of his face? The cold stung his cheeks as he got out of his truck, but the cabin he'd holed up in would soon warm.

The wind had scoured most of the snow from the path he was on, but he was ready to sit and rest. Ever since he'd hit Rock Harbor, he'd been in a state of high alert, and he needed a sanctuary, a place to gather his strength and plan his next move.

He unlocked the padlock he'd put on the door and stepped inside. Though it was still cold, at least the wind wasn't stinging his skin. He threw the new dead bolt he'd installed, then went to his cooler to pull out a bottle of beer. He popped the top and took a swig, then put it on top of the cooler and unzipped his coat before starting the propane heater in the corner.

The place was just one room with a bare wood floor, no real kitchen or bathroom, and holes in the log chinks that let in the wind. But it was well off the road, and he didn't think anyone had been here in years. There was even a back door for a quick getaway if someone came to the front. He'd hauled in a sleeping bag and cooler of food, but it was far from comfortable.

He reached up to unwind his scarf, then froze. It wasn't there.

He rushed for the door and unlocked it, then stepped out to the slanting porch and looked over the frozen landscape. No sign of the bright blue-and-black scarf. Had he worn it today? He thought back to his movements. Yes, it had definitely protected him from the wind when he was in the woods. Maybe he'd snagged it on a tree branch in his run to escape after hitting the woman.

What if someone found it? His DNA would be all over it. He took a deep breath and forced himself to calm down. Even if they found it, as long as she hadn't seen him, he would be safe. His name wasn't on it, and it hadn't even been purchased from a store. Dana had made it, so it was unlikely it could be traced to him. In a place like Rock Harbor, many people wore handmade scarves. His was hardly unique.

He reached for his beer and took another swig, relishing the way the alcohol warmed his insides. If the woman died, the law would look long and hard for her killer. He hadn't even meant to hurt her. She'd startled him, and he was just trying to escape. If she died, the fault would lie with Dana. He wouldn't even be here if not for her stupidity. He grinned at the thought of her frightened face when she'd seen him drive by.

He should try to get it back before his scarf was found, just in case. Though he dreaded the thought of going back out into that wind, he pulled on his coat and went to the door. Garret eyed the sky. He only had about an hour before it would be too dark to find anything. He'd have to take his truck at least part of the way, though he'd better try to keep it hidden.

He went to the small shed where he'd stashed his vehicle and shoved open the door. His breath steamed in the air as he turned the key. The engine stuttered twice, then caught. He pumped the gas pedal until the engine purred, then turned on the defroster.

When the windshield didn't clear after the temperature gauge registered warm, he yanked off a glove and held his hand over the vent. Cold air. He swore and banged his fist on the dash. He'd bought it after flying to Houghton, but it was a stupid piece of trash. He dug in the glove box for a napkin, then wiped the windshield, but it immediately fogged back up. There was no way he'd be able to drive without the defroster working. Not in this weather.

Frustration built in his chest, and he gritted his teeth before he turned off the engine and climbed out. He had no choice but to hoof it through the forest back to the waterfall and see if he could find his scarf. When he got back, he'd work on the truck. Otherwise he'd be stuck here with no transportation. He probably shouldn't have been watching Dana with other people around.

The wind picked up as he set off through the trees, and he flipped up his coat hood. It would take him half an hour to hike there. He didn't like how he was leaving tracks either. If someone found his scarf, it could lead them directly to his cabin. He bit down on his lip so hard he tasted blood. He should have gone along the road like he did the first time. They couldn't track him then. Maybe he should turn around.

Here he was sleeping in a filthy, old cabin that let in the snow and wind and living off cold meat sandwiches and stale chips.

But not for long. He had to leave for a few days for work. When he got back, he'd grab Dana and they'd go far away from here to somewhere warm. Somewhere with white beaches and turquoise water, maybe Kauai. The pleasant thought urged him on and kept him warm for the next few minutes until he crested the hill and made the turn toward the waterfall. It was getting dark, and finding his scarf was beginning to look more and more impossible.

He stopped to tie a shoe and heard voices. Garret ducked behind a tree and watched flashlights bobbing among the trees. Even if they weren't looking for him, this was a lost cause. He turned and plunged in another direction that would take him to the road.

CHAPTER 10

D ana couldn't believe she was actually going to do this. She'd unpacked a few boxes before coming here and should have worked all day, but the thought of being with Boone had been irresistible.

Boone's martial arts cabin sat at the end of a row of cabins with a sign designating it. A sign read *Come In,* so she opened the door and stepped into a room about twenty by thirty. A padded mat covered most of the floor, and rings and punching bags hung from the ceiling along the opposite wall. That typical gym smell immediately took her back to volleyball practice when she was in high school.

Boone kicked a heavy bag with grim determination. The beads of perspiration on his square face only added to his attractiveness. She shouldn't be here. She didn't want to feel that almost-irresistible pull toward him. He'd hurt her just like Garret had, or he'd leave her like her parents did. Love wasn't safe. Hadn't she learned that already?

Watching his fluid motions was hypnotic. Did he think about his scars all the time? Maybe he didn't realize a woman didn't notice them after the first shock. His caring manner and strong personality would attract any woman in his circle. The muscles in his thighs flexed as he kicked the bag.

As he twisted in the kick, his expression lost its focus, and he stopped to grab a towel to mop his brow. "You're early. It's only two."

"I haven't started work yet and thought I'd come on out."

"I had a bet with Allyson that you wouldn't show."

"What did you wager?"

"My favorite Arizona Cardinals sweatshirt." He shook his head. "I was sure you'd show up, but she was positive you wouldn't. I could see how determined you are to start a new life without being afraid of your ex."

"You nearly lost." She took off her boots and coat. What would he have thought if he'd seen her pacing her bedroom this morning trying to decide on sweatpants or jeans? She put on jeans and a sweatshirt at first before she forced herself to change into sweats. When she'd told Chris on the phone what she was planning, he tried to talk her out of it.

It hadn't taken long to remember how often she felt inadequate in her big brother's shadow. He'd always made her think she needed a man to take care of her, but she was through with that kind of needy attitude. If she didn't make a change now, she'd be forever stuck in making the wrong choices every time. She didn't want to feel needy, and she sure didn't want another man in her life.

Boone motioned to her to join him on the mat. "I've been thinking about what I want to teach you. Rather than pick a specific martial art like karate or Taekwondo, I think we'll focus on defensive moves. I also want to show you how to kick so you can get your leg muscles as strong as possible. Most women have better lower body strength, and you can do some damage that way with a little bit of knowledge."

"Okay. What kind of defensive moves? I sit at a desk all day, and my arms are about as strong as cooked noodles." She should be ashamed of how she'd sat on her duff in Washington and hadn't darkened the door of a gym in years. Little by little, Garret had isolated her and kept her from doing the things she used to find important. Like a frog in slow-boiling water, he gradually changed her.

She didn't recognize the person staring back at her in the mirror most mornings, but she wanted to find herself again. Maybe someday she'd be like Bree, calm and self-assured. She could dream anyway.

She practiced a calm, confident smile. "Let's do this."

He stared at her. "Let's take the mask off, okay? You're not nearly as confident as you like people to think. And it's all right."

The blood from her head rushed south. "I don't know what you mean."

"Sure you do. Right now you want nothing more than to turn around and run. You're out of your element so you're hiding behind that smile. You'd hate for someone to think you couldn't handle anything life throws at you."

Her smile faltered and died on her lips. How'd he know that? She inhaled and squared her shoulders. "Let's do this. What's your plan?"

"To start with, I want to teach you how to stand for best stability and strength." He positioned her in front of the punching bag. "Stand with your feet staggered and facing forward, not angling off to either side. Your knees should be slightly bent and fluid."

His warm fingers pressing into the flesh of her arms shot a warm tingle along her skin, but she forced herself to follow his instructions.

"Good. First thing to remember is you don't want to step closer to administer any of the strikes I'll show you in a little while. If he's too far for you to use your hands, then use your feet and give him a hard kick in his knee. To do that, you can't be afraid to kick out with all your strength. Let's practice. To kick out, turn a bit to the side and punch out with your foot like this." A loud *thud* echoed from the high ceilings as his bare foot hit the bag.

She eyed the punching bag and imagined where Garret's knees might be. Gritting her teeth, she struck out with her foot, and the impact sent ripples up her leg.

"Nice, but turn your foot a bit more so you're not hitting your toes against the knee. You have more strength in the side or blade of your foot." He demonstrated the move again.

She nodded and did it again. This time the punching bag yielded a satisfying *thud* and swung away from her.

"Great job. Now practice that for a bit and alternate your legs to get a feel for which one gives you the most stability and powerful kick." He folded his arms across his broad chest and stood back to watch her.

Her stance was probably off, but right now, she didn't care. Imagining Garret on the ground and unable to hurt her drove her on to kick and kick and kick some more. She had no idea how long she stayed at it, but when Boone finally stopped her, she was drenched in perspiration and breathing hard through her mouth. Her leg muscles ached too.

He handed her a clean white towel. "You were imagining hitting Waterman, weren't you?"

She dabbed the towel over her face and nodded. "He's likely the only one I'll ever have to take down."

"It's good to personalize it, but you have to be prepared for anyone coming after you. Someone could jump you in an alley or a parking lot. I want you prepared to handle it all."

"I'll get there." She handed the towel back to him. "I'd better get home to shower and put away more of my stuff."

"It's only three thirty. How about I show you around the camp before it gets dark? I'd even come help you unpack if you need a strong back."

She shouldn't agree, but she found herself nodding and turning toward her shoes and coat.

———

Boone watched as the boats pulled onto the shore of Lake Superior. "You ever been ice sailing?"

She looked adorable with her red nose peeking out from under her fur hood. "I've heard about it but never tried it. I saw boats in Houghton when I went to college and always wanted to try it. How long have you been taking people out?"

"About two years. I was the first outfitter here to rent out boats. Until I opened, everyone had to go to Houghton."

It had taken every bit of money and sacrifice he could muster to make a go of it at first. People in this area were more interested in renting a snow machine rather than an iceboat. His sister had created a website for him, and it had brought in tourists. Just a trickle at first, but that small stream had turned into a flood this past year.

His heart squeezed. Renee would never know how her work had helped him. She died before it had all turned around.

Dana touched his gloved hand. "You look sad again."

He forced a smile. "No one ever says that but you. I'm fine."

"No, you're not. Your eyes went all distant, and your mouth tugged down at the corners. You hunched into yourself as well."

"What are you, some kind of body language expert?" He wasn't ready to talk to anyone about Renee. It was still too painful.

She removed her hand. "A dispatcher learns to read people. Besides, as I recall, you spent some time telling me I was putting on a front. The road goes both ways, buddy."

He'd offended her, and he hadn't meant to get so prickly. "I was thinking about how my sister made a website for me. My business is successful thanks to her. And I never got to tell her." It felt good to say it instead of keeping it pent up inside.

Her blue eyes went soft, and she tucked a stray curl back under her hood. "I'm sorry. I remember how I felt when my parents drowned."

"They drowned? How old were you?"

"Eight. That's when I came to live with Chris and his parents."

He shook his head. "Wait, I thought Chris was your brother."

"Well, he is. They adopted me. But his dad was my dad's brother. Chris was my aunt's son and my uncle's stepson." She smiled. "It's complicated, I know. He was fourteen when it happened. We'd been here for a vacation and were out on Superior. Chris was with them, and I was with his parents. They beached their boat for a picnic, and they must have broken through the hull somehow because after they launched again, the boat sank.

"Chris was the only one wearing a life jacket. He tried to get the locker open to get to the other jackets, but it was locked." Her voice broke and she looked out over the lake. "He was freezing cold and frantic by the time my uncle pulled him from the water."

The scene played out in his head like a movie. What a horrific thing to experience at such a young age. "Did they recover the bodies?"

"The Coast Guard searched for four days. My uncle barely slept because he was out on his own boat. Dad was his only sibling." She rubbed her head. "To tell you the truth, I try to block out as much of that awful day as I can. It was at Copper Falls. Superior doesn't give up her dead easily."

The lake still held many a sailor in death's grip. The cold water and lack of bacteria tended to keep bodies on the bottom.

This time he touched her hand. "So you stayed in Rock Harbor and never went back to your home. Where did you live before?"

"Washington. That's one of the reasons I agreed to move when Garret asked me. I wanted to see if I remembered any old friends, to walk the same streets I did as a child, and to see the house where I'd lived for eight years. It wasn't what I expected. So much had changed. None of my friends were even still in the area, and they'd torn down the school I attended. Even the house looked different, smaller somehow."

He had a feeling she didn't talk about this much with anyone, and the realization touched him. He tucked her hand into his arm and turned her toward the main building. "I can't offer much in the way of dinner, but I make a mean deli sandwich, and I've got chips. Sound tempting at all?"

"After that workout, I could eat one of these rocks." Her rumbling stomach punctuated her words, and she laughed. "See?"

He shortened his steps to match her stride. "You nervous about starting work next week?"

"A little. I'll have to prove myself to the other dispatchers even though I've been doing it for years. A dispatcher's shift is spent praying for boredom because a true emergency can leave you scarred for life. It could be a kid who found her mother dead of an overdose or a woman screaming for help as the man who promised to love and protect her beats her brains out."

He grimaced and opened the door to the outfitter's shop. "Why do you do it then?"

Color ran up her neck. "I like to help. It's a pretty lame excuse, I know, but it's all I've got. When the worst happened to me, I wished I had someone to talk to, but everyone was so focused on finding my parents that I sat in the corner by myself for four days. I often follow up with the callers and stop by to see them. It's not much, but it's something. And isn't that all any of us can do in this life—what we can?"

Her earnest expression touched his soul. He needed to do more of that himself.

CHAPTER 11

B ree chose not to say anything about Emily's new hair color as the fifteen-year-old let her into the house. "Good morning, honey. How's Naomi doing?" It was hard to keep from staring at the pink hair.

From the entry she could see into the living room, which for once didn't look like a tornado had scattered toys. Naomi's golden retriever, Charley, tail swishing, came to greet her. Samson whined, and the two dogs sniffed noses.

Emily kept the door open after letting Bree inside. "She's fine. Cleaning up the kitchen after breakfast. I've got to run to catch the school bus. My brothers are already waiting." She tossed her hair a bit as if gauging Bree's reaction.

The girl was probably already turning heads. Slim but curvy, she had a vivacious personality that matched her usually dark curls and beautiful complexion. Today she wore leather boots over slim-fitting jeans and a pink parka that fought with her hair for dominance.

Bree might as well take pity on her. "Did you color your hair yourself? Nice pink shade."

"Mom helped me. Dad threatened to lock me out of the house,

but Mom intervened, and he didn't have the heart to say no to an injured woman." Emily flashed an impudent grin, then waved goodbye and shut the door.

Naomi's voice floated from the kitchen. "I'm in here, Bree."

Bree kicked off her boots and went to find her with both dogs trotting after her. Still in red pajamas and fluffy bear slippers, Naomi loaded the dishwasher. Her light-brown hair was in its usual long braid, and she looked bright eyed and happy.

The kitchen smelled totally yummy with cinnamon and berries. Bree snatched a partial pancake before Naomi could deposit it in the trash. "Don't waste it!" It was mostly cold, but the thimbleberry jam made up for it.

Naomi shuddered. "I'll make you a hot one."

"But the thimbleberry jam would be lost." She licked her fingers. "I'd take some coffee though."

"It's fresh." Naomi poured coffee into a pretty blue mug and handed it to her.

Bree went to the table, still sticky with the kids' breakfast. Charley and Samson lay at her feet, the picture of perfect contentment. Bree felt that way herself sitting here in the warm kitchen with her best friend.

Bree took a sip of her coffee. "Coffee always tastes better in a blue mug."

"Which is why that's all I have in my kitchen." Naomi took her own mug of coffee to join Bree at the table. "What are you doing here so early? You caught me still in my jams."

"Just checking on you. You remember anything else about your fall?"

They'd been best friends for years, and Naomi had been her right-hand girl with SAR training. They'd been each other's confidante through romance and marriage and had been there for one another when their children were born.

"I sort of remember that scarf you all talked about. I can't remember much about it. I thought for sure my memory would come back."

"Let's go through everything you remember." Bree sipped her coffee. "You parked along the road, right?"

A frown crouched between Naomi's blue eyes. "Yes, near the cutoff for the lake."

"Did you put on your hat, zip up your coat? Let's go step by step."

"I wore my red sock hat and gloves. It was super cold on the walk out to the top of the falls. When I reached the site, I–I." She rubbed her head. "It's almost there. I just can't quite grab it."

"You often drop articles of clothing on the way to where you want to hide. Did you do that or make it harder?"

"That's it!" Naomi's eyes sparkled. "I went to the top of the waterfall to drop a spare glove I'd worn the day before. I put another one back in the trees to lead them astray and make it a little harder. That's when I saw the scarf on the aspen tree branch. I started to pick it up, then I heard the dogs barking and knew I'd better hide. I went to my spot." Her smile faded. "Uh-oh."

"What's wrong?"

"I didn't fall. I heard something behind me, then it was lights out. I think someone hit me. I heard someone running toward me, feet crunching through the ice, but I didn't get a chance to even turn around."

"So it could have been Garret. Think back. What did you hear, smell, feel?"

Naomi reached for a partial piece of bacon still on the table and popped it into her mouth. Her gaze took on a faraway glint as she chewed. "I smelled wood smoke like he'd been near a fire."

Dead end. But at least Dana had identified the scarf as belonging to Garret. That might be enough.

The warm scent of something cinnamony and sweet hit Boone's nose as soon as Dana opened the door. "Whoa, what smells so good?"

She'd changed into jeans and a V-neck top in royal blue that made her eyes look deep and mysterious. Her brown curls looked still damp and curled around her head. "Homemade cinnamon rolls. I figured if you were going to work hard, the least I could do was feed you."

He deposited his coat into her outstretched hand and looked through the doorway into the living room. "Doesn't look like you've made any changes yet."

"Wait until you see upstairs. This floor is Chris's domain, and I don't want to touch it even though he said I could. I want it to still feel like his haven when he walks in."

Boone flexed his arm. "Let's get to it so I can have one of those rolls."

"Oh, I was going to give you all you wanted before I work you like a mule. They're best when they're warm." She gestured to the door to the kitchen. "Lead the way."

As he stepped into the kitchen, he heard the soundtrack to *Phantom of the Opera* playing in the background. "Music of the Night" was one of his favorites. "A Phantom fan, I take it? Is that why you named your dog Phantom?"

She shrugged. "Well, he was black and the other yellow labs shunned him. It made me think of Phantom's rejection by society."

He snagged a still-warm cinnamon roll and bit into it. "Wow, these are great."

She smiled and reached for one too. "It's my favorite movie. You'd think having watched it so much would have protected me from being attracted to a bad boy like Garret."

"So what attracted you?"

She paused, and a line of puzzlement marred her forehead. "It was his focus, I think. At first it was like there was no one in the world except me. After my aunt and uncle adopted me, I always felt just a little bit invisible. They had Chris, the golden boy who was good at everything. I was average. Average grades, average athletic ability, average looks."

Hardly average with those gorgeous eyes, but he bit back the observation. "And Garret looked harder."

"It was just an act. I found that out soon enough." She fussed with her hair again, pushing it out of her face.

"I like your curls, but you hate them, don't you?"

She rolled her eyes. "I hate the way it frizzes. How'd you know?"

"You're always shoving at it." He reached over and gently tucked a stray lock behind her ear. "You could treat it with respect. It's cute. So what about Garret? Did you realize he was one of those bad boys right from the beginning but you couldn't help yourself?"

She shook her head. "He seemed a dream come true at first."

"Sometimes the bad apples are hard to recognize."

The smile faded in her eyes. "You say that like you have experience. Maybe we have something in common?"

He wasn't ready to talk about Esther. "Maybe I'll tell you

about it someday. So what about the whole Phantom thing. Why's it your favorite?"

"Does there have to be a reason beyond the awesome music?" An adorable dimple appeared in her right cheek.

He wanted to run his thumb over it. "There usually is."

"You'll mock me."

"Never." He put his hand over his heart.

"I know it's silly, but I just love the way it portrays love as lasting a lifetime. Both men loved Christine all their lives, but one with an obsession and the other with a love that wanted what was best for her." She blew her bangs out of her eyes. "I want to make sure I know the difference."

"When you find the secret to that, let me know, okay? Like I said, it's hard to tell the difference."

Her blue eyes went somber. "I think the signs are there if we look for them. I didn't, did you? For example, I ignored how Garret only talked about how I looked on the outside. I skimmed over his insistence on seeing the movie he wanted and going where he wanted for dinner. He rarely asked me what I wanted, and the few times I voiced an opinion, he sulked for the rest of the evening. I just didn't pay attention."

Esther's beautiful face flashed into his mind. She'd been all about showing him off and talking about how brave he was to fight fires. She'd always wanted her own way too. "Good lesson." He swallowed the last of the cinnamon roll. "What do you have planned for me this afternoon?"

"What's your view on painting? Love it or hate it?"

He normally would have said he'd rather take any job but painting, but heaven help him, he wanted to see that dimple again. "Middle of the road. What are we painting?"

"My bedroom. I like the gray green color, but it's marked and faded. If I don't get it painted before I start work, I'll be stuck with it until at least next weekend."

"Lead the way."

He followed her up the stairs to her bedroom. The chests and tables sat out from the walls about four feet, but the bed was still only a few inches out. The curtains and bedding had disappeared, and the weak autumn light flooded the space.

"I couldn't move the bed by myself. I'd like to disassemble it completely so I can put down my own rug. My bed is in the other room too. I want to get rid of this monstrosity. Do we need more help to do that?"

"Heck, no." He hoisted the mattress off the bed. "Where you want this?"

She led him to the empty second bedroom. "Throw it anywhere. I'm not sure what Chris wants to do with the old furniture, but it can live here for now."

He leaned it against a wall that was painted that same ugly green, then went back for the bed frame. Without the furniture, the room looked enormous. She was on the floor opening the paint can, and he caught a glimpse of the color, a pale gray.

As he began to roll the paint on the walls, he found himself wondering where she'd like to go for dinner.

The air was cold and crisp this morning. Bree had stopped by Naomi's to check on her as well as to grab Charley to help Samson with the search for the scarf's owner. None of the rest of her team had been able to come, but she had the two best dogs. Mason and a couple of deputies waited for them.

Her breath blew out in a fog as she stood by where they'd found the scarf and held it under the dog's noses. "Search, Samson. Find him, Charley."

The dogs sniffed the scarf all over, then ran back and forth, their muzzles in the air. The dogs weren't bloodhounds but air scenters. They worked in a Z pattern until they could catch a hint of the one scent they sought. Samson's tail stiffened, and he turned and followed the tracks the man had left.

"We probably won't get anywhere," Mason panted as he jogged with her behind the dogs. "They'll track him to the road and lose him."

She and the sheriff had been friends as well as allies for many years now. His wife, Hilary, was her first husband's twin sister. A stocky man in his early forties with dark curly hair, Mason had often been the stable rock Bree needed when the whole world was quaking.

She wasn't ready to admit defeat yet. "It's worth a try since Naomi remembers being struck. It wasn't an accident."

The dogs moved fast, and her chest burned trying to keep up in the cold air. The dogs reached a clearing and stopped, nosing around again. Samson looked at her and whined. They couldn't have lost the scent yet. The tracks were still right there, and the road was about ten yards away. The dogs should at least track him to the road.

Samson whined again and came to press himself against her leg. "What's wrong, boy?"

Mason walked in a circle around the clearing. "There are tons of tracks through here. Maybe the dogs are confused."

"The tracks shouldn't confuse them." She rubbed her dog's head to comfort him. "He doesn't know which way to go. Maybe the guy circled around enough that the scent leads in several directions."

"Maybe so." Mason shrugged and turned toward the road where he'd parked his cruiser. "It was worth a try."

She called the dogs to her and had them sniff the scarf again, but they continued to mill around the clearing with no idea where to go. It definitely was a bust.

CHAPTER 12

The warm blush of sun on her arms had turned to a golden brown. Lauri stretched on the beach towel, then turned over onto her stomach. Six glorious days in paradise so far, and they had to leave tomorrow. She didn't want it to end. Peter had already come to mean so very much to her. She'd never believed in love at first sight, but she was deep in its throes now. He'd taught her how little she knew about love.

She turned her head and smiled at Peter who returned it. He was as brown as a Greek god in his bright-blue swim trunks and looked just as appealing with his skin gleaming from Maui Babe oil. The scent of kukui nut oil blended with the salty tang of the ocean, adding to her feeling of contentment. Lawai Beach was a small cove, and not many tourists were here today. They had the sliver of golden sand all to themselves except for a retired couple parked under the shade of the tree by the sidewalk. Surfers rode the waves out past the reef.

She reached across the sand to take his hand. "I never want to leave."

His blue eyes darkened, and he squeezed her hand. "Me neither. Let's just run away and stay here forever."

"If only we could. I'm even a decent snorkeler, thanks to you."

His fingers tightened on hers. "You're way more than that to me. I don't know how I lived without you in my life. I don't want to leave you."

"I'll be back in two more weeks. When will you return this way?"

"I'm not supposed to come back for a month, but maybe I can change my schedule."

They had been very much in the moment this whole week, and she realized she'd never even told him where she lived, and she didn't know where he lived. "I don't suppose your home base is in Washington state? I travel there next."

His eyes brightened. "I'm going there next too. Where are you staying?"

"In Seattle."

"I'm in Tacoma. That's not far. I can easily hop over to see you." He sat up and brushed the sand from his hands. "I'm not letting you go, Lauri. You've changed my life. I love you, you know. I haven't said it because it seems so fast, but you are everything I've looked for all my life."

Her mouth went dry, and she sat up quickly. A woman shouldn't get a declaration of love while lying on her belly in the sand. She clasped her knees to her chest. "I feel the same, Peter. I know it's fast, but the minute I saw you, I knew you were special. I don't know what I've done to deserve meeting you, but I never want to lose you."

He scooted over to her towel and put his arm around her. "Don't ever hurt me, Lauri. I couldn't take it."

"I'd rather die than hurt you," she whispered. "I'd never do it."

He tucked a strand of hair behind one of her ears with such

tenderness that she ached. Such an amazing man and he loved *her*. How could that be? Her brown hair and blue eyes weren't anything special. She had an okay figure, but it wasn't one to stop traffic.

She leaned her cheek against his chest, warm with the sun. "Why me?"

"That's what I was about to say. You could have your pick of guys. And I'm older than you. You're what—twenty-three?"

"Yes."

"I'm thirty-six, old by comparison."

"You're not old. You're so strong and handsome you take my breath away."

His white teeth flashed in a smile. "I like to hear that. Would you consider a lifetime with me?"

Her breath caught in her throat. Was he saying what she thought he was saying? Her gaze searched his face, and the love in his eyes brought tears to hers. "I–I feel like I've come home when I'm with you. Wherever you are is where I want to be."

"When things are right, you just know. And I know I want to marry you, Lauri. We'll have a great life together."

His warm arm left her side, and he reached for the beach bag he'd brought. His hand dove inside and emerged with a small white box. Lauri couldn't tear her gaze away. She couldn't think, couldn't breathe. How could her life change so dramatically in a week?

He got on his knees and took her hand. "Lauri, will you marry me?" He opened the box to reveal a diamond ring.

The stone looked enormous to Lauri. Other diamonds twinkled around the platinum setting. A band of rose gold with platinum bands on either side made it unique. "It's the most beautiful ring I've ever seen," she whispered. "When did you have time to get it?"

But there was no lack of jewelry stores on the island. She reached for it, and he snatched it back with a teasing grin. "You haven't answered me."

She threw her arms around his neck, and they both nearly toppled to the sand. "Yes, yes, of course!" Tears made hot tracks down her cheeks. "I'm so happy, Peter, so incredibly happy."

He plucked the ring from its home and slipped it onto her finger. It twinkled in the bright sunlight. A bird landed nearby as if drawn by the ring's glitter. Lauri felt just as mesmerized as the bird.

Peter brushed a kiss across her lips. "Happy?"

"Deliriously. I can't wait to tell my brother and his wife."

His blue eyes darkened. "They might think I'm too old for you."

"Oh don't be silly! They will love you as much as I do. You're not old, and that's final!"

"My friends will say I have a trophy wife. And I do." He nuzzled her neck. "You smell so good. What do you say we bust out of here and go to my place? We can order in sushi and watch a movie. I'd take you out tonight, but I don't want to share you, not tonight when I have to leave tomorrow."

"I can't think of anything I'd rather do," she whispered.

Dana's first day of work. The Rock Harbor Dispatch office looked like most: lots of desk areas with banks of computer screens and the incessant sound of phones ringing. The American flag hung on one wall and county maps covered a perpendicular wall. At least this office had windows along one side that let in the sparkle of sun on the snow outside. The odor of fresh paint permeated the room and overlaid that of sweet perfume worn by one of the dispatchers.

Three other dispatchers looked up briefly when Dana came in. They sized her up before returning to their screens. It must be a busy day, probably people in the ditches from last night's snowstorm. One station was free, so she slid into the office chair and logged in. The radio was already live, crackling with static and voices. The hubbub died down as she put on her headset and rolled her chair up to the keyboard.

"You must be Dana." A woman in her fifties sent a smile her way. Her graying brown hair was cut in a stylish bob, and she wore just enough makeup to enhance her hazel eyes. Her khaki slacks held a precise crease, and she'd topped it with a navy lace top. "I'm Karen Patton, senior dispatcher."

Dana felt decidedly underdressed in her jeans and sweatshirt. Mason had told her the department had casual dress. "Dana Newell. Nice to meet you."

Karen waved a plump hand sparkling with rings toward the woman to her left. "That's Tracie Pitt, also known as 'Babelicious' by the guys." She dropped her voice to a whisper. "Don't let her see you trying to cut into her territory. She's apt to sabotage your computer."

Dana vaguely remembered meeting the younger woman the day she'd interviewed. She sent a smile toward her. Tracie didn't seem to notice the introduction and kept her gaze on her screens. About twenty-five, she had straight black hair. Her high cheekbones and coloring hinted at some Native American in her heritage, though her skin was as pale as if she never went in the sun. Dana could see why the guys hung around her.

The man on Dana's other side stood and stretched. In his early forties, he was about five-ten and stocky with dark hair that hadn't started graying yet. When he held out his hand, she caught the glint of his wedding band.

He shook her hand. "Mark Johansen. You probably don't remember me, but Chris and I used to go ice fishing together."

"I thought you looked a little familiar."

"Tell him to call me the next time he's in town." Mark headed for the door. "See you girls later. It's quitting time for me."

Dana waved as she answered another call, just a breakdown in the county that she reported.

Tracie finally turned from her screens. "So you're the new girl." Her smile didn't reach her eyes. "The guys told me I had competition." Her tone implied she didn't see it herself.

Dana forced a smile. "I'm not even in the running."

Tracie sniffed, but the glint in her dark-brown eyes faded. "You're married?"

Dana shook her head as her phone rang. "Nine-one-one, what is your emergency?"

"My husband! He yelled and fell down. I think he's having a heart attack." The woman was sobbing so hard it was difficult to understand her.

Dana looked at her screen and rattled off the address showing there. "Is that your location? And are you Helen Grayson?"

"Yes, yes! Please send an ambulance."

"I'm sending one now. Please stay on the line with me." Dana opened her mouth to ask the woman if she could pray with her, then pressed her lips together. She didn't want to get off on the wrong foot at her new job.

Once the ambulance was dispatched, she had Mrs. Grayson kneel beside her husband. "Is he breathing?"

"Y-Yes, I think so. But he's not waking up." The woman's voice held a tighter edge of hysteria. "Is he going to die?"

"He's still breathing so that's good. Do you know CPR?"

"No." Mrs. Grayson began sobbing again. "I should have taken a class. We're getting older."

Dana heard the reedy wail of a siren. "The paramedics are almost there. Go to the door and open it so they can get in right away."

"Okay."

The phone clicked in Dana's ear before she could remind Mrs. Grayson to stay on the line, but the paramedics should be walking in the door now. She logged in the details of the call. It felt good to be back in her element, doing what she loved most. The call center fell silent for nearly an hour.

Her phone rang again, and she glanced at the screen as she answered. The cell phone call's coordinates showed on her monitor. "Nine-one-one, what is your emergency?" She looked closer. The cell phone belonged to Allyson.

"He's going to kill me next." The harsh whisper was barely audible.

"Allyson, what's wrong? Where are you?" Dana quickly keyed in the coordinates to send help. "Who is going to kill you?"

Allyson didn't answer, and Dana checked the connection. She hadn't lost it, not yet. "Allyson, are you there? Can you see anyone who might help you? What's happening?" Barely aware of standing, she realized she'd raised her voice. All the other dispatchers were staring at her.

Was that wind on the other end of the line? She stared at the coordinates and tried to make out their location. As near as she could tell, it was close to where they'd trained the dogs yesterday. Had Garret hurt Allyson? Was that what she meant by *next*?

Shudders worked their way down her spine at the continued silence on the phone. "Allyson!" She'd given up hoping for an answer when she heard a choked scream, then the line went dead.

Dana frantically called the sheriff's line to request assistance. But every fiber of her being knew it was too late.

CHAPTER 13

H is nose up, Spirit leaned into the wind. Boone pulled in the mainsail and manipulated the front steering runner to turn the boat. Wind stung his face as he rounded the lake and headed into the breeze. Clouds of snow clung to tree branches from last night's snow, and the only world he cared to know right now was white and cold. He resisted an impulse to stand and shout into the wind. Nothing compared to being out on the ice. The scrape of the runners on the ice was the most melodious sound he'd heard in his life.

He saw a quick movement up ahead, a parka-clad man running for the shore. The guy disappeared into the thick scrub of the tree line. He'd probably been ice fishing, so Boone slowed his boat in case an ice hole lurked ahead. As the boat slowed, he saw something on the ice. Not a hole but what appeared to be a pile of blankets or something.

He took off his sunglasses to see better. Wait, that wasn't a pile of material. A person's face turned up toward the blue sky overhead.

He managed to get the boat stopped in time and yanked down the sail. Boone anchored the boat and stepped out onto the ice.

"Hey!" The person on the ice didn't move, and an icy certainty formed in his gut as he neared.

A woman, her wet hair spread out on the ice, lying on her back. He gasped. "Allyson!" His chest squeezed at the paleness of her skin.

Slipping and sliding on the frozen lake, he managed to reach her side. Blood pooled by her head from a cut on her forehead. There was an open hole beside her as if she'd been ice fishing, but she was soaking wet from her hair to her chest.

He tried to find a pulse in her neck. Nothing. "Allyson!" He tried again to find a pulse at her throat, then moved to her wrist. When he didn't get a heartbeat, he unzipped her parka and put his head onto her chest to listen.

She couldn't be dead. He stared into her beautiful face and began CPR. "Breathe, Allyson!" *Pump, pump.* He counted off the compressions, then blew into her mouth twice before repeating the routine. After several rounds, perspiration dripped from his forehead. There was no response.

What had happened? Maybe she'd fallen. He gave a slight shake of his head. She was wet like she'd been in the water, but if she had, she'd never been able to get out by herself. *That man.*

Half-rising, Boone turned toward the tree line but saw no movement. He yanked off his gloves with his teeth and pulled out his cell phone to call the sheriff. He'd keep doing CPR until help arrived. A sob forced its way past the constriction in his throat, and moisture flooded his eyes. Spirit whined and licked his face.

Before he could dial, he heard the *whup-whup* of a helicopter overhead.

He waved both hands in the air and shouted, "Here!"

The chopper dipped a bit as if to acknowledge his wave, then descended to the ice. The fierce wind from the rotors bit into his cheeks, but he continued the CPR. The helicopter finally settled, and the rotor rotation slowed. Two paramedics disembarked followed by Mason's familiar bulky form. How had they heard about this? Maybe the guy Boone had seen called it in.

Sliding on the ice, the paramedics manhandled the stretcher to Allyson's side. Boone stepped out of the way, though in his heart he knew they were too late.

He took several steps to meet Mason. "I–I think she's gone. I tried CPR, but she's not responding." His voice wobbled, and he knuckled the moisture out of his eyes.

The paramedics checked her, then grabbed the defibrillator. One of them opened her coat and rolled up her shirt to get to her skin.

"Clear!" The paramedic administered the electric shock several times, but Allyson never responded.

Boone sank to his knees and let out a groan. "She's gone."

Mason's big hand came down on Boone's shoulder. "You know what happened?"

Unable to speak again, Boone shook his head.

"Did she call you too?"

Boone lifted his head. "Too? She called for help?"

"She called dispatch. Dana Newell took the call and reported it."

Boone turned and stared at the paramedics as they loaded Allyson onto a stretcher. Their lack of urgency told him everything he already knew. His throat closed tighter again, and he clenched his fists as he struggled to get his grief under control.

"I'm sorry, Boone. Did you see anyone out here who might have done this?"

Done this. Boone raised his head. "You think she was murdered?"

"She called Dana and said, 'He's going to kill me next.' Dana tried to get more information, but the connection ended."

Boone gestured toward the shore. "I saw a man running into the trees. That was before I saw Allyson's body. I didn't think much about it at first, and when I saw the chopper, I assumed he'd gone to call for help."

Mason's hazel eyes sharpened. "What'd he look like?"

"I was too far away to tell. He wore a black parka and snow pants. I'd guess him to be about six feet tall. That's about all I saw because he was so covered up." Boone turned and pointed. "I was back there by the curve when I saw him. I'm not even positive his parka was black. It was just an impression."

He started toward the shore, but Mason grabbed his arm. "This is my job, Boone. Let me handle this."

"You're here by yourself. You can use some help." He held Mason's gaze until the sheriff finally nodded and released his arm. Boone did Mason the courtesy of lagging back to let him take the lead. Spirit loped along beside him.

Mason walked to the side of the large tracks leading into the woods. "I wear an eleven shoe. This looks a little bigger, maybe a twelve."

"Yeah, I wear a twelve. Looks about the size of my print. You recognize the tread?"

Mason knelt and looked more closely at the footprint. "No, but we'll get a mold of it and see what forensics can tell us." He rose and headed for the trees again. "Did you yell at the guy?"

"No. I had no reason to when I saw him. I thought he'd been ice fishing." Why had he assumed that? Boone tried to remember if the man had carried any fishing gear. "I think he might have had something in his hand that I assumed was a pole, but I was too far away to see it."

They reached the trees and followed the prints to the road where the snow was mashed down. "Looks like a four-wheel drive," Boone said.

Mason nodded. "Yep. He's gone."

Bree's head throbbed from crying so much. She sat on the sofa with Kade's arm around her and Samson pressing against her leg. The fire flickered in the hearth, but nothing could penetrate the cold permeating her. How could Allyson be dead? It didn't make sense.

Dana, pale and red-eyed, stirred in the armchair across from Bree. "I should go home." Chris was back from Florida and would want to know what had happened.

The doorbell rang, and Bree sprang to her feet. She half tripped over Samson as she went to the door. Kade would have gotten it, but she wanted to *do something* and get out of her own head. Through the window in the door she saw Boone's bowed head. Her chest squeezed as she yanked on the doorknob and opened the door.

There were no words, so she didn't try to fill the silence with anything. Her eyes filled again as she pulled him inside and shut the door against the wind before embracing him.

His shoulders shook, and he clutched her hard. He exhaled harshly, then pulled away. "Sorry to come so late. I've been with my aunt and uncle. They're devastated."

Allyson's parents owned the local jewelry store and had always been kind to her. "Of course they are. I wanted to see you." She took his coat and hung it in the closet. "Any break at all in the case?"

He followed her into the living room. "No. That guy I saw, his vehicle tracks merged with the road. I drove around aimlessly all afternoon and stopped half-a-dozen people in SUVs and trucks to see if they'd seen anything. It was a dead end."

"When will the coroner rule on cause of death?" Dana's voice wobbled, and she pulled her knees up into the overstuffed chair.

"A few days." He dropped into the other chair beside Dana.

Bree went back to her spot beside her husband. "You look exhausted. Want to stay here tonight with us? The spare room is all yours."

"I have to go home. There's a full day with tourists tomorrow, and I'll need to arrange someone to take my place."

Bree nodded. Boone was never one to neglect his duty.

Kade poured coffee from the carafe into a fresh mug and leaned across to hand it to Boone. "If you need someone to take your place on a hike or ice climbing, I can take a group. I've got some vacation time coming."

Boone shot him a grateful look. "I might have to take you up on that, Kade. I am shorthanded right now."

"There's some new ice out at Copper Falls. I saw it today. I could take a group out there."

"Let me make some calls and see what I've got." Boone set down his coffee and pulled out his phone, then rose and walked into the kitchen. The low rumble of his voice came a few seconds later.

Bree tucked her hand into Kade's arm. She had a good man right here. Not many would jump to help the way he did. "Have you seen Lauri today? I don't think she's come home from the airport yet. I'd feel better if she were home."

"She called and said she was running late."

His tone was resigned, and she knew he'd given up trying to

monitor his sister's life. At sixteen Lauri had been a handful, and now at twenty-three, she held her own life firmly in her hands and brooked no interference. All the worry in the world couldn't corral her even though her headstrong ways had brought trouble her way in large doses over the years. Being with Lauri was like being on a seesaw—one minute you were up when seeing signs of maturity and the next minute you hit the ground because she didn't seem to possess common sense.

The door in the hall banged open, and Lauri called out, "Kade, Bree, you guys here?"

Zorro leaped to his feet with an excited bark and raced to greet her. Still dressed in a parka and knee-high leather boots over slim-fitting dark jeans, she appeared in the doorway with her dog by her side. Her smile faded as she looked them over. "What's wrong?"

Bree held her gaze and told Lauri what had happened. The happy smile and high color drained from Lauri's face. "We don't know for sure what happened, but I'd appreciate it if you texted and let us know where you are until this guy is caught. I was worried when you didn't come home straight from the airport."

Lauri shrugged out of her coat revealing a figure-hugging red turtleneck. She was so beautiful, and a wave of warmth settled in Bree's middle. Even when Lauri was difficult, she belonged to them, was part of them. Bree wanted to keep her safe, to see her grow up and have kids they could spoil. Sometimes she didn't think it would ever happen.

Lauri laid her coat onto the ottoman. "I'll let you know. I didn't mean to worry you." Her eyes sparked, and she tossed her head.

The lamplight glittered on something on Lauri's hand. Bree reached over and caught Lauri's hand. "I-Is that an engagement ring?"

Lauri snatched her hand away, but a smile lifted her lips. "It is. His name is Peter Lovett and he's wonderful."

"I didn't realize you'd been dating anyone. How long have you been seeing him?" Kade asked.

"I don't tell you every single thing I'm doing. I'm an adult, Kade, even if you haven't figured it out yet."

Time to tamp down the antagonism. Bree smiled and took her sister-in-law's hand again. "It's gorgeous, Lauri. And you know we only want you to be happy. Where'd you meet him?"

Lauri shrugged. "What does it matter? I think you'll like him. He's mature and settled with a great job. He's a pharmaceutical rep. Blond with the bluest eyes you've ever seen. He's so kind and sweet to me. Can't you just be happy for once and not grill me over every little thing?" She tugged her hand free again, then petted Zorro.

"Of course we're happy for you." Bree rose and enfolded Lauri in a hug. "Congratulations. When do we get to meet him?"

Lauri's returning hug was perfunctory. "Soon, I hope." She pulled away. "I'm going to bed." Her dog at her side, she stalked off.

Bree sank back on the sofa. "Here we go."

CHAPTER 14

The wind whistled through the trees and whispered along the rocks, and snow had begun to fall as the promised storm moved in. Boone stamped his feet on the snow-covered ground to warm them, but he couldn't bring himself to leave his vigil by the murder site. His friends had wanted to help him, but nothing could numb the pain splitting his chest wide open.

He stood well outside the yellow crime-scene tape and stared at the dark stain gleaming in the moonlight. He should have done something to prevent this. Desperate to bring his sister's killer to justice, he'd egged Allyson on in her investigation. If he'd left this in the professionals' hands, his cousin would still be alive. He knew this into the farthest reaches of his soul.

This was his fault.

A branch snapped behind him, and he whirled. "Who's there?"

A shadow moved from the cover of the trees, and the moonlight illuminated Chris Newell's face. He wore a blue parka and knit cap. "I went by your cabin, and when I saw the lights were out, I thought I'd find you here. Dana told me what happened. I'm really sorry, buddy."

The tension eased from Boone's shoulders. He and Chris did the man-hug thing. "Thanks, Chris. I can't believe she's gone."

Chris stepped back and shoved his hands in his parka's pockets. "I know there's nothing I can do, not really, but I wanted you to know I'm here if you need anything." He gestured back the way he came. "I brought you a beef pasty. You probably haven't eaten."

"Not since breakfast." The thought of food turned Boone's stomach, but it had been thoughtful of Chris to bring something. "Thanks." He took one more look at the stain. "The hole froze over."

"It's twenty below. Wouldn't take long in that kind of weather. Did she stumble on an ice fisherman out here? Maybe she caught him doing something illegal. The sheriff should come out to explore the area under the ice. Maybe she found a guy stashing drugs or something."

"I hadn't thought of that. I wonder if Mason has? It's a good idea." But Boone's gut told him Allyson had died because of her investigation. He hoped he was wrong. It would help ease the guilt squeezing the air from his lungs.

Chris clapped a gloved hand on Boone's shoulder. "Let's get you out of this wind. You look lousy."

"I had hoped the killer would come back tonight."

"I think that only happens in the movies. Why would he run the risk of getting caught?"

"Sick thrills." Boone's blood heated at the thought of some monster gloating over what he'd done here. Allyson deserved justice. So did his sister. He tore his gaze from the murder scene and looked at Chris. "You glad to have your sister here?"

"Yeah, and happier yet she's away from that lowlife Waterman, though I'm beginning to wonder if she's any safer here. I never wanted her to go off with him in the first place and did everything

I could to talk her out of it. She didn't listen, but she knows now I was right."

"You seen him around? We saw him drive through town in a pickup the other day. She thinks he might have done this."

Chris shook his head. "I don't buy it. He's not bright enough to do something like this. He's the kind who strikes boldly in broad daylight and doesn't care about who sees him. The guy who did this was clever and didn't leave any clues."

Boone rubbed his forehead. "Maybe you're right. Waterman tried to drown Dana so Allyson thought he was worth checking out."

Chris went still. "Waterman tried to *drown* my sister?"

"Maybe drown is too strong a word, but yeah, he dunked her face in the kitchen sink. Ask her about it."

Chris clenched one gloved hand. "I'll find out if he's still around. Is the sheriff tracking him down? If he isn't, I will!"

Boone adjusted his knit cap over his ears. "Right now I hope he's looking for a killer."

"We could check it out too, you and me. You have the notes Allyson made on her investigation? Maybe we could start there."

"They're probably in her cabin." He'd given Allyson a cabin at his place to call her own while she was in town. "The sheriff told me to stay out until he had a chance to inspect it."

"If he gets those notes first, we're out of luck."

Boone nodded. "Let's go back to my place and take a look."

He and Chris plunged back through the trees to the road. The fifteen minutes to drive home seemed way too long. Would law enforcement have taken everything by now? A sinking sensation in his gut started the minute he approached his cousin's cabin. There should have been crime-scene tape across the door, but access appeared free and clear. He saw a wadded-up length of yellow tape in the trash barrel by the road as he stepped onto the sidewalk.

Chris joined him. "You have the key?"

"Yeah, but I don't think it will do any good. They've processed this already."

"Let's check to be sure."

Boone punched in the lock's master code, and the door opened. The cabin was a one-room studio. The last time he'd been in here papers and a laptop computer covered the small wooden desk in the corner. That desk was bare now. No computer, no papers. Every drawer had been pulled out, and the bedclothes lay tangled on the floor in a heap. The deputies had been very thorough.

Boone picked up a hair tie that still held a few strands of Allyson's brown hair. "We're too late."

The lights shone out the windows of the lighthouse home, creating a pretty picture. Garret crouched behind the neighbor's shed and watched Bree standing on the back deck as her dog nosed through the snow in the backyard. Once she was gone, all he'd have to do was drop his little gift over the fence into her yard.

"Hurry up, Samson," she called.

Garret had expected her to let the dog out before bed, but he didn't think she'd stay out watching him. The animal was a menace and had nearly led her and the sheriff to his hiding spot. The threat was easily neutralized by the little gift at his feet. Maybe she wouldn't be so eager to poke her nose into someone else's business. And it would teach Dana a lesson as well.

"Go inside," he muttered.

The dog paused, nose up. He swung to face Garret's direction. A low growl carried on the wind, and Garret winced. Surely the mutt couldn't smell him from this far. Dana had prattled on about how a search dog was trained, but he'd tuned her out most of the time. Still, hadn't she said they were air-scent dogs? Maybe the mutt really could tell he was over here.

"What is it, Samson?" Bree came down the back steps and stepped into the circle of illumination from the security light.

Ruff raised on the back of his neck, the dog ran to the fence, barking with urgency. Garret could almost feel the dog's dark eyes fixed on him, though he knew it was too dark for the animal to see him.

"Kade, there's an intruder!" Bree called over her shoulder, then took a couple of steps into the yard. "Is someone there?"

The moon came out from behind the clouds and illuminated the landscape with ghostly light. Garret shrank farther behind the shed and sidled to the other side where he was sure he couldn't be seen. But he could no longer see the Matthews's backyard. Bree could be opening a gate and heading his way for all he knew.

Stupid dog had ruined everything. Garret peeked around the side of the building. Kade exited the house and approached a gate at the back end of the yard. Garret had no choice but to run for his truck. As he ran back along Negaunee Street, he stopped. What an idiot. He'd left the cooler behind. At least he'd been wearing gloves.

Morning sunlight poked through the blinds in Boone's bedroom window. He groaned and threw his arm over his eyes. The bedding had been kicked into a tangled mess by his restless night, and he doubted he'd gotten even a full hour of sleep. Every time he closed his eyes, he saw Allyson's face.

His ancient heater kicked on and blew out some warm air to moderate the cool room temperature. He rose and went to the desk under the north-facing window. Spirit followed him and lay at his feet. After the snowstorm last night, there were likely some cancellations to today's excursion. If there were two or more, he would just call off today's hike to the waterfall. He fired up his e-mail and began to sort it. Yep, three cancellations as expected. He texted the remaining two hikers and told them to reschedule for later in the week. Both were locals so they'd likely call him for another time.

He paged down through his e-mails, then saw Allyson's name on one. It was like a punch to the gut to know she'd sent that e-mail when she was still alive and smiling. His eyes burned, and he gave a harsh exhale before he clicked on the message.

Hey, Cuz! I tried to stop by your cabin this morning, but you were already up and at 'em. Typical! I found some interesting information about Faith Rogerson's death, and it ties in to Renee's in interesting ways. Call me when you get this, and I'll come over.

I know I'm being a little paranoid, but I thought I heard someone outside my cabin last night. Just in case, I'm attaching all the notes I've made on my investigation. I'd hate for all this work to go to waste if someone stole my laptop! I've got a backup, but you just never know. So here it is.

Call me!

A

He pressed his fingers against his temples. Spirit rose and whined, then thrust his nose into Boone's lap. He petted him. How he wished he could pick up the phone and call her. He'd never hear her cheery voice again. With a quick command he renamed the file and saved it under Cancellations. An intruder wouldn't be likely to look there. He couldn't read her notes, not yet.

He closed his computer and pulled on jeans and a sweatshirt, then went to the kitchen. He fed Spirit first, then filled the pot with water. The enticing aroma of coffee filled the room, and he whipped up a bacon-and-cheese omelet, then poured himself a mug of coffee. He flipped on the news. When the local TV station showed the scene on the lake, he turned it up to see if law enforcement had found out anything new, but the reporter just repeated the same old information.

When the knock came at the door, it was only seven. Spirit huffed but didn't bark. Boone was still barefooted and hadn't combed his hair. Through the window he caught a glimpse of Dana's brown hair. He swung open the door, and Phantom immediately touched noses with Spirit before pushing past him.

She studied him. "You look terrible."

"Hey, come in. Your dog already is."

"He has no manners." She stepped inside. "Sorry it's so early. I couldn't sleep. Seems like you didn't either."

"I didn't. So I decided to get up and have breakfast." He held up his mug. "Coffee?"

"Sure." She took off her coat and boots, then followed him to the kitchen and perched on a stool at the breakfast bar. "Nice light granite and white cabinets are my favorite. And oak floors. It's gorgeous. Did you do the work yourself?"

"Yeah, except for the granite." He poured a mug of coffee. "Cream?"

"Just black." She accepted the coffee and curled her fingers around the mug.

He liked the way she looked sitting in his kitchen. Her hair appeared soft enough to touch, and her blue eyes reminded him of Lake Superior on a summer day. Blue and mysterious.

"I bet you're wondering what I'm doing here so early."

The compassion in her eyes told the story. He would have been more surprised if she hadn't shown up today to check on him. To his surprise, he realized he already thought of her as a close friend. That was dangerous. "It crossed my mind, but I figured misery loved company."

She took a sip of the coffee. "I was thinking about Allyson's investigation into Renee's murder. The way she said he was going to kill her next made me assume it was whoever killed Renee. I want to talk to Garret and see if he might have had something to do with it, but I don't want to go alone. I don't trust him."

"You mean, see him today?"

Her lips flattened in a determined line, and she nodded. "I thought I'd see if you'd go with me. I could ask him to meet me somewhere. Garret might not talk if he knows someone else is there, so you could be out of sight but ready to step in if need be. If I hadn't come here, maybe Allyson would still be alive."

"You don't know that." He thought through the plan. While he didn't know this Garret Waterman, he had every confidence in his own ability to handle anyone. "I'm in. What about work? Aren't you supposed to be there already?"

"Mason told me to take the day off. Any idea where we could set it up? Somewhere you can hear yet can't be seen."

"What about Bree's SAR building? No one is using it today, and there's a small storage room just off the office area where I could hide out."

"Great idea! I'm sure Bree would give me the key."

"She never locks it. A hiker nearly froze one winter and managed to get inside her building. It was the only structure around for miles, so she looks at it as a safe haven in the winter." Boone shook his head. "I wouldn't tell her about this until it's all over. She wouldn't like you putting yourself in danger."

"But you think it's okay?"

"Only if I'm there." He gulped the last of his coffee. "Give him a call and let's see what we can find out."

CHAPTER 15

No part of her wanted to ever see Garret's face again. Dana squared her shoulders and pulled out her old phone. She hadn't touched this phone since she got to Rock Harbor. "I reactivated my old phone so he'd recognize the number. Wish me luck."

Boone put his hand on her shoulder. "I'll do more than that and pray for you."

"Even better." The coziness of his living room with its log walls and warm blue rug exerted some calming influence as she settled into a chair by the fire. Phantom plopped down beside her and rested his head on her foot.

The place was small, and she imagined drinking mugs of hot chocolate by the fire and sharing a bowl of popcorn while watching a movie on the big-screen TV over the fireplace. She wanted to plant her head in a face palm for such a crazy notion. She barely knew Boone, yet somehow she felt she knew him well. And hadn't the relationship with Garret taught her anything?

Her hand shook as she called up Garret's number. For a moment she wondered if he would answer, then gave a slight shake of her head. Of course he would. He'd be delighted to taunt her in any way possible.

The phone rang once in her ear before he picked up. "Dana!"

The joy in his voice took her aback. Their relationship had once seemed very special. The deep timbre of his voice always had the power to melt her defenses, and she grabbed the tail of her courage as it turned to flee. "Hi, Garret. Am I bothering you?"

"Of course not. You can call me anytime, day or night. You should know that."

"I–I wondered if you'd want to get together to talk. I'm going through a hard time right now."

"Where and when?"

"Are you still in Rock Harbor?"

He paused before speaking. "You saw me, didn't you?"

She forced a carefree laugh. "You didn't try to hide."

"I guess not. Yeah, I'm close. Not really in town but close."

She didn't blame him for his cautious tone. He had to be wondering about the call. "I have a friend who owns a building out of town." She gave him directions and the address. "Would you meet me there?"

"I can find it. It will probably take me fifteen minutes to get there. What time?"

She glanced at her watch. It would take her only five minutes to get there. "Let's make it in half an hour." He'd likely head there immediately, but so could she. They'd have time to get Boone lodged in the storage room, and she could have her hand on her bear spray in case Garret lost his temper. Hearing his voice started a tremor in her gut that wouldn't go away. He was so unpredictable.

"I'll be there. I'm so glad you called, honey. We can work this out."

It was all she could do to get her numb lips to move enough to mouth, "See you soon." With the call ended she leaned back in the chair and let the phone drop into her lap. "He's going to meet me."

"You sure you want to do this? You're as white as the snow outside." Boone stood over her with his socks in his hands.

The sunlight shone on his scarred cheek, and she hardly even noticed it now. She couldn't say the same for the tanned skin covering sleek muscles and the thick thatch of black hair still standing on end. Even his bare feet were sexy. There was something so intimate about being in a room with him. What would he do if she got up and slipped her arms around his slim waist and leaned her head against his chest?

Heat soared to her cheeks at her wayward thoughts. Either lack of sleep plagued her or sheer insanity.

"What's wrong?"

"Nothing." She rose and grabbed for her coat. "We'd better get over there. He'll want to arrive before me, so I'm sure he's heading to his car now."

He nodded and sat down to yank on his socks and slip his feet into boots. "We'll take my truck. It's got four-wheel drive, and the road out there might be bad."

"We can't. He'll be looking for my Prius. Dolly will get us there."

He lifted a dark brow. "You named your car?"

"Doesn't everyone? And she looks like a Dolly, don't you think?" She pulled on her coat and lifted the hood. "Dolly has never let me down. You'll see."

He grinned and slid his arms into his parka. "Whatever you say. You scared?"

"Terrified. Wouldn't you be?"

"We don't have to do this. We could call Mason and have

him pick Garret up at the building. You wouldn't even have to see him."

"He won't tell the sheriff anything. I want to see if I can get him to admit he killed Allyson. He's a braggart. If he did it, he's likely to let it slip." She called Phantom to her. "You'd better leave Spirit here. He's liable to whine or bark when Garret comes in."

"Yeah, that's what I thought. Stay," he told the dog. Spirit sank to the floor with a mournful expression. "I won't be long, you crazy dog."

"He doesn't believe you." She delayed long enough to give Spirit a belly rub. "Come on, Phantom." Her dog let out a happy bark and danced around her, then raced for the door.

"You sure you want to take him?"

She headed for the front of the cabin. "He doesn't like Garret. I figure Phantom is one more layer of protection for me. He'll guard me with teeth bared."

"You don't think Garret would shoot him?"

That brought her up short. "He's more apt to use his bare hands. He's proud of his strength."

Boone reached into the closet as she stepped to the door. His hand emerged with a pistol. "I'll take this along just to be safe."

———

I have to be crazy for doing this. Dana could hardly hear over the blood pounding in her ears.

The cold metal edge of the desk in Bree's office steadied Dana as she leaned back against it. Various search boxes sat along the concrete floor, and harnesses and leashes hung from hooks on the finished walls. The ceiling of the metal pole building was ten feet overhead, and lights shone down brightly, erasing any possible shadows. It held the scent of Pine-Sol Bree used to clean the floors.

No sound or movement came from the storage room where Boone had hidden away. Phantom whined and pressed against her leg, and she reached down to rub his head. His ears went to alert, and the hackles on his back stood at attention, the dog's usual reaction to Garret's presence.

She listened for a moment to the wind whistling around the windows, then heard the unmistakable sound of a vehicle door shutting. Her gut tightened, and she swallowed hard.

She'd left the door unlocked. He would come in without knocking. She stared at the doorknob until it began to turn. The door opened a crack, then slammed into the wall. Garret strode into the large room as if he were a CEO taking charge of a meeting. He often treated her like a subordinate obligated to obey his commands.

Her spine stiffened. He wasn't going to order her around any longer, and she wouldn't allow herself to fall back into subservient behavior.

He wore a black parka over jeans and boots, and he ran his hand through his thick blond hair and shot a grin her way. "There you are. I wasn't sure if you'd be here or not."

When he started her way, it took all her strength to stand her ground and not dart for the other door. "Hi, Garret."

His smile faltered at her cool tone. "I was glad you called me. We can work this out, Dana. Remember the night we first met? I took one look at you and knew you were the one."

"Lee Greenwood was singing 'God Bless the USA.'" The words were out before she could choke them back. She shook off the memory and stared into that face she'd once loved so much. He'd made her feel alive and desirable. He'd actually *seen* her. At least it had seemed that way for a time.

Phantom growled and bared his teeth when Garret took a step closer. He grimaced. "Why'd you bring that mutt? He hates me."

She grabbed the dog's collar as he lunged. "Where were you yesterday afternoon?"

He stepped away from Phantom and blinked at her abrupt question. He took another step closer and reached one hand toward her. "Why do you want to know where I was? None of that matters. We're meant to be together, and you know it."

She evaded his touch. He sounded way too smug so he knew exactly why she was asking. "Did you know Allyson Hegney?"

A glower settled over his face, and he dropped his hand. "That's why you asked me to meet you, isn't it? You actually think I killed that woman. I didn't even know her. You'd like to railroad me for that crime too?" Ignoring the dog, he stepped closer again. "Let's forget this foolishness, Dana. You still love me. I can see it in your eyes."

Lord help her, even now she felt the pull of his charismatic personality. He was the first man who'd ever made her feel truly wanted. After losing her entire family, she never felt safe, never felt truly part of her adopted family even though they treated her well. On one level it would be so easy to forgive him and take him back, but this kind of leopard never changed his spots. The next time he might kill her too.

Suddenly chilly, she hugged herself. "You'd better go, Garret. I'm not going anywhere with you."

He laughed, but it was a sound as cold as the wind howling outside. "If you think I'm leaving here without you, you're delusional." In the next moment he pointed a gun at Phantom. "Lock your dog up over there." He gestured toward the storage room. "We'll get out of this hick town and back to civilization where you can think more clearly."

She couldn't look away from the gun aimed at her dog, and she plunged her hand into her pocket to curl her fingers around the bear spray. "Put that gun away!"

"Not until you secure the dog. You're coming with me."

She bit her lip and looked down at Phantom. It would take very little provocation for Garret to shoot him, and she wasn't close enough to use the bear spray, or any of the moves Boone had taught her. Holding firmly to the dog's collar, she half dragged him toward the storage room.

Boone would help get her out of this.

CHAPTER 16

Phantom was growling and snarling on the other side of the door. Boone's hand crept to the butt of his Glock, then he shook his head. A gunfight was apt to spray bullets in Dana's direction, and he wouldn't risk harming her. He'd have to rely on his martial arts skills along with the element of surprise.

The hinges on the door creaked open, and he caught a glimpse of her pale face. Phantom struggled as she pushed him through the door. Behind Dana, Garret waved a gun toward her.

Boone moved behind the door where he couldn't be seen. He grabbed Phantom's collar and dragged him into the room, then thrust the dog behind him. He motioned for Dana to come inside too.

Her eyes wide, she rushed through the doorway, and he closed and locked the door. Garret wouldn't have a key to get in.

"Hey!" Garret twisted the doorknob. "Open this door or I'll shoot the lock."

"Shh." Boone held his fingers to his lips, then went to the back of the space. He opened the window, then slammed it shut. Garret would go outside thinking she'd escaped that way. Sure enough, he heard quick footsteps toward the door, then the sound of it opening.

He eased the storage door open and stepped out. "Call 9-1-1 and have them send a deputy. Come out of there in case he tries to get in through the window. Lock the front door behind me until I tell you it's safe."

The room was empty, and the entry door stood ajar by a couple of inches. He moved quickly to the door and peered out. Gun in hand, Garret stalked the snowy yard with a grim expression. He disappeared from view around the corner of the building.

Boone motioned for Dana to join him. "This won't take long."

He stepped outside and waited until he heard the lock click behind him. The biting wind carried the scent of the lake to his nose, and he thought he detected male cologne as well. Peeking around the edge of the building, he saw Garret grunting with effort to raise the window. Had he figured out the ruse already?

Boone ducked back around and thought through his options. The best idea would be to take the man by surprise but how? An expanse of yard stood between here and the window. Garret would see him quickly. Maybe he could lure him this way.

He picked up a stick from the ground and tossed it against the far wall of the building. The grunting around the corner stopped, and footsteps tromped his way. Hands up, he crouched in ready position.

The tip of the gun barrel in Garret's hand appeared first, but the guy was no dummy. He paused and listened before proceeding past the corner where Boone waited. Boone held his breath, not daring to make a sound.

Garret inched forward a bit more. Boone needed just a few more inches of arm and he'd be able to disarm him.

More, more, just a little farther.

Just as Boone's arm came down, Garret seemed to realize something was up. He jerked his arm back. Boone sprang after him, but he tripped over another branch on the ground and hurtled to his knees.

Garret sprinted for his truck. After opening the door, he threw himself under the wheel, and the engine roared to life. In the distance a siren wailed, but Garret's truck spun on the snow for a moment, then took off in the opposite direction. As he passed, his glare at Boone promised retribution.

"Bring it on," Boone muttered. "I'm taking you down."

He returned to the entry door and rapped his knuckles on it. "It's me, Dana."

The door opened and she peered past his shoulder. "He's gone? The sheriff should be here any minute." Phantom pushed past her legs and nosed Boone's hand.

Boone petted the dog's ears as the siren grew louder in the distance.

"I'm not sure he had anything to do with Allyson's death." She pushed a curl out of her eyes. "But if he didn't kill her, who did?"

"He's still the best suspect we've got." The trouble was, how did he prove it?

She'd tricked him. Garret kicked a soda can across the cabin's rough floorboards. And she had that creep with her. Was she seeing someone else already? His rage burned and he drove his fist into the wall. Pain shot up his arm, and he howled with frustration.

He'd come here because he loved her. She *belonged* to him.

He sucked an oozing cut on his knuckles and grimaced at the coppery taste. If she thought she could walk away from him, she was mistaken.

A distant sound soaked into his consciousness, and he realized he'd been hearing the drone of a snow machine for several minutes. He darted to the dirty window and looked out into the yard. Nothing moved but a few hardy dry leaves clinging to the barren tree branches surrounding the property. Just in case, he grabbed the backpack and cooler, then pulled on his coat and stepped out onto the rickety porch.

It was probably sportsmen out on their machines, but after today's fiasco, he needed to make sure. The truck engine still ticked as it cooled from his run over to the SAR building, and it fired right up when he started it. He'd replaced a heater hose, so warmth blew out from the vents as he headed out a secondary fire road to the highway.

As he pulled onto the main road, a snow machine carrying a county deputy zipped by him. He floored the accelerator. The truck fishtailed on the slick road, then the tires grabbed hold and carried him away.

He knew in his bones the law was out looking for him. His hide was about to be exposed, and he'd have to find another place to lay low. He wasn't leaving, not without Dana. She wasn't going to blithely move on to another man, and he wasn't going to live without her.

He turned onto another fire road, slick with ice and snow. The trees were so close on either side that branches brushed against the truck's sides. Though he had no idea where this dirt track led, he followed it as it wound through evergreens and stands of aspen.

The trail broke off in different directions, and he took the one to the right. It narrowed even more, and he had to slow the truck over massive potholes. No one had been down this way in ages. He found a narrow spot to turn around and went back out the way he'd come.

He pulled back onto the road. What if he found a summer home as a base to come in and out of? Not a cabin, but a nice place with a garage and heat. Should be plenty of them around. He just had to find one. He retrieved a map of the county from under the seat and looked it over. The most likely place to find a vacation house would be along Superior's lakeshore. People with money out of Chicago or Wisconsin wouldn't want to brave the winter Michigan weather.

He studied the map, then pulled out onto the highway and drove north from Rock Harbor to a curving bay southwest of Houghton. It should be far enough away from Rock Harbor to escape detection but close enough that a short drive got him to Dana. A road sign indicated a boat launch site, so he turned and followed it around to the water.

Several roads split off from the boat launch, and he turned left and followed the road to its end, passing several homes along the way. None of them appeared occupied, and he grinned and did a fist pump.

"You can't outsmart Garret Waterman," he muttered.

At the end of the road he turned onto a driveway that led into the woods. He soon came to a palatial mansion. Pay dirt! This place would be perfect. Secluded by the forest and obviously occupied only in the summer. Now to find a way in without triggering an alarm or breaking a window.

He parked in front, then walked around the house. Its alarm system would be no problem for him. He went back to the truck and grabbed his computer from the backpack. He logged onto his phone's hotspot and set to work. It only took him half an hour to break into the network and disarm the alarm system. A few more minutes, and he had the code for the door.

He slung his backpack over his shoulder and picked up the cooler. The front door opened easily with the code, and he stepped onto oak floors. The place was spotless. The owners had left the heat on fifty-five, much warmer than he'd endured in the old cabin. He'd be very comfortable here, even if he didn't turn up the heat.

The sweeping staircase led to a second floor containing five bedrooms but no master, so he went downstairs and found it on the other side of the house. It was massive, a good thirty by twenty feet with a marble bathroom that was bigger than most bedrooms. This would do quite nicely.

He dropped his backpack on the floor, then took the cooler to the kitchen. Rows of canned goods and boxes of pasta and cereal lined the shelves in the gigantic pantry. He wouldn't go hungry here. It would all be waiting when he got back from his work trip.

CHAPTER 17

The spicy aroma of lasagna filled Bree's kitchen. Dana had already set the table, and Bree put her to work making garlic toast while Boone made coffee. The sun had set an hour ago, but the bright lights in the kitchen pushed back the shadows.

Usually Bree loved nothing more than having her friends and family with her like this, but sadness and tension hung in the air. Kade would be home from work any minute, and Davy was playing hide-and-seek with Hannah and Hunter. Or rather, Dave, as he often corrected her. It was still impossible to think of her eleven-year-old as anything other than Davy.

Boone turned on the coffeepot. "Once Mason finds Garret, he'll be headed to jail for attempted kidnapping. I saw the whole thing so it's not just Dana's word against his."

"I bet he leaves the county," Bree said. "He knows now that Dana won't go with him willingly."

Dana shook her head. "He doesn't give up that easily. I fear Boone is on his radar now too. Probably all my friends are. The more he sensed me pulling away, the more he followed my every move back in Washington. I was at a coworker's house one night, and he left a dead rat on the doorstep."

Bree suppressed a shudder. "How do you know he did it?"

Dana slid the sheet of garlic bread under the broiler. "He bragged to me about it later. He said to stay away from Michelle or the attacks would escalate. That's why I thought he might tell me the truth about Allyson. And maybe he did, even though it seems he's the most likely person to have killed her."

"Creep. He won't scare us off." Grief squeezed Bree's chest. Allyson deserved justice. If Garret killed her, he had to pay.

Dana tucked a curl behind her ear and shut the oven door. "I'm worried about your kids, Bree. He's not above scaring them if he thought it would affect me."

This time Bree couldn't hold back the shudder that ran up her spine. After Davy's ordeal when he was four, she knew she tended to be too protective, but she found it impossible to stop. If any of the kids were out of her sight for more than a few minutes, she was out looking for them.

Boone lowered coffee mugs from the cabinet over the pot. "He'd actually harm a kid?"

"I don't know, but he's not above scaring the daylights out of them. He's so unpredictable."

Bree slipped on oven mitts and carried the pan of lasagna to the table. She placed it on the hot pads and turned as Kade's voice called out from the front door.

"We're in here."

He greeted the children before he appeared in the doorway from the living room. His cheeks and nose were red. He'd shed his boots and jacket but still wore his khaki ranger uniform.

He smiled when he saw the group. "Hey, looks like we've got a crowd."

She lifted her face for his kiss and palmed his cheeks. "Your skin is cold. The coffee is nearly ready."

"Dinner smells awesome. I didn't get any lunch. We were all out searching for Waterman."

Dana straightened from checking on the garlic toast. "He was out on forest land?"

Kade nodded. "We had a report he might be staying in one of the summer cabins along the Ottawa, so we were out on snow machines. We found signs of a squatter in the last one, but if it was Waterman, he had already gone."

"You think he left the area?" Dana's voice held hope. She moved the garlic toast from the baking sheet to a plate.

Kade shrugged and went to pour himself a cup of coffee. "No way of knowing, but the cabin was warm, and I smelled kerosene. It could have been kids. That happens all the time. Though I only found one sleeping bag." He took a sip of the steaming coffee. "A report described his truck, so I think it was him. He'd have heard all the snow machines going from house to house and probably skedaddled."

Kade bit into the crunchy bread and sighed. "Man, that's good. I'm famished."

Bree carried the glasses of iced tea to the table. Her anxiety level had been rising through the dinner preparation. Would Garret be likely to target any of them because of their friendship with Dana? Samson growled softly at her feet, and she glanced down at him. He was looking at the door.

She set down the glasses and touched the top of his head. "What is it, boy?" But she knew. He had an uncanny way of knowing when they were in danger. Someone was outside.

She glanced at Kade, and he went to the back door and peered through the window into the dark night. "The light is out. It was all right last night."

"Maybe the bulb is burned out." She hoped that was it.

He frowned and reached into the top cabinet by the door for a flashlight. "Come on, Boone."

"You bet." He followed Kade out into the wind.

Bree started to follow, but her husband shook his head. "Stay inside, honey. We'll check this out. Keep your phone handy and call Mason if you need to." He snapped his fingers. "Come, Samson." The dog was only too happy to leap after them.

She grabbed her phone from her purse before going to the window to watch the beam of the flashlight bob along the backyard. The shadowy figures of the two men went to the garage, all along the fence toward the crashing waves of Superior. The light paused for a while, then came quickly toward the back porch.

Kade opened the door for Boone and Samson, then shut and locked it once they were all inside. "Someone shot out the light." He held out his hand and a .9mm casing lay in his palm. "We'd better call Mason." He stared at Bree for a long moment. "I didn't want to worry you needlessly, but Martha found a cooler with two chunks of steak in it behind her shed. I had them checked, and they both contained poison."

Naomi's mother, Martha, owned the bed-and-breakfast next door. Bree caught her breath. "There *was* someone out there Monday night."

"Looks like he planned to poison Samson. Maybe Phantom too." He held up the bullet casing again. "And now this. I want you to be careful, honey."

What she wanted to do was run Garret to the ground and see him behind bars. "We have to get that man jailed."

"And we will," Kade promised.

The scent of an apple-spiced candle hung in the air when Dana let herself into the house. She could hear Chris's low voice in the living room. Who was here? She slipped off her boots and hung her coat up in the closet, then went to find out. Her stockinged feet slipped on the polished oak floor, but she made no noise. Maybe she should. He might think she was spying on him.

She deliberately tromped on the boards a bit as she moved toward the flickering glow of the TV in the otherwise dark room. As she paused in the doorway, she made out Chris's figure sitting on the sofa. He had a phone to his ear.

"Hey." She moved on into the room.

"I wasn't expecting you yet." Chris cupped the phone closer to his mouth. "Listen, I'll call you later." He ended the call, reached over and flipped on the table lamp, then got up to throw another log on the fire.

Dana blinked at the sudden glare of illumination, and it took a second for her eyes to adjust. "I went to Bree's for dinner. We, uh, we had things to discuss."

Maybe hearing what Garret had done today would get Chris moving on her behalf. Garret was his friend, or had been. If anyone had a chance of getting Garret to leave her alone, it was Chris.

She headed for the recliner opposite the sofa. "I talked to Garret today."

Chris took the remote and clicked off the television. "Are you okay?" His gaze raked over her as if he expected to see her bloody and beaten.

The sweet scent of the candle relaxed her, and she settled back against the chair. "He tried to make me go with him. To be honest,

I kind of set him up." She launched into how the meeting had come about and what she hoped to accomplish. "So it sounds like he didn't kill Allyson. Do you think he could have had an accomplice?"

Chris shrugged and went back to his seat on the sofa. "I can't see him trusting anyone enough to be in cahoots on a murder. I'm glad you're home and away from that creep."

Dana grabbed the fluffy red throw from the pile by the fireplace and snugged it around her legs. Home. This place had quickly become her sanctuary. If she could, she'd stay inside the rest of the winter and emerge when spring did. Maybe Garret would be gone by then.

But she couldn't hide from this. He'd already proven he wasn't one to easily give up. Even with all the law enforcement looking for him, he was still in the area. She could feel him.

"It's my job to take care of you. You're my baby sister. I like being your knight in shining armor." He gave a short laugh.

"You've sure rescued me enough." She shuddered. "The night I got locked in the hull of the abandoned boat was the worst night of my life. It kept creaking all around me, and I was sure monsters dripping with seaweed and slime were slithering out of the water after me."

He grinned. "I always regretted not getting to you sooner."

She was twelve and had foolishly thought Chris's friend Kory liked her. He'd invited her to come with them to roast marshmallows in the abandoned shipyard, and she'd gone with high expectations. Instead, the kids ignored her, and she was locked into a boat's hull overnight. Even now the thought of being in a tight, dark room made her chest tight.

"How'd you find out where I was anyway?" She'd asked Chris before, but he never really answered her.

His blue eyes darkened, and he looked toward the fire. "You'd already been through so much. It was just plain mean to pull that when you'd barely buried your mom and dad."

Her smile faded at the memory. "I sure got over my crush in a hurry."

He grunted. "Lousy person to have a crush on."

"He was your friend, and I thought you were Superman and Captain America all rolled into one. He took on some of your glamour." She laughed and rose. He wasn't going to tell her how he found out she was trapped, even after all these years. Had he beaten it out of Kory? Overheard him? She would never know. Kory didn't move in Chris's circles after that. He'd seemed almost afraid to talk to her and probably feared she'd tell the sheriff.

She wasn't a tattletale though. Pressing charges against Garret had been impossible.

Chris rose and held out his arms. She went into them and laid her cheek on his chest. His love and care for her was the one steady thing in her life.

CHAPTER 18

B oone settled on the recliner with his laptop and called up the file his cousin had sent him. Reading her breezy e-mail was a knife stab to the chest, but he owed it to her to find out what had happened. He opened the file, then blinked. It was all gibberish.

"What the heck?"

He went back to her e-mail, saved the file again, but got the same result when he tried to read the newly saved document. A conversion problem from the e-mail, or had she protected it in some way? Maybe Mason had figured it out after taking Allyson's computer.

He glanced at his watch. Only nine so it wasn't too late to call the sheriff.

Mason answered on the first ring. "Boone, how you doing?"

"Hope I'm not interrupting anything, Mason."

"Nope, just got Zoe down for the night. Hilary is working on a campaign speech, and I'm sitting here trying to decide between watching *Fixer Upper* or a ball game. What can I do for you?"

Hilary wouldn't have any trouble winning reelection for Rock Harbor mayor. "You have Allyson's computer, don't you? At least I saw it was gone from her cabin."

"Yeah, for all the good it's done us so far. Most of her files are encrypted. I have our computer guru trying to figure out the password she used in the program so we can access them. Why?"

Boone told him about the e-mail from his cousin. "So she knew she was in danger. She must have stumbled on the identity of whoever killed my sister."

"Whoa, Boone, you're jumping to conclusions. She was poking around a lot, but she could have seen something else that got her killed. Maybe she ran into a smuggling operation."

Boone gripped his phone more tightly. "You have evidence of that?"

"There was the hole in the ice. I've got divers going in there tomorrow to see if they can find anything. But it's hard to say what happened. We have to look at all of it objectively."

"Do you have cause of death yet?" Boone wasn't sure he was ready to deal with the mental images that were sure to come, but he had to know.

"Yeah. The coroner found water in her lungs. She drowned."

Drowned. Just like Renee. "And you still think it wasn't that guy she called the Groom Reaper? Come on, Mason."

"I admit it looks suspicious, and I'm going to get to the bottom of it. I have a call into the detectives in charge of both of the other cases Allyson was investigating, including your sister's. But again, let's not leap to conclusions. Good police work means we don't get set on an answer until we examine all the evidence."

Boone knew Mason was right, but as far as he was concerned, everything pointed to whoever had killed Renee. Allyson had figured it out, but why hadn't she called immediately and told him? It didn't make sense.

Boone closed his laptop lid. "Any unusual phone calls? Like

from someone out of town? Maybe she called whoever she sus-pected of being the killer, and he came after her."

"I thought about that too. We've got a court order in to get her phone records, but they haven't come through yet. I've got orders to check the phone's location too."

Boone rubbed his forehead. "Man, everything takes forever."

"I know it seems like it when you want answers, but it's only been a day and a half."

"It seems like weeks."

"I'm sure sorry, Boone. Just be patient. I won't stop looking until I find out who did this."

"I know you will, Mason." The words felt like a lie on his tongue. The detective in charge of Renee's case had promised the same thing, yet here they were three years later and no closer to an arrest.

"I'm actually glad you called. I was going to stop by in the morn-ing. I don't want you or Dana to pull another stunt like you did this afternoon. That could have gone south really fast with a man as vola-tile as Waterman. He had a gun, and I doubt he was afraid to use it."

"He had it out. I had a firearm too, but I couldn't use it with Dana in the way."

"And that would have put you at a disadvantage. You could be dead right now. Do I have your word that you'll leave the investiga-tion to law enforcement? If it makes you feel any better, I've called in the state boys to help. This case has everyone's full attention."

"That's good." Boone couldn't bring himself to make the promise.

"Boone? I want you both to stay out of it."

"I'll do my best to at least notify you if I find anything."

Mason heaved a sigh. "Just focus on your business and let me do my job. I've got resources you don't have."

"Will you let me know if you figure out how to decode those files? I'd like a copy of them. Something in them might trigger a lead. I knew her better than you."

"True. Okay, I'll let you know what I find out."

"Thanks, Mason. Have a good evening." Boone ended the call and opened his laptop again. Maybe he could figure out the encryption. But nothing he tried worked.

Too restless to give up, he changed into his swim gear—a wetsuit, neoprene hat, boots, and gloves—then called Spirit. A cold-water swim would enhance his mental focus. Spirit barked and wagged his tail, then ran to the door. Boone jogged to the beach where he left his towel and waded into the water, then dove into the waves.

The shock of being submerged in icy water brought him sputtering to the surface before he found his determination again and set off for the rocky outcropping twenty yards out into Superior. He reached it, grabbed the rock to catch his breath for a moment, then turned and swam back to shore.

The wind pierced his wetsuit, and he grabbed his towel and wrapped it around him. On the way back to his cabin, he saw a bobbling light in the window of Allyson's cabin.

Someone with a flashlight was inside.

He took off at a run, but as Boone went in the front door, he heard the back door slam. By the time he got there, the intruder was long gone.

———

Most people Dana talked to thought a dispatcher had the inside scoop on everything going on in the sheriff's office, but the truth was, most of the time the dispatchers made an effort to gain that information. The moment a dispatcher sat in front of her bank of computer screens, the new day's emergencies pushed yesterday's out of the way.

Today was no different, and though she desperately wanted to know about the investigation into Allyson's murder, she found herself answering a host of calls ranging from a dog attack to a kid hitting a tree on his sled.

Her shift was nearly over by the time she got a chance to take a break. She rose and stretched. "I'm going to get a snack. Need anything?"

Her coworkers shook their heads, and only Karen spared her a glance.

Dana escaped the stuffy room with its cacophony of phones and keyboard noises. She stopped at the break room long enough to grab a bottle of water, then headed for the sheriff's office down the hall. Mason's door stood open, and he sat at his desk tapping at his keyboard.

She rapped her knuckles on the door frame until he looked up. "Hope I'm not bothering you."

"Nope, come on in. Settling into the job?"

It had been three days, and she already felt at home, though her coworkers had done little to make her feel welcome. "Fine." She advanced to the desk. "Um, I wondered if there was anything new on Allyson's murder."

He nodded and leaned back in his chair. "Here's a shocker— she had water in her lungs. That maniac held her head in that hole until she drowned." His eyes narrowed, and his lips flattened. "I'm going to find him and make him pay."

Drowned. Dana clenched the back of the chair in front of the desk to steady herself. She licked her dry lips. "Um, did you know

Allyson was investigating two murders in other states? One in Washington and one in Oregon."

Mason frowned and reached for his keyboard. "Hang on a second. Let me get down anything you have to say. The state boys want anything we know available to them online." Lines appeared between his eyes, and he grunted. "Stupid computers have ruined good investigations." He looked up. "Okay, so about these other two murders. Are you talking about Renee's murder and the Rogerson case?"

"Of course Boone would have already told you. Allyson thought they might be connected and that the killer was the same man."

"Did she talk to you about it at all? Maybe she told you something she didn't tell Boone."

Dana shook her head. "Not really, but she was killed the same way they were. And when she called emergency dispatch she said, 'He's going to kill me next.' So that makes me wonder if the killer found out she was on his trail and made sure she didn't talk." Did she mention Garret's name?

"Blasted computer," he muttered and resumed his typing. "You're sure she said 'next'?"

"Positive. That's why I think she found out something about the Groom Reaper."

He lifted a brow. "I'm sure you know Boone told me all this. Why are you really here?"

She had to tell him. "She was looking into my ex-fiancé. H-He tried to drown me once, and he travels all over the country. Both of the murdered women's fiancés were pharmaceutical reps. And Garret often traveled to both states in which the women were murdered, and he could have pretended to be with pharmaceuticals to conceal his true profession."

Mason frowned and shook his head. "There are thousands of

reps in the country, maybe tens of thousands. And plenty of abusive boyfriends, unfortunately. You'd think Allyson had more to go on than that." His scowl deepened. "Still, he's here in town, or at least he was. So that scoots him up a notch on the suspect list. Have you heard from him this week?"

"Not since Tuesday when Boone and I confronted him."

"So he could be gone." He grabbed the phone. "I'll get a search warrant to check his cell phone records. That will tell us if he's still in the area." He paused. "Thanks for coming in, Dana."

"I guess I didn't have all that much information for you. I hope it's not Garret. I feel like it's my fault she's dead. If I'd never come here, she might still be alive." Her voice quivered, and she swallowed.

"You get that out of your head. You didn't turn him into a killer."

She started to answer, but he spoke into the phone and gave her a wave of dismissal. As she walked back to the dispatch room, she tried to talk herself out of her funk. The sheriff was right. She wasn't responsible for Garret's actions. But even though her head knew the truth, her chest tightened and her eyes burned. But who could he be working with? She ran through the list of his friends she'd met, and she couldn't imagine anyone killing Allyson.

Maybe she was on the wrong track altogether, and her suspicions were just that—unfounded suspicions.

CHAPTER 19

Work would give him something else to think about. Boone packed his climbing gear in a bag and glanced at the clock on the wall of his office. Barely seven. The Gordon party of two was going out today, a man and a woman. He rose as a vehicle's tires crunched on the gravel in the drive outside. They were early.

The rest of his crew should be arriving anytime, but he hadn't been able to sleep so he'd come in at five. He opened his office door and went to greet the customers. They hailed from Arizona so he'd have plenty of conversation points.

The first person through the door was a tall, dark-haired man whose cold-weather gear and boots gave off the scent of money. Boone recognized the Yuki Expedition parka the guy wore and suppressed a sigh. His rich clients always expected nature to bow to their whims like everyone else did, and it didn't work that way.

Boone held out his hand. "Mr. Gordon? Boone Carter." His smile died as he saw a face over the man's shoulder. A beautiful face he still sometimes saw in his dreams—or more accurately—his nightmares.

"Buck?" His former fiancée went white as their gazes locked.

Esther Stanton hadn't changed much other than her hairstyle. A short bob had replaced the long blonde hair he'd loved to tangle his fingers in. Her eyes were still as blue as he remembered and her legs just as long and enticing. A million emotions swarmed in his chest each vying for attention. Love, hate, terror, shame, and an overwhelming desire to hide his scarred face.

He started to raise his hand to his face, then dropped it. Her horrified gaze was already on the ridges of his cheek. Lifting his chin, he turned so she could get a good look.

Neal Gordon gave a long look at Esther, then back to Boone. "You two know each other?"

Esther's laugh was breathless and high. "A long time ago. Um, Buck and I were engaged."

It was all Boone could do to hide a wince. "Buck was my smoke jumper nickname. I go by my real name now, Boone Carter. I left that life a long time ago." *And Esther's fickleness.*

Understanding lit the man's face. "The smoke jumper who was burned. Why didn't you ever get that fixed? Plastic surgery can do wonders these days."

Rude question. Boone chose to ignore it. "Come on in. The guide I have going out with you isn't here yet, but I can give you the briefing."

"I thought you were taking us out. Aren't you the owner?" Gordon shut the door behind Esther who hadn't recovered her color yet.

"I think you're blocking the drive, and my employees will be arriving any minute. Could you move your SUV to the parking lot?" Boone pointed it out.

Gordon's lip curled, but he inclined his head and went out the door.

Esther's hands fluttered. "I–I had no idea this was your business. You've done well for yourself. This is very different from Arizona."

"I like it." He wanted to stare at her and see if she showed signs of shallow character and lack of heart, but it was too painful to see her perfect skin and figure. Her beauty had always left him breathless. It just hadn't been more than skin deep.

"I–I still cringe when I think of what I did to you." She took a step closer and her oh-so-familiar perfume wafted up his nose in a heady rush. "You were my first love, and I've never gotten over you, not really. Do you ever think of me?"

He stepped back. "Sure. I remember your cruelty most of all." He didn't care if she flinched. "When I needed you most, you were only too happy to walk away. You taught me a lot though. You showed me that women can't be trusted and that beauty has a dark side."

She gasped and put her hand to her mouth. Her eyes filled with tears. "You're very bitter, Buck. You've never forgiven me, have you?"

"You've never asked for forgiveness." But as he spat the words, he knew it wasn't her fault he'd nursed his anger. He'd held it close to his heart and let it define him. Was that all he'd become—an embittered man scarred more by his anger than by the fire?

The thought tightened his chest, and he turned to check out the window for his employees. There was no way he was taking her out with her new boyfriend or whoever he was. If Gordon didn't like it, Boone would refund his money. No amount of cash would be worth that torture.

He turned back around to face her. "You married to this guy?"

She nodded. "For three years. He's the son of my dad's business partner. We have a lot in common."

"And he's filthy rich. I never made enough money for you, not really."

He saw it all clearly now. When she dumped him, she'd saved them both a lot of grief. He'd always thought she'd eventually settle in and realize he wasn't made of money, but that never would have happened. Status and nice things were important to her. He'd been like a fancy bracelet on her arm or an expensive set of diamond earrings. Something to be shown off to her friends like a tame tiger. She'd loved his muscular form and his handsome face as well as the danger of his profession.

He exhaled and some of his anger escaped with his breath. It was all for the best.

———

Cars, trucks, and SUVs crowded the small parking lot at Carter's Cabins. A group was just piling into a white Carter van by the office, and Dana looked to see if Boone was driving, but a young woman was in the driver's seat.

A handsome man with a set jaw skewered the driver with an imperious gaze as he slammed his door shut. In the back a woman was biting her lips as she looked at her lap. Maybe the guy was forcing her to go out today, but she didn't look happy about it.

Dana parked in the last space, then hurried through the gusty wind to the office with Phantom on her heels. She should have called to make sure they were on for self-defense practice today, but she'd decided to take a chance and run out anyway. He could be gone for all she knew. Head down against the wind, she dashed across the frozen ground. The bell over the creaky door jingled when she stepped through onto the rough wooden floor.

Boone looked up from manning the counter. "Hey, I thought about calling you."

Spirit, tail wagging, came over to greet Phantom. Dana glanced around the room and saw no one else. "You the only one running the counter today?"

"Just for a few minutes. Kacie is on a break. You're off today?"

"Yep."

"Ready for a lesson?"

"Ready." She eyed him. He seemed different this morning, distracted. He wore a haunted expression as well. "What's wrong?"

A redhead, obviously from a bottle, came down the hall. "I'll take over now, Boone."

"I'll check in with you in an hour or so." He grabbed his coat from a hook on the wall and slipped it on, then took Dana's elbow and steered her toward the door. Phantom wagged his tail for a pet, but Boone didn't seem to notice. Both dogs followed them outside.

The wind gusts took her breath away, and she didn't repeat her question until he ushered her into the workout room. She took off her coat and hung it up. "What was that all about?"

Boone ordered the dogs to lay down in the corner. "What?"

"Avoiding my question and rushing me out of there. I'm not an idiot. Something happened this morning. Did Garret come by or call you?"

"No, no, nothing like that." He hung his coat up beside hers. "Did you see the group leaving when you arrived?"

His tone was too casual so she thought back to the people she'd seen before and nodded. "The woman didn't look happy about the excursion, and the guy with her was the type to make sure everyone does it his way. Another Garret."

"I hadn't seen her in a while."

"The woman, you mean?"

He nodded. "Yeah, it's been years. I'm still a little rattled, I guess."

She studied the pain lurking behind his eyes. "She's the one, isn't she? The one who dumped you because of your scars?"

He shrugged. "Any woman would have done the same."

"They would *not*! It's just a scar, Boone." She stepped closer. "The scars don't define you. Who you really are inside is what matters. Any woman with real depth would know that. You're a handsome guy. The scars don't change that." She longed to touch his face, but he'd probably resent her attempt at comfort.

His Adam's apple bobbed and he turned away. "It doesn't matter. It was a good thing I saw her. I realized we were never really suited for each other. She was always more interested in showing me off to her friends than she was in who I really was. I bet she doesn't even know what my favorite color is."

"It's dark red."

He turned and lifted a brow. "How'd you know that?"

"It's a Cardinals color. You wear it all the time. Even your sock hat is that color."

"Well, she wouldn't have known if you'd asked her. Once the novelty wore off of being engaged to a smoke jumper and her friends quit oohing and ahing, she would have moved on to greener pastures. I never would have fit with what her parents wanted for her either."

"And you would have hated taking anything from them."

He shot her another quick look. "Yeah, exactly."

Anyone with half a brain could see he was the type who liked to make his own way in the world. He'd never had anything handed to him, and he would refuse it if it were. She liked that about him.

"Look, let's change the subject. It's over. She's gone, and I don't have to deal with her again. You didn't hear anything more from Garret this week, did you?"

"No. I got home and talked to Chris awhile, then went to bed. I've been at work the last two days and he hadn't called. How about you?"

He took off his boots and socks and motioned for her to do the same. "I tried to look at the files Allyson sent me, but they're all encrypted so I called Mason to see if he could read them straight from the computer. They're all gibberish for him too. He's got an expert working on them though so maybe he'll crack them."

"Did Mason say if he had any suspects?"

"He doesn't, not really. Divers were supposed to be out there on Wednesday to look for any clues under the water, but I don't think they found anything or Mason would have called me. He's pretty ticked we talked to Garret on our own. He wanted us to promise not to do that again." A light danced in Boone's eyes.

"You didn't promise, did you? I can see it in your eyes." She laughed. "So what do we do next, Kemosabe? You have any ideas?"

He grinned. "Does that mean I'm the Lone Ranger?" He pulled off his socks and stepped to the mat in bare feet. "I'm going to try to call Renee's fiancé again. He's dropped off the radar and hasn't even called Detective Morgan in months. I think it's suspicious."

"Anything I can do?"

He held up his hands in a ready pose. "You can learn to kick butt and take names."

She put her fists up. "I'm ready, big guy."

CHAPTER 20

Mount Rainier rose in the distance, its peak visible for once on this fine, clear day from where Lauri stood on the observation deck of the Space Needle. She glanced at her watch. Peter was over an hour late, and he hadn't even texted her. Should she worry? Their relationship was still too new to know whether or not he was commonly late.

She pulled out her phone and stared at it again, but doing so didn't make a text suddenly appear. She turned back to the fabulous view of the city bathed in the colors of the sunset. Wasn't this just a little bit like *Sleepless in Seattle* where Meg Ryan met Tom Hanks at the top of the Empire State Building? She only hoped her happily ever after turned out like that movie.

"This is ridiculous." Her fingers jabbed the screen of her phone. *Where R U?*

The least he could do was to let her know he'd be late. She had just gotten into town and hadn't had a chance to even shop for groceries for the condo. The aroma of steak wafting from the nearby restaurant made her even crankier. She could have grabbed something to eat during the hour she'd been waiting.

She glanced at her phone. Nothing. Maybe he was driving and

didn't use his phone while at the wheel. A good practice but not when she was waiting here for him. She drummed her fingers on the railing. The sun was going down, and lights blinked on all over the city. Even that gorgeous sight failed to ease the tension in her neck and shoulders.

She'd wait fifteen more minutes. If she didn't hear from him, she was out of here and he could come to her condo if he really wanted to see her. He hadn't called the past two days either, and that neglect fueled her anger. Maybe anger was too strong of a word. More like hurt and disappointment.

A couple glanced at her and giggled. Heat flooded her cheeks. They probably thought she'd been stood up, and she should probably admit she had been. She shifted her purse higher on her shoulder as her stomach grumbled again. He was ninety minutes late now. She'd waited long enough.

She started for the elevator when the doors opened, and she caught sight of the gleam of his hair in the lights. She didn't know whether to kiss him or slap him so she lifted her hand and waited where she was for him to join her.

His grin widened as he saw her, then faltered as he neared. "What, no hello kiss? What's wrong?"

She dutifully lifted her face for a kiss. "You're late. Like extremely late. Why didn't you call me?"

He held his hands palms up as he shrugged, the picture of bewilderment. "I told you I wasn't positive what time I'd get here but would try to make it by five."

"You did not! You just said to meet you here at five. I rushed straight from the airport with no food." Aware her voice sounded like a petulant child, she made herself shut up. "Sorry, but I'm tired and hungry. Plus I was worried."

His frown deepened, and his fingers bit into her arm as he moved her away from spectators interested in their argument. "Don't try to make this my fault. I told you I wasn't sure what time I'd be here."

Had he told her? She tried to remember everything he'd said when they set up this meeting, but she was so tired that everything was a jumble. Maybe she was wrong. "I'm sorry. It's been a crazy-long day with delayed flights and no food. Can we forget it and go get dinner? I'm so hungry I feel light-headed."

His deep-blue eyes softened, and he cupped her face. "How about a proper greeting?"

As he lowered his head, she tried to put her anger away and give herself over to a real kiss. She loved him. Really, she did. But every couple had their spats, even Bree and Kade. No relationship was without conflict.

She wrapped her arms around his neck and kissed him back. The scent of his Bornéo 1834 enveloped her and made everything better. He smelled good, he tasted good, and he *was* good.

She mouthed a small protest when he pulled away. He tucked her hand into the crook of his arm. "Let me feed you before you turn into a tiger again. My meeting ran late, and I dashed to my car. Then I got caught in a traffic jam and time just got away. Forgive me?"

"Of course. I hope you'll forgive me for biting off your head."

He touched his head. "I think it's still there. Let me make it up to you with the biggest, most expensive steak on the menu."

"Now you're talking my language!" She went with him toward the elevator.

He punched the button and smiled down at her. "I just want to remind you of what you said in Hawaii. You said you'd rather die than hurt me. Your words hurt me. Just giving you fair warning."

What on earth did he mean by that? She managed to hold on to her smile as they stepped onto the elevator. "And I meant it." But what a strange comment for him to make.

———

"Who are you going to call first?" Dana carried a plate of peanut butter sandwiches to Boone's table. "This isn't much for lunch, but your pantry is bare."

Her red sweatshirt was a bright pop of color in his gray and white kitchen. Her face was pink from their workout, and her hair looked adorably messy. Boone dragged his gaze away and turned his attention back to his laptop in front of him on the table. "I'm trying to find Tyler." He reached for a sandwich and bit into it.

"I thought that number had been disconnected or something."

"I thought maybe I could find him on the Internet. I was relying on the detective, but he's never called me back so I'm going to take it into my own hands." He leaned forward and scrolled down the myriad links. "Tyler Dixon is a fairly common name."

"Try some other search parameters." She leaned over his shoulder, and her arm brushed his.

He caught the scent of her perfume, something sweet and vanilla scented. "Like what?"

"Pharmaceutical sales."

He added the phrase to the search, the list narrowed. "Still twenty-seven thousand links. Holy cow."

"Try adding the name of the company."

"Good idea." He shook his head. "Too far the other way. Nothing came up."

"Nothing?" She squatted behind him. "That would seem to

indicate he never worked for them. Did you try calling Lincoln Pharmaceuticals?"

"The detective said he was going to try that." He took another bite of his sandwich. "I should try calling Morgan and see if he got anywhere at Lincoln. No sense in spinning my wheels if he's run into a dead end." He called up the detective's number.

"Detective Morgan."

"It's Boone Carter. Sorry to bug you again so soon, but it's important."

"What can I help you with?"

Boone told him about Allyson's murder. "She was investigating Renee's death, and I think she stumbled onto the identity of the man who killed Renee and Faith Rogerson."

"You're assuming it was the same person. I'm not sure where you're getting such a strong link."

"Allyson was drowned too, Detective. You don't find that more than a little odd?"

Morgan went quiet for a moment. "What do you want from me? I can confer with the lead detective there and see if we have any links."

"That'd be great, but I was mostly wondering if you called Lincoln Pharmaceuticals and found Tyler Dixon."

"I did call, but I didn't get anywhere. The HR person I spoke with told me they'd never had a Dixon in their employ. I spelled it several different ways, but there was no person with that last name, male or female. That got me even more curious, so I tried to contact Justin Leyland, Faith Rogerson's fiancé. His phone had been disconnected as well. I spoke to the detective in charge and asked what company Leyland worked for. Get this—it was Lincoln again. So I called the woman in HR back, and she told me they had no Justin Leyland either."

Boone shot to his feet and paced. "That has to be more than coincidence!"

"I believe so, yes. And we are pursuing every option open to us. However, both men seem to have vanished."

"I think they're one and the same man."

"Unfortunately, we can't prove that. We have no engagement pictures."

"What about friends? Maybe a friend took a picture. Did you ever speak to Tyler in person?"

"Oh yes, right after the murder. I could get a police artist in here to do a sketch of him from my memory. I think I remember him well enough to create a fairly accurate one."

They were close on the monster's tail. Boone barely resisted giving a fist pump. "If we could compare that composite with Justin Leyland, we might get somewhere."

"We might," Morgan agreed. "Do you have the contact there in Rock Harbor for me to talk to?"

"Yep, it's Sheriff Mason Kaleva." Boone called up Mason's number and rattled it off to the detective. "The investigation is in its earliest stages here. He's called in the state police, and he should be able to give you their contact information. And a copy of the autopsy."

"I'll get on it. It may take a few days to get a composite. We've got an FBI forensic artist instructor coming to town next week to train our officers, and she's the best in the country. I'll arrange for her to compose the drawing."

"By then, Mason might have more information as well."

"Thanks for calling, Mr. Carter. This investigation just took on new life."

Boone ended the call and told Dana what he'd learned. "I have to wonder if any of Renee's friends have a picture of the guy. Surely they went out together with her friends."

"Do you know who you might call? Who was Renee's best friend?"

His elation leaked away. "Allyson. She never met him."

"Coworkers, other friends?"

He tried to think. "Someone from church maybe. I'll call her pastor and see if he has any idea who might have gone out with them." He caught her by the wrist and stared up at her. "You've been a rock through this, Dana. Thanks for being here for me."

Her cheeks bloomed with pink, but she didn't look away or pull away. "Anytime, Boone. I—I feel like I've known you forever. It's nice to have an instant friend."

In that moment he realized he wanted more than friendship from her.

CHAPTER 21

Dana assembled all the ingredients on Boone's counter and took out her container of sea salt. Working on the light granite counters was pure pleasure, and while there weren't many of the white shaker cabinets, they were well organized and held everything she needed for preparing fish tacos.

Boone stood by the red Blendtec blender. "What do you want me to mix up in here?"

"Two limes and a poblano pepper. I'm going to marinate the fish in it before we grill it." She handed him a small container of sea salt. "Use a little of this. Sea salt is healthier. I started using it when I went to work as a dispatcher. Sometimes I wouldn't get in enough fluid and would get dehydrated. Sea salt keeps my electrolytes in better shape."

Boone turned back to his task of peeling the limes and cutting up the pepper. She should get to work on the rest of the food, but watching him was way more fun.

He wrinkled his nose, then pulled the blender jar from its stand to add the ingredients. "I think it would be easier to go to the café."

She grabbed an apron from a drawer, then came up behind him

and whipped it around his waist. "But I wouldn't get to see you in an apron." The consternation on his face as he turned around brought laughter bubbling to her lips. He started to untie it, and she grabbed his arm. "Don't you dare. There's nothing more appealing than a man in an apron."

His hazel eyes lit in a smile, and his hands dropped back to his sides. "In that case . . ."

The laughter died on her lips as she stood near enough to him to catch the scent of his aftershave. The attraction swirled between them like an approaching storm. His Adam's apple bobbed, and he took a tiny step closer. The breath caught in her throat as she held her ground. His pupils dilated as he stared down at her.

Somehow she knew she'd have to be the one to make the first move. He had that weird idea that his scars made him unattractive. She sidled closer by half a step and brought up her right hand to touch his chest. Standing on her tiptoes, she reached up to brush her lips across his firm mouth.

His arm came around her, and he pulled her closer to deepen the kiss. A maelstrom of emotions rose in her chest as something in her recognized and responded to his deep need for affection and approval.

He started to withdraw when her hand caressed the scar on his right cheek, but she tightened her grip on him. He wrapped both arms around her like a drowning man grasping at a life preserver. All thought left her head as she welcomed the emotion bubbling in her chest.

What am I doing?

She dragged her mouth away and stepped back on trembling knees. "I told you there was nothing more appealing than a man in an apron." Her hand shook as she pushed the curls away from her face. "But we'd better get to work or I'll be fainting from hunger."

He gave a crooked grin before he returned to his task. She stared at his broad back for a moment. Garret would never have deigned to help in the kitchen. He never cared what she needed or what made her happy. In only three weeks, she'd come to recognize how different Boone was from many of the men she'd met. He cared about other people, and his integrity shone through every moment she'd spent with him. When he looked at her, she knew he saw the real Dana Newell, the person inside who often felt invisible and ineffectual.

This emotion she felt when she looked at him she couldn't quite name yet. It was already so much bigger than anything she'd ever felt for her ex-fiancé. It would be easy to run to someone strong to protect her from Garret, but that wasn't what this was. Boone's character would draw her even if she didn't have to worry about Garret.

———

What was Anu's shop doing open so early? Nicholls's Finnish Imports had been one of Dana's favorite places since she was a teenager. Stacks of Finnish sweaters were on display at the front of the store, and the scent of dye and fine wool was a familiar one. Another table held Marimekko linens, and Dana touched a coverlet as she passed.

Anu Nicholls, Bree's first husband's mother, owned the place. She made the best *pulla* in town, and the aroma of cardamom and raisins wafted from the kitchen at the back of the building. Dana hadn't been to see her since she got back, an oversight she was eager to remedy.

Anu looked up from attaching price tags at a table of Kalevala jewelry. "*Kulta,* at last I see you! I had heard you had returned to us."

In her sixties now, Anu was still as slim as a girl, and a few gray strands glimmered in her short blonde hair. Her blue eyes twinkled out of a mostly unlined face, though the lines around her eyes showed some of the sorrow her life had endured. She'd raised two kids by herself and had built a well-known business in the Upper Peninsula.

Dana stepped forward to hug her. "I know I've been neglectful. It's good to see you. I was surprised to see your lights on so early. I was on my way to the Suomi for breakfast before work and saw you moving around in here. I thought you might have spared some *pulla* and coffee."

"It's still hot."

Dana heard the clicking of dog nails on the scarred wooden floor, then Samson, followed by Bree, exited the kitchen at the back of the store.

"I thought I heard your voice." Bree handed her a piece of *pulla.*

"Ooh, that's what I was hoping for." Dana took a bite and nearly groaned as the delicious flavors hit her tongue. "I've missed this."

Anu glanced out the windows at the windswept street. "I have tea and coffee in the back. Come."

When they stepped into the kitchen, the warm aromas wrapped Dana in a cherished embrace. She'd spent many an afternoon here with Anu and Bree. Anu's worn Bible lay on the counter, and Dana's gaze lingered on it. Much of what she'd learned about how to live a Christian life had come from Anu. Seeing her again brought back so many memories as well as shame.

"You look sad, *kulta.*"

"I'm just thinking of how much I've failed. God, myself. My life hasn't turned out like I'd hoped."

Bree touched her shoulder. "Failure isn't fatal. Giving up is."

Dana smiled at her. "I often forget that." She slid onto one of the kitchen chairs and accepted the cup of coffee. The light roast was a Finnish tradition, and the mild taste seemed foreign to her palate, which had adjusted long ago to a bolder flavor. "Yummy."

Anu leaned against the counter. "As Bree said, you haven't failed. You are still here, still moving forward. God has a plan for you."

"I'd sure like to know what it is." Dana studied her face. "You never seem to hesitate to encourage someone in the Lord, even customers. That's how I first met you. I was buying a skirt for my parents' funeral, and you noticed I was crying. You hugged me and quoted Psalm 116:15."

Anu nodded. "'Precious in the sight of the LORD is the death of his saints.'"

"Don't you worry you'll offend someone when you do that now? I mean, the world is so different from what it was even five years ago. How do you know where to draw the line between offense and help?" The words came out in a rush. "I get terrible calls some days. I want to share a Scripture with them or pray, but I get all tongue-tied thinking about what my coworkers will say and if I'll get in trouble with my boss."

Anu's gaze probed hers. "Deep down you know when to speak and when to be quiet, but you are afraid to trust your instinct. And only God knows if your words will have impact. We are not told to decide who or who will not benefit from the words that point to life. We are just to be faithful with our lives and our words. If the Holy Spirit prompts you, then be faithful to what he has told you."

"I wanted to start over here, to be a better person, but I've found myself falling right into the old ways at my job. At my last job, my boss told me I wasn't allowed to say anything about God to people who call in, even when I felt like I should pray with them as they are waiting for help. Some have asked me to pray, but I was afraid of losing my job."

Anu nibbled on a piece of bread before answering. "I have no boss but the Lord. Has your current employer told you that you may not offer comfort to those in distress?"

"No." Dana glanced at Bree who sat across the table from her sipping coffee. "You know Mason better than me. Would I lose my job if I spoke up with a caller?"

Bree smiled. "Mason is a good Christian man. Why not ask him directly?"

Dana wanted to slap her forehead. "Of course. I was assuming the worst because of my past experience. Edmund Burke said, 'The only thing necessary for the triumph of evil is for good men to do nothing.' I've felt helpless lately. I guess I'm really not."

"We are far from helpless. God hears all prayer, even silent ones. It is the biggest power we have," Anu said. "Remember 2 Timothy 1:7."

"I will." Dana glanced at her watch. "I guess we'd better get to work."

CHAPTER 22

For God gave us a spirit not of fear but of power and love and self-control." Today was a new beginning. Dana was determined to cling to the verse Anu had given her.

Her muscles were pleasantly sore from the martial arts workouts she'd been doing. She hung her coat on a hook by the dispatch office door and went to her desk. The aroma of fresh coffee perked her up, and she glanced toward the snack station to see it wasn't quite finished brewing.

Tracie barely grunted when Dana greeted her. Dark circles rimmed her eyes, and her skin had a sallow tone.

"You okay, Tracie? Anything I can do for you?"

Tears filled Tracie's eyes, and she shook her head. "Rough night is all."

Dana started to walk past her, but her new determination to speak up stopped her. "Can I pray for you? I'd like to help you."

Tracie's eyes widened, and red washed up her neck. "I'm *fine*. Just leave me alone. I don't need your pity."

"It's not pity I'm offering." She put her hand on Tracie's shoulder and kept it there even when the other woman tried to shrug it off. "I'm here if you need anything."

She left Tracie and turned to meet Karen's speculative gaze. "Ready for a busy day?"

Karen sighed and her hazel eyes went flat. "I hope it's not like yesterday. You're lucky you weren't working. We had vandals going around town breaking windows and painting graffiti. The phones were nuts."

Dana wrinkled her nose. "Let's hope today is calmer."

Karen rolled her eyes. "Don't count on it." She studied Dana a moment, then glanced at Tracie and lowered her voice. "You're wasting your time with that one. She wouldn't want religion to interfere with her fun."

"I think she's beginning to realize her life isn't all that enjoyable."

Karen sniffed. "I doubt it."

Mark rolled his chair a little closer. "I'm sorry about your friend's death. You holding up okay?"

The sudden sympathy made Dana's eyes fill, and she swallowed hard. "Thanks."

Mark spared a glance at his computer, then focused on Dana again. "You think the serial killer she was tracking found her?"

"Did you know Allyson?" As far as Dana knew, not many people were aware her friend had been an investigative reporter or that she'd been pursuing what she believed was a serial killer.

Mark shook his head. "No, but you know how stuff gets around here in the sheriff's department."

Dana balled her hands into fists. This wasn't something she'd wanted to get around, not until they discovered who was responsible for Allyson's death. And she didn't care for the avid curiosity in her coworker's eyes.

She sat in her chair and swiveled it closer to her screen as a call came in. "Nine-one-one, what is your emergency?"

"That wasn't nice, Dana." Garret's deep voice rumbled in her ear. "You set me up. Is that guy your new man? Who is he?"

Her throat tightened, and she quickly tried to pinpoint where the call originated. He was on a cell phone on the outskirts of Rock Harbor. Even as she watched, the location moved. He was in a vehicle. Since Karen was on another call, Dana motioned to Tracie to come help her.

She pointed to the monitor and jotted on a paper *Tell the sheriff Waterman is on the phone.* Tracie nodded and grabbed her phone. Dana turned her back so Garret couldn't hear Tracie's call. "Why are you still hanging around?"

He let loose a string of curses. "I love you, Dana. That's the only reason I'm here. Nice job deflecting my question though. What about the new boyfriend?"

"He's Allyson's cousin, and he was helping me out." Remembering last night's kiss, she touched her lips.

"By trying to trick me?"

"We both just wanted to see what you knew about Allyson. We found your scarf by Naomi. Why did you hit her?"

"I'm not going to answer your crazy accusations. I just called to let you know I'm leaving. I'm through with you and your devious ways. Have a nice life."

The connection ended in her ear with a click. The location of the call winked out on the screen. Was he telling the truth? Was he really leaving town?

The sheriff burst into the room. "I sent deputies to the location. He signed off?"

Dana nodded. "He says he's leaving town."

"Not if I can help it." He waved a photograph in his hand. "I've had my men plaster posters all over town along with a description of his truck."

Tracie's face paled. She swiveled on her chair. "Can I see that a second? He looks familiar." She took the poster from Mason and studied it. "He told me his name was Jarret Mannon." Her voice choked off.

"Where'd you see him?" Mason demanded.

"At my brother's bar. I work there a few nights a week. This guy came in just after you moved to town. We started talking. H-He didn't have a hotel room, so I offered him m-my spare room." She looked away.

She is lying. Dana watched her shuffle and twirl a pen in her fingers. "You look frightened."

Tracie's hand went to her neck, and she pulled away the silk scarf. "H-He choked me. I think you can still see the marks a little bit. They were really dark, almost black, after he grabbed me."

The faint traces of bruises marred her creamy neck. Chills shuddered down Dana's skin. "Garret tried to kill you?"

Tracie's cheeks flushed, and she put the scarf back in place. "He got mad for some reason. I couldn't figure it out, but I think I just did. We were talking about you, and even though I didn't mention your name, I said the new hire was being stalked by some nutcase. He got all bent out of shape and grabbed me."

Mason scowled. "And you didn't report it?"

Tracie looked away as she fiddled with a strand of her black hair. "He said I'd be sorry if I did. I believed him. He's a scary dude."

"I'll need a deposition from you," Mason said.

"Did he spend the night?" Dana asked.

"No, he left with a final warning. I didn't ask where he was going—I was just glad he was out of my house." She turned back toward her screen as a call blinked. "I really thought for a few minutes that he might kill me on the spot. His eyes were soulless."

"I hope he really is leaving town," Dana said.

"I'll notify the state boys to keep an eye out for him. If anything, this shows you're not the only woman in danger from him." Mason headed for the door.

Dana turned back to her screen as another call came in. She should feel relieved, but an unsettled sensation had lodged in her belly.

———◆———

The aroma of pot roast, potatoes, and carrots still filled Bree's kitchen after the service for Allyson. Bree's eyes felt gritty from crying. The small church had been packed with grieving people, and Allyson's poor parents had been devastated. Only the Lord could bring comfort in a situation like this.

Her lips compressed, Lauri slammed the drawers and cabinets as she helped clean up the supper mess. Zorro lay in the middle of the kitchen not far from her. Bree exchanged a commiserative glance with Dana over Lauri's bad humor.

Bree put the last plate in the dishwasher. "You're free. Dana and I can finish."

Lauri still looked about sixteen instead of twenty-three in her skinny jeans and red sweater. She'd kicked off high heels before helping clean the kitchen, and her bare feet made her look even younger.

She tossed the dish towel onto the counter. "I don't know why you made such a big deal out of my engagement. I'm not a kid anymore. You and Kade are smothering me."

"Kade is just looking out for you. He's done it too long to stop now. Peter is a lot older than you."

"Thirteen years older isn't all that much." Lauri slipped her heels back on and turned toward the living room. She paused and turned back to face Bree a moment. "You'll see how perfect he is once you've met him."

"I'm sure he's a nice guy." But Bree wasn't sure. Not at all. Lauri had a habit of always picking the worst guys.

While she'd love to see Lauri happy, Bree wasn't sure she was grown up enough for that kind of lifelong commitment. Maybe in another three to five years, Lauri would be settled enough to think about a serious relationship.

"I can see the wheels turning," Lauri said. "What aren't you saying?"

Bree dried her hands, then hung up the hand towel. "I just think you're awfully young."

Lauri turned to Dana. "You haven't been stuck in this backwater all your life. What do you think?"

Dana's cheeks turned pink. "I'm sure Peter is a great guy, and from the size of that ring, he must have a good job. I see Bree's point though. You're just barely out of college, and Peter is mature. What if you get bored with him after a while?"

"You think I'm immature." Lauri spun on her red heels and stalked for the living room, her heels clacking on the floor all the way. Zorro padded after her.

Dana sighed. "I didn't handle that well."

"It was the truth though. I think that's my major hang-up about it. I love her, but she's spoiled and willful. She's used to getting her own way. This Peter might not really know what he's in for." Bree forced a laugh, but she felt like crying. Lauri had just gotten that new job where she had a chance to build a career and make a real change in her life. If she got derailed by a doomed romance now, it could set her back years.

"Maybe he'll be good for her maturity. These kinds of romances often work."

"Lauri was so excited about this new job because she got to get out of Rock Harbor. She craves new experiences and excitement."

"They met at her new job, didn't they? I thought that's what she told me."

Bree nodded. "Right off the flight in Kauai. But I need to stay out of it. She's right—it's not my business, really. She's an adult, and I keep forgetting that."

"You and Kade are still supporting her. She lives here, doesn't she? I bet she's not paying room and board. So that does give you some authority to speak into her situation. And you love her. She can hardly kick about that."

"We've never asked for money from her. Kade feels an obligation to her. Their parents died when she was in her teens, and he took over as a father figure. She's always resented that some. I think she didn't make the shift from seeing Kade as her brother to seeing him as an authority figure very well. I bet she'll move to her own place now that she's making decent money."

The thought of Lauri moving out seemed something to both rejoice in and despair about. Would Bree feel this way about her kids as they grew up and didn't need her anymore? Lauri was like her own sister. If she were sure she was ready for such a drastic new step, Bree could accept it. Or could she? She was beginning to realize how much she disliked change.

She forced a smile. "We can't solve this one. We'll have to leave it in God's hands. How's the new job working out?"

"Good. I feel right at home." Dana's smile faltered. "Garret called me at work yesterday and told me he was leaving town."

Bree studied her friend's downcast face. "Why aren't you smiling from ear to ear then?"

Dana's gaze came up. "I don't trust him, Bree. He says things to get your guard down, then moves in for the kill."

"Did you ever put a restraining order on him?"

She shook her head. "Everyone urged me to, but I just wanted to get away. And besides, it wouldn't stop him. Do you have any idea of how many times I sent cops out to stop a man with a restraining order? And Garret has always done whatever he wanted."

Boone's deep voice carried from the living room as the men cheered a touchdown for the Arizona Cardinals. Bree arranged homemade fudge on a tray. "And speaking of romance, what's up with you and Boone?"

"I don't know what you mean."

"Don't play dumb with me. I'd have to be blind not to see the way you look at him. Come on. Spill it."

Dana's cheeks went pink and she pushed a stray curl out of blue eyes that had suddenly gone soft and tender. "I think he's pretty wonderful."

"Well, of course he is. He's kept women at arm's length since he's been here, but he looks at you like you're wearing a Cardinals jersey."

Dana's laugh was breathless. "You really think so? He was really hurt by Esther."

"Esther was the name of his fiancée? It says a lot that he's told you about that."

Dana snatched a piece of fudge, and Bree realized the probing was making her a little uncomfortable. She picked up the tray of chocolates. "Let's go see what everyone is up to."

CHAPTER 23

The weather was clear and a bit warmer on Monday, a nice respite from the constant wind they'd had. Boone waved good-bye to the last of his customers around four, then glanced at the sky. He had time for a swim in Superior before darkness fell, and the lack of wind might make the experience a little more fun. After locking the office door behind him, he started for his cabin but paused when Dana's blue Prius pulled into the parking lot.

He waited for her to reach him. She wore a lighter coat today with no hood, and her light-brown curls glowed in the late-afternoon sun. "You just getting off work?"

She nodded. "I should have called, but it was a gorgeous day and I thought I'd drive out and see if you wanted to go for a hike. I've been cooped up all day and felt like doing something strenuous."

Would she be game? "I've got a better idea. Come with me."

She fell into step beside him. "What do you have in mind?"

"Swimming."

"You have an indoor pool?"

"I've got something better." He gestured to the deep-blue lake. "Superior."

She stopped and shook her head. "No way, big guy. You have to be crazy if you think you're going swimming in forty-degree water."

"I do it all the time. The benefits of cold thermogenesis are well known. It will be good for you. I've got a wetsuit that will fit you, and we'll only go in for a little while since it's your first time. You'll jump out of there feeling like you just won a marathon."

"I'll jump out the minute I put one toe in it."

He took her arm and turned her toward his cabin. "I take it that means yes you'll give it a try?"

She chewed on her lip, then sighed. "It's not a good thing for a relationship when a man can talk a woman into something that extreme."

Relationship. Did that mean she had feelings for him? He kept reliving that moment she kissed him and had come to no firm conclusion. When she'd actually touched his scar, he hadn't known how to react. No one had put a finger on that ugly ridge other than himself when shaving, yet she'd caressed it like it was the most attractive thing about him. He hadn't been able to forget it.

He opened the door to the cabin, then steered her toward his bedroom. "There are wetsuits hanging in the closet. You'll need a small. I'll change in the bathroom and meet you in a few minutes." Before she could back out, he retreated and closed the door behind him.

His wetsuit was hanging by the wood stove. It had dried overnight, so he carried it to the bathroom and tugged it on. He'd need to find her a hoodie, shoes, and gloves. How many women would do something like this? Renee had but not many would. He'd wanted to talk to Dana about that kiss ever since it happened, but he was afraid she'd say it was just a whim, that she only thought of him as a friend.

That kiss had been much more than friendship.

He yanked on his cap, then went to rummage in the storage chest for the rest of her equipment. The bedroom door creaked, and she stepped out in the wetsuit. His mouth went dry. He knew he was staring, but he couldn't help it. Maybe this wasn't such a great idea. She wasn't one for tight jeans and tops, but the neoprene suit showed off her curves and long legs.

"I look like I'm a cat burglar." She tugged on the sleeve of the suit. "All I need is a mask and I could steal the crown jewels."

"I've got the hat right here." He held it out.

Her smile faltered as her gaze locked with his. Her lips parted a bit as she stared up at him. He should make the first move this time. He took one step in her direction, but his cell phone rang and it broke the magic of the moment.

He snatched it from the coffee table and glanced at the screen. "It's Detective Morgan." He answered the call on the third ring. "Boone Carter."

"Mr. Carter, I told you I'd let you know if I had any news. There's a couple of things going on here. I checked with DMV to see if I could get hold of any photos of Leland or Dixon. Neither had a driver's license."

Boone inhaled. "Fake names."

"It appears so. And I had Gwen Marcey do a composite as part of the class she taught here on Friday. I faxed it up to the detective in charge of the Rogerson case. He remembered interviewing Faith's fiancé and said it looked like it might be Justin Leyland. He couldn't say for sure since composites aren't exactly pictures, but he was certain enough to say he believes there's a 90 percent likelihood that we're dealing with the same killer."

Goose bumps ran up Boone's spine. "So Allyson was right. There's a serial killer out there."

"Well, a budding one anyway. A serial killer is defined as someone who kills at least three people with at least a month of cooling off between murders. These murders were a year apart."

"What about Allyson? She makes number three."

"True, though she was never engaged to the creep. Her killing was likely more out of fear."

"But he drowned her," Boone reminded the detective.

"And that's reason enough to call in the FBI. Thanks for the tip on this. We might have a chance at stopping him now that we know he's operating out there. I'll have the Feds cross-check against the database for any other murders with a similar MO."

"Thanks for calling, Detective. Please let me know if you hear anything else."

"You got it."

Boone tossed his phone onto the sofa and told Dana what the detective had learned. "So at least they have a rough description. With the FBI on the case too, we have a better chance of finding him."

"Good news for sure. I say we get dressed and go have pizza to celebrate."

He tugged the cap onto her head, then began to tuck in the curls. "You'd throw away all the hard work of getting that thing on for pizza?" Her hair was as soft as bunny fur, and he wanted to linger with his fingers in those springy curls.

"You're right. That was about the hardest thing I've done. Besides, if I do this, I'll have bragging rights to being the toughest one on the dispatcher team."

He reluctantly dropped his hands back to his sides. "Stay in for ten minutes, and I'll spring for squeaky cheese."

"Now you're talking my language." She tucked her hand into the crook of his elbow, and they went toward the door.

Instead of heading to Rock Harbor, Boone had driven to Houghton to Pilgrim River Steakhouse, a place Dana had only heard about. The food had been amazing, and the moon glimmering on the treetops on the trip home had made it feel like a fairytale night. She didn't want it to end.

Boone parked his truck beside her Prius in the parking lot and shut it off. "I'm almost too full to move."

"Me too." She touched her curls, which were still a bit damp. "I think my hair is nearly defrosted."

His laughing scoff was soft. "Come on, you loved it. Admit it."

"It was the longest ten minutes of my life, but worth every moment with a meal like that." She shifted in her seat and released her seat belt. "But I will say my skin still tingles from the cold water. I'm sure it was good for my circulation."

"I think you should do it several times a week. It's good practice."

"For falling overboard in the winter?" She could sit here for hours and just banter and talk with him. Had she ever been this relaxed with anyone? He made her feel she could let down her guard and totally be herself with him. That he liked everything about her and wouldn't judge her. Her hair and clothes had never been perfect enough for Garret.

"You never know." His seat belt clicked as he unbuckled it.

She didn't want to get out of the truck. "Did the detective say what his next move was?"

"Just calling in the FBI. I'd like to do something myself, but I don't know what it might be. The FBI will be taking it over, and I doubt they'll be as tolerant of my pushing and questions as Morgan has been."

"Have you heard anything from Mason on getting into Allyson's files?"

"Not yet. He mentioned that the diver didn't find anything under the ice though. And there wasn't anything strange in her phone records."

"Maybe you and I can monkey with the files a bit. We could give it a try after my martial arts lesson on Wednesday."

"I don't know how far we'll get, but I'd like you to come over. I like having you around." His voice went husky at the end.

She licked suddenly dry lips as he slid toward her on the bench seat. His arm went around her and gently tugged her closer to him. Closing her eyes, she inhaled his clean, masculine scent as she tipped her head under his chin. They sat like that in companionable silence for several long moments. Dana almost didn't want to breathe in case it upset the contentment she felt.

His fingers found her chin and tipped it up just before his lips swooped down on hers. She curled the fingers of her right hand around the zipper of his jacket to drew him closer. Too soon he lifted his head, and she made a small mewl of protest and pulled him back for another kiss. He chuckled and tugged her onto his lap, then kissed her until she was breathless.

"We can't stay in the truck and neck all night." His words were a soft growl at her nape.

She ran her palm down the scars on his cheek and stared into his eyes. "Are you sure? I'm game if you are."

"What am I going to do with you? You're way too tempting to resist."

"You could try falling in love with me," she whispered. Her hand flew to her mouth. Did she say the words aloud? "I'm sorry, that was a stupid thing to say." She tried to scramble from his lap, but he held her cradled in his arms while she died inside. How could she say something like that?

He pressed his lips against the side of her head. "I didn't think I'd ever love anyone again, but you're making me doubt the truth of that. I'm willing to see where this relationship goes if you are."

Was he just saying that because she'd been so bold? Her eyes burned. "You don't need to pity me."

He stiffened. "Who said anything about pity? If anything, I'm the one who should wonder if your attention is because you're sorry for me because no other woman would look at me."

She managed to scoot off his lap. "You're an idiot! Any woman would want you, but you think this scar," she touched it, "disfigures you. It doesn't at all. I think you're incredibly handsome, but more than that, you're *good*. You make me want to be better, to care more about other people, to make more of a difference."

"You're already doing that, honey." The outrage went out of his voice. "Look, let's start this over. You want to explore the relationship, yes or no?"

"Yes," she whispered.

"Shew, you had me scared for a minute." He cupped both her cheeks in his palms, then leaned forward for one more brief kiss. "We're friends first as we figure out where this might lead. Okay?"

"Okay." Her chest felt like it might burst with the spurt of joy and disbelief that filled it. "Bree won't be surprised."

"I know. She said something to me about it the other day and told me I'd better not hurt you."

"What'd you say?"

"I told her it wasn't me she had to worry about. That I was more afraid of you trampling on my heart."

She put her palm against his chest and felt his heart pounding against it even through his coat. "I'd never do that."

"We'll see. I'm willing to risk it if you are."

CHAPTER 24

The house, lavish and comfortable, felt like home, but Garret couldn't quell his urge to pace and look out the windows at the snow blowing across the lake. Everything in him wanted to jump in the truck and grab Dana on her way home from work tonight, but he had a quick business trip to take care of first.

He took out his cell phone and glanced at it. Even texting Dana would be a bad idea. She was liable to track his location. Nothing said he had to stay here though. He could get lunch in Houghton or maybe go up the Keweenaw Peninsula to Calumet where he could text her before he got on the plane.

He grabbed his coat and slung it on, then took his keys and went out through the garage where he'd parked his truck out of public view. The truck engine fired as soon as he turned the key, and he backed out, then hit the remote on the garage door opener. His tires crunched on the frozen snow as he drove slowly to the driveway exit. No other vehicle was in sight, so he quickly gunned his truck out onto the road before anyone noticed which drive he'd exited.

His cell phone buzzed, and he glanced at the screen. Chris's picture showed. Should he answer it? Chris might be checking to see if he'd really left the area. Still the challenge of outsmarting his old buddy was enticing.

He slowed the truck and swiped the screen. "Hey, Chris, it's been a while."

"I wasn't sure if you'd talk to me." The noise in the background made it sound like Chris was in a store or somewhere public.

"Hey, we're still friends, regardless of what went down between me and Dana." There was no way Chris would buy that. He'd been antagonistic with Garret ever since he'd caught Dana's eye, and especially after she moved to Washington to be closer to him.

"Yeah, sure."

Garret lifted a brow at the nonanswer. What was his deal, and why had he called? "You back in Rock Harbor now?"

"I will be this weekend. I'm about to board my plane. I thought we might get together if you're still in town."

Garret didn't trust his former friend enough to even think about being honest. "Sorry, I'm back in Washington. When you headed that way? Maybe we could meet for a drink."

Chris swore under his breath. "I didn't think you'd give up so quickly."

"Hey, Dana made it clear we were through. No sense in beating my head against a fence post. I know when I'm not wanted. Still, I have to say I'm surprised you called. Why would you even want to see me? You've made it pretty clear you didn't want me dating your sis."

"I was probably wrong about that. I want her to be happy."

"And you think I'd make her happy?" Garret's chest expanded. Finally, someone else who saw he and Dana were meant to be together.

"She's sure not happy now."

Was he talking about Scarface? "He's an ugly dude for sure. But what can I do about it? She won't even talk to me."

"I'll work on her a bit. Any chance you could come back to Rock Harbor if I can get through to her?"

"Well, sure, as long as you get the cops off my tail. Dana has them out for blood."

"I think I can manage that. I'll talk to her and have her call them off. It's good to talk to you again. We used to be best friends, and I've missed that."

"That was all you, Chris. I never pulled away."

"I know, I know. I'm super protective of Dana, and I can't help it. Listen, I have to go. Talk to you when I have things worked out on my end."

"See you soon." Garret ended the call and tossed the phone into the other seat as he accelerated the truck toward Houghton. There was more to the call than it appeared. Chris never did anything without a motive. He must really have something major against Carter. *Scarface.* He couldn't stop the grin at the thought of that nickname.

Maybe he should have told Chris he was still in town. They might have hatched something together to get Dana to listen to reason. He picked up his phone and started to call Chris back, then shook his head and dropped it back in the passenger seat. Until he was sure of what was going on, it would be better to keep his whereabouts to himself. He didn't trust Chris, not really. He'd been too moody when it came to Dana. For all Garret knew, Chris would turn him in to the sheriff.

Something was going on with Newell, but what? Chris had a hard side. Garret had seen it in Afghanistan. "Trust but verify," according to the old Russian proverb Reagan used to quote. It was worth remembering when it came to Chris Newell.

Everything would be all right now that they were back on the island where it all began. Lauri dried and curled her hair, then went out on the balcony to wait for Peter to arrive. This had become her favorite spot on Kauai, right here on her own balcony watching the crabs fight for dominion on the lava rocks below. Wasn't that just like life? You fought and scraped to stake out your own little piece of happiness, then had to fight off contenders.

Such a cynical turn of her thoughts when she was waiting on the man she loved. She twisted her engagement ring around on her finger. Staring into the depths of its sparkling facets, she felt her spirits lift. So they'd had a little rough patch since he'd been late in Seattle. It was no big deal. They'd weather this.

The doorbell rang, and she sprang to her feet. Her heart pattered as fast as her steps to the door. She flung it open and threw her arms around Peter's neck. "I'm so glad to see you!"

His blue eyes were tired, and he looked his age. "That makes up for a long flight." He gestured to his suitcase. "Let me drop my things off in my condo. I wanted to let you know I was here before you wigged out again."

She pressed her lips together. "I'll come with you. I grabbed you some groceries. I'll bring them over."

He blinked and the tension around his mouth eased. "How sweet of you."

She went to the small kitchen and pulled out the bag of items she'd purchased from Big Save. He'd gone on to his apartment when she returned to the door. Was he still peeved with her? She didn't get it. She grabbed the key to the door, pulled it shut behind her, and went across the street to his place. The door stood open so she entered and headed straight for the kitchen.

The place had the same closed-up smell hers had when she'd gotten there. She set down the bag and began to empty it into the fridge. He must be in the bedroom putting his things away.

"I got you eggs, bacon, milk, butter, bread, and some lunch meat," she called. "Also some yogurt and soda. I figured we could grab anything else you wanted tomorrow. I have dinner in the oven. I thought you might be too tired to go out."

When he finally appeared, he'd changed from his suit into shorts and an aloha shirt. The stress of the trip was gone as well, and his smile seemed real this time. He hadn't lost any of his tan in the time they'd been apart.

He approached and slipped his arms around her. "Thanks for getting the groceries. The last thing I want to do tonight is go out. You thought of everything. I'm starving. What did you fix?"

"Lasagna and garlic bread."

His eyes narrowed. "Garlic bread?"

Taking one look at the displeasure on his face reminded her of her gaffe. "Oh no! I forgot you're allergic to garlic. I'm so sorry."

His mouth flattened, and the sparkle in his eyes dimmed. He pulled away. "You trying to kill me, Lauri?"

"Of course not. I just forgot! Give me a few minutes to whip up something else." Her mind scrambled for what she could fix that didn't have garlic. "I could make some omelets. I've got a ton of veggies in my fridge. Or I could do toasted cheese and soup. I've got tomato soup. No, wait that might have garlic too. I'll have to check the ingredients." She told herself to stop babbling because it wasn't helping. He seemed to draw more and more into herself the longer she went on.

She put her hands on her hips. "What would you like? I can even run to the store."

He stared steadily back at her. "Fix whatever you like. I'll just go out."

"Y-You mean alone?"

"You clearly don't really want to be with me."

She caught his arm. "That's not true, Peter. We haven't known each other long. You can't expect me to know everything about you in such a short time."

"I would have thought you'd pay attention to something that might kill me."

"I was tired. Everyone loves lasagna, or so I thought." She tugged at his hand. "Come on, honey. Let me fix you something else. I'll dump the lasagna in the trash so the smell doesn't bother you. Better yet, I'll bring the food over here and fix it." Tears stung her eyes, and she blinked them back. Why did she always mess up the good things in her life? She should have remembered something so important.

His blue eyes examined her face and he finally nodded. "Don't cry, Lauri." He pulled her into his arms and rested his chin on top of her head. "We'll muddle through getting to know each other better. I'm expecting too much too soon. You're very young. I'd thought that might make it easier, but that was a silly assumption on my part."

Make it easier? What did that mean? Sometimes he confused her so much. Maybe it was the difference in their ages, the way they saw things. They'd learn each other's ways and thoughts. It was a learning process for everyone.

"What sounds good for dinner?"

"The omelet idea would be great. Lots of veggies and bacon. Don't throw the lasagna away. That's wasteful. Give it to a neighbor or keep it for your lunches this week. You could even take it to work and let everyone else eat it."

He was a good man, always thinking of other people. She nodded. "Let me get the food. I'll be right back."

She hurried back to her place but couldn't quite squelch the feeling that something was very wrong.

CHAPTER 25

It was nearly bedtime, but Boone didn't want to have another sleepless night so he made no move to head to bed. Last night he'd lain in bed and listened to the clock hum as he relived every moment of the evening with Dana. The old fear had risen up and mocked him like an unrelenting bully. Dana seemed so different from Esther, but was she really? Was any woman? He'd called up every Bible verse he knew about being fearless, but he still shuddered when he thought about being hurt like that again.

A knock at the door startled Spirit, and he barked. Boone put down the book he was reading and went to the door. Who would be out on such a blustery night, especially at this hour? It was nearly ten. He flipped on the porch light, then opened the door.

Esther stood in the wash of light spilling from the entry. She wore what looked like a real fur coat and slim jeans tucked into leather boots. Time crawled to a stop as he stared into her beautiful face and the full lips that had once enticed him. He'd thought she was long gone with her husband.

Her smile held a trace of nervousness. "Don't look so surprised. Surely you knew I'd come by to talk."

"We said all there was to say years ago." And it had been four days since she and her husband showed up. He stood aside to let her in, which was probably a mistake, and looked past her to her empty SUV. "Where's your husband?"

"Dead drunk and asleep. He won't wake up until morning." As she sashayed past him, her perfume wafted in her wake.

How did he get rid of her? And why was she even here? He reluctantly gestured toward the fireplace. "Have a seat."

She took off her fur coat and settled on the sofa, then patted the spot beside her. "Nice little cabin. Cozy. I never expected you to leave Arizona."

He ignored her invitation and sat in the chair across from her. "I needed a fresh start."

"You ever see your old buddies? Tess, Flint?"

"Tess and Chase are as happy as two cubs in a cave on their ranch. They have two kids now, both boys. Chase is still fighting fires from one end of the country to the other. He comes this way on occasion." She'd never cared about his smoke-jumper friends before, so he wasn't sure why she'd bothered. Maybe she felt the awkwardness between them like he did.

"That's good." She wet her lips and looked down at her clasped hands.

He shot a glance to the clock on the wall. "Why are you here, Esther?"

She looked up then, her eyes luminous with tears. "I never got over you, Buck, not really."

"So you said. And the name's *Boone*." Hearing his old smoke-jumper nickname roll off her tongue hurt like the dickens. Once upon a time, the sound of his name on her lips lifted him to the heights. No more.

Her blonde hair shimmered in the firelight, and she turned those big blue eyes on him. "I still love you, honey. I never stopped. I tried to move on with my life, but you're my knight in shining armor, the strong man who would risk it all for others."

His pulse leaped, just a little, and he squelched it. "You're married."

She flicked her fingers. "That's easily remedied." Her lips curved in a smile. "We could be together the way we should have been from the start. I know it's all my fault. I have the money to get your face repaired. You won't have to live that way any longer. Neal never asked for a prenup so I'll get half of everything he has. You can sell this crummy old outfitting business, and we can travel the world together. You've always wanted to see Rome. That could be our honeymoon trip."

Bile burned his throat, and he fought it back down. How had he ever loved someone so shallow, so focused on money, so faithless? "What makes you think I still love you after the way you treated me? And you're talking trash about your husband, the man you promised to love forever. What kind of woman does that?"

Her smile faltered. "You love me. I know you do." She rose and stepped to his chair.

When she reached his side, he again caught the scent of her perfume, a familiarly sweet scent that tightened his gut and brought memories flooding back. He flinched and turned his head away when she leaned down to kiss him.

She reached out to touch his chin, and he grabbed her wrist. "I'm not interested, Esther. Whatever I felt for you was over long ago. I have a great life now, a life that doesn't include worrying whether or not I meet your standards. We are like oil and water. I was too naive to see it back then, but I should have known you weren't the sticking kind. You just proved it. I pity Neal."

Her eyes flickered, and she straightened. "I was young and didn't understand things of true importance. As a Christian, you have to forgive me."

Funny how she flung that in his face when she used to roll her eyes at his faith. "I forgive you, but that doesn't mean I'm going to have any kind of relationship with you. As I said, you're married. Even if I felt anything for you, I would never break up a marriage."

"So you *do* feel something for me!" She reached for him again.

He leaped to his feet to evade her. "I don't love you, Esther. I'm not sure I ever did. I didn't know you very well, and I was just as guilty of looking on the outside as you were. Go back to your husband. He loves you."

"He's a drunk." Her voice trembled, and she tucked a blonde lock behind her ear. "If I were a bottle of vodka, he might notice me. Most of the time he barely knows I'm in the room."

So she'd just come looking for comfort from her home situation. He had to admit he was relieved that her feelings didn't run any deeper than that. "I'm sorry, but you married him. I had nothing to do with it."

"I went looking for someone the opposite of you—someone who would always do what I wanted, who would give me what I wanted. I never dreamed that wasn't what I needed at all. He has no true character and doesn't stand up for much of anything. I suppose he might get angry if I hid his whiskey, but he doesn't love me. Not really. I'm just a bauble at his side."

"Kind of like I was to you."

Her eyes widened, then she nodded. "Touché."

He started for the entry, then turned the doorknob and opened the door to the blustery wind. "Have a nice life with your husband, Esther, but don't come back. We have nothing more to say to each other."

She grabbed her coat and followed him. She paused as she neared the door and reached for him, then dropped her hand. "I suppose you're right. Good-bye, Boone. I hope you find whatever you need to be happy." She pulled on her coat and stepped into the opening.

"What makes you think I'm not happy now?"

She gestured to the tiny cabin space. "You were never meant to be alone. I hope forgiving me will at least heal the scars on your heart enough to find someone else."

The door closed on the silence she left, and her last words reverberated in the room. Her vehicle lights flashed through the window a moment, and as he watched her pull away. Maybe he was able to forgive her after all.

———

Dana felt sweaty and sticky from the martial arts workout on Wednesday afternoon. Boone had been quiet and intense through the lesson, and she was beginning to wonder if he regretted Monday night. They sat in the warm sunlight streaming through the kitchen window as if they'd done it a thousand times. The aroma of freshly brewed coffee would have made her feel right at home if he'd shown the least bit of romantic interest in her. She'd thought he might at least kiss her after he tossed her to the mat, but he'd just held out his hand to hoist her to her feet.

She took a bite of the turkey sandwich slathered with mayo and piled high with lettuce and tomato. "Good," she mumbled past a mouthful. "I was starving."

"Me too." He took a sip of his coffee. "I was thinking about the encryption problem. The easiest way to get into Allyson's files is to access the software she used and figure out her password."

"That doesn't sound easy. How can you possibly figure out her password?"

"If I had her computer, I might be able to guess it."

"It will do no good to ask Mason for it back." She shook her head. "It's an active investigation. He's not going to give it up."

Boone ran his hand through his thick black hair, and it stood on end. "What if we cloned the hard drive? Then I could play around with it just as if it's her computer."

Surely he understood his request was highly unlikely. "Mason won't want you poking around in his investigation."

"Could you get into the evidence room and clone it?" He held up a large tanned hand. "Look, I realize I'm asking you to do something that could get you fired. It's not like we're tampering with evidence though. I just want a copy. If I discover the password, Mason will thank us for helping him out with the case."

She cared way too much what he thought about her. This had been her downfall all her life. She wanted to be liked and admired. If she did this for him, he'd think she walked on water and envisioning that made her heartbeat speed up. She liked her job though, and she wanted to play fair with her employer.

She gave a slow shake of her head. "I can't do that, Boone. I'd like to help you, but it wouldn't be right."

He sagged back in the chair. "I didn't think you would. I'm sorry I asked, but I'm desperate. I don't think the sheriff will be able to figure this out without my help."

Dana took a sip of her coffee. "I have an online backup of my entire computer. Do you think Allyson had anything like that?"

His hazel eyes brightened. "I hadn't even thought of that. I know she was crazy about making sure she didn't lose any files, but Mason didn't mention a hard-drive backup. Maybe she did."

"This isn't a hard drive. It's a backup in the cloud. We could try several popular services. You'd have to know what password she used for that too, but it would be a place to start. Login is usually the person's e-mail."

He grabbed his plate and coffee. "Come with me."

She took the rest of her sandwich and followed him down the hall to a small bedroom. It was scrupulously neat and held only a pine log bed, matching dresser, and a small corner desk with a laptop. A blue-and-red Ohio star quilt covered the queen-size bed. An oval rag rug was on the right side of the bed closest to the closet. The room held Boone's scent, an enticing aroma of man and spicy cologne. The top of the dresser was bare except for a picture of a pretty young woman who looked vaguely like him around the eyes and mouth.

She stopped and stared at it. "Your sister?"

His mouth twisted, and the sunshine streaming through the window threw the scar on his face into sharp relief. "Yes, that's Renee."

Dana's chest squeezed. She'd been so young. "She was beautiful. I love the laughter in her eyes. I bet she was one of those people who lifted your spirits whenever you were around her."

"She was." His voice was choked, but he strode past the dresser and went to the laptop. "What are some of the online backup services?"

She named the top one and watched him call up a window. "Just click forgot password and see if it accepts her e-mail address. Do that until you find a service that recognizes it."

"Good idea." The computer keyboard clacking stopped. "Not that one. What's another one?"

She named another. "That's the service I use."

He called it up. "It recognized her e-mail!"

"Try the most likely password. I know they say not to use the same password for multiple sites, but it's tempting to do so you remember it."

Intent on the screen, he didn't look at her and nodded. "Maybe her birthday." He tried that and shook his head. "I should have known that was too easy."

They tried several other passwords, but nothing worked. Boone stared at the screen. "It's going to lock us out after another failed attempt."

Dana felt a sense of déjà vu. Some hint was so close to being able to remember. She and Allyson had been friends a long time. In high school they'd all called her Ally Cat. Dana moved to his side and tried to ignore his scent. "Try AllyCat, no space between the two words and capitalize the first letter of each word. Add the last two digits of the year she was born."

He nodded. "That's it, Dana. You did it!" He grabbed her and pulled her into a hug on his lap.

His lips brushed her cheek and the corner of her lip. Time stuttered and slowed until all she saw was the gold flecks in his hazel eyes. She could drown in those eyes.

His grin faded, and he leaned forward a fraction. Her lids fluttered and started to lower until his arms came around her waist and he set her on her feet.

"Let's see what we can find out now."

His impersonal words were as cold as a rainy November day. What had happened between Monday and now?

CHAPTER 26

W hat had he been thinking? While seeing Esther had allowed
him to forgive her, it had also been a reminder of what he
might experience again if he let Dana get too close. The hurt in her
eyes when he'd turned away had been a knife to his chest though,
and he called himself every kind of coward under the sun. But he
still couldn't bring himself to look at her.

He scrolled through the list of files in Allyson's backup. "I don't
remember that nickname. None of the family called her that."

"It was just in high school, but when I called her that at the
café, she smiled and said she didn't think anyone remembered that
old nickname." Dana's voice held a wobble.

Untouched and forgotten, their sandwiches sat on the desk.
They were going to find something from this. They had to. He
leaned forward and let out an exultant cry. "I can just download this
entire backup to my computer. It will restore all her programs and
files."

"Will it overwrite your files though?" Her voice regained its
usual timbre, well-modulated and polite.

"I can create a new user, then download it all as if it's her." He
went to System Preferences and created a new user, then started

the download. "It's going to take a while. Let me get you a new sandwich and freshen your coffee."

"I should get going. I'm sure you have t-things to do." There was that wobble in her voice again.

"If you happen to have a change of clothes in the car, you can shower here. I mean, it would be great if you were here long enough to rejoice when I crack the encryption." He wouldn't blame her if she turned and rushed out of the cabin and never came back.

The workout had caused her dark-blonde hair to curl all over her head. "I've got some clothes in the car. I'll grab them and shower while it's downloading." Her gaze searched his before she turned toward the door.

How did he even explain what he was feeling? For so long he'd felt stuck in a time warp, determined to be alone, but now he was beginning to imagine another kind of life. One that included Dana. The thought terrified him.

He shoved the emotion away and went back to his computer. For the next fifteen minutes he sat and watched the files copy. It seemed an eternity before the patter of the shower ended. When the bathroom door finally opened, she brought the scent of his soap and shampoo with her.

He swiveled in the chair as she came back into the bedroom. "Sorry I only had guy shampoo."

Dana looked even more beautiful after her shower with her wet hair slicked behind her ears and her skin flushed all over from the hot water.

She smiled as she approached him. "It was fine, and I feel almost human again."

He forced his clenched fist to relax and reach for the keypad. "We're only at 10 percent. This could take all day."

"Probably not." A dimple showed in her cheek when she smiled. He turned his attention back to the computer. It was at 25 percent. Maybe another half an hour and he'd have it. Then what? What if he couldn't figure out the encryption password? He doubted Allyson would have been able to figure out his passwords if she were on this end of things.

But maybe she would. His preferred password was EsthersFool. Maybe it was time he changed it and moved on to something more positive. She had no power over him any more. He could clearly see her now, and he was lucky to have escaped.

Dana's blue eyes were shadowed when he looked up and caught her gaze. He'd put that hurt there. What was wrong with him? One step forward and two backward. "So you mind staying and working with me on this? I promise to whip up something better than sandwiches in a little while."

"I don't have anything else to do. Phantom will like hanging out with Spirit."

"We might actually crack this thing by bedtime."

"Let's not get too crazy. Her password might not be the same." She leaned over to look at the computer.

His shampoo smelled much better on her. He had to heal this chasm that suddenly yawned between them. His stupidity had put it there, and he needed to figure out how to bridge it.

She tapped the screen. "I was thinking about the encryption program while I was in the shower. The password might have something to do with the investigation. She might have used your sister's preferred password. Do you have any idea what it might be?"

What might it be? Renee had been the sweetest person he'd ever known. She had a passion for people, kittens, and chocolate, in that order. As far as he knew, she didn't have a nickname. He shook his head. "No clue." He looked back at the screen. It would still be a while, and there was time for him to make amends.

"Listen, Dana, I don't want to hide anything from you. There's something I need to tell you."

She straightened. "Okay."

"Esther came to see me last night."

"Your former fiancée?"

He nodded. "It was nearly ten. She said she still loved me and wanted me back."

Dana backed away as hurt overtook her face. "So that's why you're being so cold." Her head bobbed as her eyes filled with tears. "I totally understand. Don't think any more about it. You've loved her a long time."

Love? It hadn't been real love at all. It was more like some kind of fever that had gripped him. He rose and stepped toward her. "It's not like that. I told her to leave, but I'll be honest. It scared me to realize what might happen."

Her eyes were huge as she stared at him. "M-Might happen?"

He ran his fingertips over the rippled ridges of his scar. "I'm not sure I'm ready for a relationship. You'd have to look at this a lot of years."

The stricken expression in her eyes intensified. "That boulder you carry around is going to break your back, Boone. Would you walk away if I had a scar?"

For a moment he tried to imagine her with a scar. Would it change this pull he felt toward her, the way he loved being around her? "Well, no. It wouldn't change who you are or how beautiful you are."

"Then why do you keep harping on that stupid scar?" She touched his cheek. "I stare into your eyes and I can't look away. It's like we have this connection that happened from the first moment we met. You see me on the inside. I don't think anyone has ever even noticed how much I love *Phantom of the Opera* or that I hate the way my hair frizzes. You pay attention. You *care*."

Her fingers made their way up to his hair and tangled there as she pulled his head down. Her sweet breath enticed him, and he lowered his lips to hers. She twisted her fingers more tightly in his hair, and her eyes were still closed when he lifted his head.

"You make a lot of sense."

"Of course I do." She took her time to stroke his cheek, then stepped back and turned toward the computer. "Looks like the download is finished. Let's see what we've got."

He moved reluctantly back to the chair and called up the encryption program. The pressure built in his chest as he typed in the *AllyCat* password. The spinning beach ball swirled for a moment, then the program opened. "That's it, we're in! I'll print out all the pages."

———

The flames in the kindling caught and flared. Boone added more wood and stepped back as the fire settled into a soft crackle. "Let's split up the pages. What I've read so far is background I know all about."

The dogs lay together on a rug near the fire, and the cozy picture it brought made Dana sigh. Would she ever feel true safety and peace in her life like the dogs snuggled so close together?

Dana pulled a red chenille afghan from the back of the sofa over her feet and legs. "I don't know much so I'll be reading it with a fresh eye. Let me have the early stuff and you take the ones from the past few weeks." She took the pages Boone handed her and spread them out on her lap.

"Good plan." He sat on the floor in front of the sofa.

His shoulders touched her knees, and she had to resist the urge to plunge her fingers into his thick hair. *Focus, Dana.*

She inhaled and picked up the first of the pages. They were mostly a recap of what Allyson knew about Renee's death. A vein in Dana's neck pulsed at the description of the murder scene. How did Boone bear it? What must it be like for him to know some sociopath held his beloved sister's face in the water tank? And what would he do when he discovered the identity of the murderer?

She couldn't stop herself from reaching for him and resting her hand on his shoulder. He swiveled his head to look at her with a question in his eyes. "I'm sorry." Her throat felt thick. "This has to be hard for you."

"No matter how many times I've read it, I can't keep the mental images from forming with every word."

The sorrow in his eyes broke her heart. She removed her hand and went back to reading. The only way she could help was to find the killer. She flipped to the next page. It held only one line of text.

November 15. What really happened to Dana's parents?

Her eyes widened, and her breath caught in her throat. "B-Boone?"

"What's wrong?"

Wordlessly, she held out the page to him. "Where was she going with this?"

He took the paper and stared at it, then looked back up at her. "I don't know. She never mentioned it to me. Your parents died on a boat, didn't they?"

The mental images slammed into her—their bodies floating in

the water at the foot of Copper Falls, the smashed-up boat, the way her cries echoed through the canyon. *Focus.* "Why would she be asking a question like that? It has nothing to do with this investigation. And the date is the day I came to town. I don't understand."

His frown deepened. "And why is it mixed in with the pages detailing Renee's murder? It's like she went back to that spot and inserted it though it had nothing to do with Renee."

Her world seemed to shift and take on shadows she'd never seen before. This was all mixed up, and she didn't know how they could be expected to figure it out.

Boone put down the sheaf of papers. "Tell me what you remember of the day your parents died. Maybe someone was there who is connected to Renee."

"I told you the other day how their boat went down."

"Yes, but let's talk about before. Earlier in the day. What happened?"

It was a time in her life she hated to think about. Had her desire to fit in, to please everyone, started with that bright summer day with the sun blazing down and reflecting on the blue water? Maybe. Nothing had been the same after that, nothing.

"I'd been spending the whole summer with my aunt and uncle in Rock Harbor. My dad had gotten a new job, and Mom thought it would be easier for me not to be there when all my things left the house."

He rose and settled on the sofa beside her. "You didn't want to move?"

She shook her head. "I'd lived in that house my whole life. I was going to change schools too, and I was worried about leaving my friends. For weeks I'd been able to forget the shadow looming over my life. Mom and Dad came to pick me up. They were staying a week before we all left to go to our new place. The last day of our vacation was a little blustery and cool, but Dad had been hot on the trail of a big steelhead. He wasn't about to lose his last day of fishing." She smiled at the memory.

"Did you have a fishing guide? Did you stop at an outfitter before going out? See anyone or anything unusual?"

She thought back. "We went to the bait shop. Dad also got some new tackle and lures. Tommy Whitaker waited on us. We'd gotten to be friends that summer. He had a bad feeling about us going out that day and tried to talk my dad out of it. He thought there was a big storm coming."

"Some people have always thought Tommy was a little bit of a seer. He's warned me off the water several times, and he's always been right."

Tommy was born with Down's syndrome, but a sweeter, gentler person didn't walk the face of the earth. "You're not saying Tommy had something to do with the accident?"

"No, no, nothing like that. I just mentioned it in case it triggered a memory."

She nodded. "I hadn't even remembered it until now. Mom didn't want to go. She wanted to stay home and pack, but Dad coaxed her into going. Chris too, and she could never deny him anything. She loved Chris like he was her own kid. So she packed a lunch and we went."

"Did you stop to get groceries?"

"Yes, some peanut butter and bread as well as chips and soda."

"So you saw quite a few people that day." His arm crept around her shoulders.

"I guess you're right. But what does that have to do with Renee?" She leaned her head against his arm.

He sighed and removed his arm. "I don't know, but I think we should look at the old records of the accident and see if we're missing anything." He scooted back to the floor. "Back to work."

"Here's something," Dana said a few minutes later. "Allyson mentions that Faith Rogerson's best friend says Justin had food allergies and that Faith had to be careful about what she cooked for him."

"What kind of food allergies?"

"She notated that she was going to call Renee's friends and see if anyone knew. It doesn't look like she did."

Boone reached for his phone. "I'll check with her pastor to see if he knows anyone she was close with other than Allyson. I'm sure there are others. I'll call Pastor Saul Rigney. It's only six in the evening on the West Coast. I'll put it on speakerphone so you can hear too."

"Boone, how you doing, my friend?" Pastor Saul's voice boomed out.

"We've got more trouble, Saul. You probably haven't heard about Allyson."

"Your cousin?"

"Yes." Boone told him about the murder and what they knew so far about the connection. "Do you know anyone in the church who might have double-dated with Renee and Tyler?"

"Renee and Shana were pretty close, and we went out for burritos a few times on Friday night."

"So you met him! Do you know if he had any food allergies?"

"Strange question, but yeah. I can't remember what it was though. Something kind of common. Shana's at a ladies' meeting right now but should be home by nine. I'll shoot you a text if she remembers. And I'll be praying for you, Boone. I'm really sorry about this."

Dana jotted down food allergies on a notepad. What kind of common item might be at a Mexican restaurant? Corn maybe. Wheat, dairy. Lots of things it could be.

"Thanks, Saul." Boone ended the call.

She showed him the note of possible allergens. "So maybe it's another indication that the two men are one and the same." She yawned and looked at the clock. "I need to be getting home." Phantom's ears perked at the word *home* and he rose and stretched.

"Looks like your dog is tired too." Boone stood and helped her slip her coat on. He grabbed the front of her jacket and pulled her in for a kiss. "Saying good night is a good excuse for a kiss."

She smiled up at him. "I don't think you need an excuse."

CHAPTER 27

Another day, another city. Why had Lauri once thought the travel would be glamorous and exciting? She sat at a table for two in The Eagle's Nest atop the Hyatt Regency and looked out the window at the city lights of Indianapolis. At least Indy was a clean, safe city that had a friendly Midwestern vibe. A server carried a steaming steak past her, and the aroma made her mouth water.

Peter should be here any minute, and she smiled at the thought of seeing him again. She'd missed him terribly. She flipped over her left hand and studied the glittering ring on her finger. They still hadn't set a date. Maybe they could do that tonight. She was impatient to begin her new life with him. Where would they live, and did he have a house already? They'd discussed so little of their backgrounds.

She saw his familiar blond head and waved. His easy grin lifted her spirits even more. Dressed in khaki slacks and a navy blazer over a crisp white shirt, he was incredibly handsome. Several women in the restaurant shot him admiring glances. And he was all hers.

She lifted her face for a kiss and soaked in his spicy scent and firm lips. It was much too brief. She opened her eyes as he moved to his seat across from her.

"Did you order for me?"

She shook her head. "I wasn't sure what you wanted, and I thought you'd better stress to the server how serious your allergy is to garlic."

He smiled across the table at her. "I've missed you. Have you had a good week so far?"

She shrugged. "I was lonely without you."

The server arrived, and they both ordered the center cut filet without garlic. She reached across the table to take his hand. His fingers squeezed hers gently, and warmth flooded into her chest. She was so lucky to have him. On impulse she grabbed her phone and came around to crouch beside him. She lifted the phone to take a selfie.

He knocked her arm down. "What are you doing?"

"Taking a picture of us. I don't have a single one which is crazy."

"I don't like having my picture taken." He scooted his chair away.

So it was going to be one of those kinds of nights. Suppressing a sigh, she moved back to her seat and put her phone away. She picked up her water glass. "Have you thought about where we'll live when we're married? We really haven't talked much about the future."

He shrugged. "I haven't thought about it."

"Where do you live now? You've never really said."

He traced circles on her palm with his thumb. "I actually don't have a place. I gave up my house about two years ago since I was never home. It seemed a waste to spend the money on a house that sat empty."

"What about your belongings?"

"I got rid of most everything. I have a small storage shed here in Indianapolis I visit from time to time."

Uneasiness rose in her chest at the thought of having nowhere to call home. "That's no way to build a marriage though. We'll want something that's our own where we can establish a home base. I'll want to have my things there to be able to trade out clothes. It's important to build a sense of family and connection. I don't want to live out of a suitcase every single day of my life."

He withdrew his hand, and his lips flattened. "It seems silly, Lauri. We both travel so much that it would be a waste of money. Still, if that's what you want, I can think about it."

His secrecy was driving her crazy. They had to talk about things—their past, their lives, their families. "I live in Michigan in case you're wondering. You've never asked. I have an older brother, and both my parents died when I was a teenager. How about you?"

He cocked a brow. "I like Michigan. Where do you live?"

Was he being deliberately secretive? She stared at him trying to read his hooded expression. "You wouldn't have heard of it. I'm in the Upper Peninsula, a little town called Rock Harbor. It's between Ontonagon and Houghton."

He sat back in his chair. "I've been there. Cute town."

"I'm surprised. Hardly anyone knows where it is." A thread of tension tightened around his eyes. She studied him, trying to figure out what he was thinking. "What if we bought a house there? Or an apartment. Real estate isn't expensive. That way I'd be able to see my family on the weekends. You'll love them! My brother, Kade, is a park ranger, and his wife runs a training center for search-and-rescue dogs. They're lovely people."

And she missed them. She hadn't realized it until she started talking about them.

He loosened his tie and released the top button of his shirt. "I thought being with me would be enough, Lauri. Are you going to be just like most women who want the moon? Give me this and give me that. Stay near my family. I thought you were different."

Her pulse ratcheted up. "Anyone would want a home base, Peter. You're being unreasonable. How would we even be together without a home?"

"We've been together most of the time since we've been engaged."

"What about kids?" she shot back. "We won't always be free-spirited and able to travel the country week after week. We'll eventually need to settle down."

"You want kids?" His voice rose a bit.

She saw people looking their way and tried to tamp down the discord. "Well, sure, don't you? I just assumed."

"That's an assumption you shouldn't have made. What if I can't have kids? Or you can't? You're painting this rosy picture of the perfect family in your head, and nothing in life is guaranteed. I didn't have that kind of perfect life, did you?"

"Well, it was mostly that way until my parents died. Kade did the best he could, but I never really got over losing them. I guess that's why I'm looking to have my own family unit." She reached across the table to take his hand again. It was stiff and unyielding. "Don't you want that too? Why marry me if you don't intend to be a family unit?"

His blue eyes were like chips of Superior's frozen waters. "I'm beginning to wonder how well suited we are, Lauri. I thought you were a free spirit like me and would want to continue our lifestyle. I want us to be able to travel the world and see exotic places like Cambodia and Bali. If we're locked down with the so-called American dream of two-point-four kids and a house, we'll turn into someone just like Kade and Bree."

"There's nothing wrong with that. They have a good life." She pulled her hand back as the server brought their food.

She might have made a big mistake.

Boone banked the fire for the night, then turned off the lights and turned to go to his bedroom. While he still wasn't totally ready to let go of any fear he had about a new relationship, Dana was becoming more and more important to him. In his heart of hearts, he knew she was nothing like Esther, but it would take his head a little while to fully accept it.

His cell phone lit up with a text message from Saul that read *Tyler allergic to garlic.* Boone shot back a message of thanks, then grabbed the files from Allyson's computer and started down the hall. Tail wagging, Spirit followed him.

When his cell phone rang, he assumed it was Saul calling to talk more about the murders, but it wasn't him. "Detective Morgan, I wasn't expecting to hear from you again so soon."

Harry's smooth southern voice held a trace of weariness. "Sorry to call so late, Mr. Carter, but I thought you'd want to know the FBI has found two other cases that bear remarkable similarity to the murders of your sister and Ms. Rogerson. The case is getting high priority. A team of federal agents is going to be working the case."

Two more cases. He flipped on his bedroom light, then sat on the edge of his bed. Spirit leaped atop the quilt, then lay down beside him and stared at him with mournful eyes.

He needed to answer instead of just sitting here in shock. "I'd be happier if it weren't for realizing how evil this man truly is. Allyson was right all along. Up until her death, I'd poo-pooed her conviction Renee's death was tied to the Rogerson one. But she was right about everything."

"I'm afraid so. If not for you and your cousin, his existence would still be a mystery, and he'd be preying on innocent women in the shadows."

"He still might be," Boone said. "He's not in custody yet."

"There may be even more cases. It's a little too early to tell, but these other two cases had exactly the same MO—brides drowned the night before their weddings and no pictures of the mysterious fiancés. And while we don't have him in custody yet, we'll be able to compare notes between the cases and see what we turn up."

Boone looked down at the sheaf of papers beside him. "I found out something along that line tonight. In Allyson's notes, she mentioned that Dixon was allergic to something. I called Renee's pastor and found out he was allergic to garlic. Have you discovered Leyland's allergy yet?"

"It's also garlic." The detective's voice held satisfaction. "One more clue to follow, Mr. Carter. I'll be in touch."

"Thanks for calling, Detective." Boone turned off his phone and picked up the papers he'd printed from Allyson's files. He forgot to mention Allyson's question about what had happened the day Dana's parents died, but it probably wasn't relevant.

Bright LED lights flooded the records department with enough light that it was easy to forget it was in the basement. Deputy Doug Montgomery hiked his pants up over his big belly and gestured at the rows of beige metal cabinets. "The files are all here. They are arranged by year. When did your parents die?"

Dana shifted a bit closer to Boone who had joined her at the end of her shift. Her lunch was still a hard lump in her stomach, and she wasn't sure she was ready to look at details of the accident that killed her parents. "Twenty years ago."

Montgomery stopped and peered at several cabinets before yanking open the fifth one in the row. The metal screeched to a halt. "Help yourself. I'll be in my office if you need me. A copier's in the corner there by the table if you need it."

Dana wet her lips and nodded. "Thanks."

Montgomery closed the door behind him leaving them alone in the cavernous room that suddenly felt hot and stuffy. She wiped her clammy palms on her jeans and forced herself to step to the files. She found the file labeled NEWELL about halfway back. It almost felt hot in her hand, though she knew it was just her trepidation. She'd spent most of her life trying to forget that day, and now here she was plunging headlong into all the facts.

Boone's hand, warm and comforting, came down on her shoulder. "I'll be right here with you. Let's just see if anything's here. It's probably nothing. I can look for you if you'd rather not read it all."

She shook her head. "I have to face it." The file was ominously thick in her hands as she carried it to the wooden library table. Boone pulled out a chair for her, and she settled onto it, then opened the file. The picture on top was of the wrecked boat, and she shuddered.

He touched her shoulder again. "You okay?"

She couldn't tear her gaze from the picture. "I'm fine. It's just hard to think about that day."

"You were eight, right?"

"Yes."

"A hard age to lose your mother."

All these years she'd tried not to think about her mother. It was as if grief had blanketed her life, the dark folds muffling the feelings and memories of her first eight years of life. Now that she was staring at the picture, it felt wrong that she'd allowed it to happen. Her parents had loved her and her brother, Aaron. Snippets of events flooded her head: Aaron protecting her from a bully at school, Mom discussing their favorite movie, *Phantom of the Opera*, with her, Dad taking her to fish for the first time.

It was hard to catch her breath with the crushing weight in her chest. What was wrong with her? Why had she blocked out so much of it? Those had been good times not bad. Her hand trembled as she moved the picture to the other side of the file.

A close-up of her father's dead face was next, and she slammed her eyes shut and stood, nearly knocking the chair over. "I can't do this."

"Let me do it." Boone's hands steered her away from the table. "There's a coffeepot by the copier. Get some coffee while I take a look at it all. If there's anything I need to ask, you'll be close by."

Miserably aware of her cowardice, she nodded and headed to the coffeepot. It shouldn't be this hard. Coffee sloshed over the side as she poured it into a cup. She took a big gulp and grimaced. It tasted old and burnt, but the acrid flavor steadied her and anchored her here to this place and not to the events of a lifetime ago.

Her hand was steady as she walked back to the table. She wouldn't look at any pictures. Maybe the details of what the investigators found wouldn't be so traumatic. "Find anything?"

Boone held up a paper. "Were you familiar with the boat they took out that day? A storm washed it ashore, and they were able to examine it. The investigation stated that it wasn't owned by your uncle but by a neighbor, Owen Cork."

"I'd forgotten that. Mr. Cork owned a marina, and he was my uncle's best friend. Since there were so many of us who wanted to go out that day, he loaned him a fishing boat. Mr. Cork had just repaired it and put a new motor on it."

"Looks like an eighteen-footer with three seats. So that's why you went with your uncle and his family?"

She nodded. "They had a big boat that held six. We were short a seat for all of us to go, and no one wanted to stay home."

"The report mentions that the hole caused by the log going through the hull might have been preexisting. Cork swore it was sound when it went out though, so that avenue of questioning appears to have been dropped."

She detected the suspicion in his furled brow as he looked back at the report. "You're not sure?"

He shrugged. "I know boats, and the description sounds fishy. The hole was too perfectly round. It sounds like it might have been a plug that got knocked out. It could have happened in the impact, but I'd love to take a look at it myself."

"It's probably in a boat graveyard." She suppressed a shudder.

His gaze sharpened. "Something wrong with going to a boat graveyard?"

"I was trapped in the hold of an old boat overnight. It belonged to Mr. Cork, strangely enough. I was twelve, and I haven't been on a boat since." Again, it was something she tried not to remember.

He made a copy of the entire file, then took her arm. "Let's go see Mr. Cork."

CHAPTER 28

Broken and abandoned boats stretched for four acres. Boone had been to Cork Boat Salvage before, but it had been several years. A layer of snow coated the hulls, but no amount of snow could cover the stoved-in holes in some of them. Busted motors rusted away in the elements, and rats had torn the stuffing from boat seats and left them as deflated as an abandoned inner tube.

Dana looked a little pale as she got out of his truck and tucked some errant curls back into her sock cap. "It looks smaller and sadder than I remember. When I was a girl, this was a fun place to play hide-and-seek. It seemed to go on forever too."

"Perception is a funny thing. I fell out of a cherry tree once and sprained my ankle. I crawled for what seemed like miles to the back door. When I look at the yard today, it's only about twenty feet."

She looked around. "I don't see Mr. Cork. Wasn't he supposed to be here somewhere?"

"His wife said he was wandering around looking for a part to repair a boat." Boone caught movement from his right side and turned to see a stooped figure rummaging through the remains of what appeared to be an old Lund boat. Grizzled hair stuck out from under a blue knit hat. Bundled up in a down jacket, Cork appeared heavier than he really was.

The man caught sight of them and straightened. A grin broke out on his thin, weathered face. "Boone Carter, is that Miss Dana with you, eh?" His broad Yooper accent stressed the first syllable of every word.

Dana stepped past Boone. "It's me, Mr. Cork. Good to see you again."

The old man approached and shook hands with them. "I heard tell in town that you'd been spotted about. You here to stay?"

He was about eighty-five, but he looked about twenty years younger, probably from staying active. Boone saw him around town most weeks. He was often carrying equipment that would cripple a younger man.

"Planning on it. I'm working as a dispatcher."

Cork's alert brown eyes twinkled. "That's good, that's good. You should stop over and say hey to the missus. She has fond memories of baking cookies with you and your mama."

Dana's smile looked forced. "I'll do that."

The old man appeared to be waiting for them to state their business, so Boone obliged. "You remember the day Dana lost her family, I'm sure."

Cork's smile vanished, and he nodded. "Ya. Hard to forget such an awful thing."

"Do you still have the boat that went down with them?"

He blinked, then nodded again. "What you be wanting with that old heap? It won't tell you much except its sad story."

Boone hesitated, unsure if he should tell the old guy he suspected he was lying about the previous damage. Before he could make up his mind what to say, Dana took a step forward.

She held out her hand toward him in an appealing gesture. "There's so much I've forgotten about that day. So much I've blocked out. I need to come to terms with what happened."

The suspicious glint in Cork's eyes faded. "Ya, I can see that." He turned and pointed toward an old grain bin whose roof was partially caved in. "It's in yonder building. Mind your step though. The old grain bin could fall if you give it a good shove. The boat is on the north end under an old tarp. I'd go with you, but I've got a doctor appointment. Wife's been harping on me to get a checkup. Foolishness, I call it, eh."

"We'll be fine by ourselves. Thanks, Owen." At least they wouldn't have to hide their interest in the hull.

The old guy gave them a nod, then walked off toward an old barn where a gray pickup sat. Boone led the way in the opposite direction. Birds fluttered away in indignation as he stepped into the leaning building. Sky showed through in multiple places in the roof, and bird nests and spiderwebs covered the interior walls. It didn't appear anyone had been here much over the years.

"There it is." Boone picked his way through the assortment of boat parts toward a tarp covered shape. He tugged the canvas off the boat, and a mouse squeaked and ran in terror.

Dana's gulp was audible. "I hate mice."

"You don't need to come any closer. I know what I need to see." He leaned over the side and lifted two torn life cushions out of the way to reveal a gaping hole in the hull. Just as the report had stated, the hole wasn't jagged but as round as if someone had used a hole saw on it. "There it is." He took out his phone and snapped some pictures.

Dana stepped closer and peered over the side. "What do you think?"

"Looks like someone might have repaired it by making a hole and filling it with a wooden plug that came loose during the impact."

"So it likely didn't really have anything to do with the accident?"

"That would be my guess, but I think we need to find out where this boat came from and if Cork knows who repaired it."

"Why bother if it isn't likely to have caused the accident?"

"I'm giving Cork the benefit of the doubt, but it's possible someone did a shoddy job and the repair came out. Maybe the boat was filling with water, and your dad couldn't control it well enough. Steering a boat filled with water is like trying to guide a log in the rapids."

Her blue eyes clouded. "You still wonder if someone did it deliberately and killed them, don't you?"

"I don't think that's the case, but Allyson obviously wondered so we need to pursue that thread until we're sure. You game?"

She squared her shoulders and nodded. "Let's go talk to the Corks."

"I'm starving. Let's grab a pasty at the café first. By then Owen will be back from the doctor's." Was his motive purely hunger, or was he just eager to see that lost expression in her eyes vanish for a while?

———

The Cork residence was as familiar as if Dana had been there yesterday. The big house, built in the 1800s, was in pristine condition. Bright-blue shutters contrasted with the white siding, and the wide wraparound porch was just as inviting as she remembered. The swing moved gently in the wind, and two big pots on either side of the door held the frozen remains of mums.

The two-car garage sat next to the road like most in the U.P. Boone pulled into the drive next to it, and she got out almost before the truck rolled to a stop. Boone had taken the lead with most of this, and it wasn't fair to him. This was her family who had died. The accident was more than an unlikely clue—it was where her entire world had shifted on its axis. She didn't think she would ever be whole until she faced what had happened. It was time to get her head out of the sand and examine her life in all its pain and trauma.

With Boone on her heels, she marched up the wide painted steps to the blue door and pressed the doorbell. No answer. Boone reached past her and rang it again. Moments later a familiar female voice called, "Coming."

Jane Cork threw open the door and drew Dana into a hug. "Owen told me he'd seen you." She pulled away and held Dana at arm's length. "Let me look at you. Ya, I see you have the look of your mama just like Owen said." She tugged on her arm. "Come in, child. I want to know what you've been up to."

Jane hadn't changed much. Her hair was still dyed the most gaudy shade of red imaginable, and her brown eyes sparkled with the joy of life. She wore enough necklaces to drown her if she fell overboard, and Dana was sure she'd seen the tie-dyed blue-and-purple skirt fifteen years ago. Jane was barefoot and wore a shapeless blue sweater over the skirt.

Dana had always loved her free spirit, and warmth spread through her chest. At least some things never changed. She kicked off her boots on the rug in the entry and handed Jane her coat. Boone did the same. Jane's house was always spotless, and she liked to keep it that way.

"I've got coffee on," Jane said. "And I just took snickerdoodles out of the oven. I know they're your favorite."

"I haven't had a snickerdoodle since I left here." The scent of cinnamon made her mouth water.

"I gave you my recipe," Jane scolded. Her bare feet slapped on the wood floors as she led the way to the kitchen table where a tray of cookies awaited.

"I know. They aren't as fun to make or eat without you there."

"Have a seat and I'll pour the coffee. Owen is washing up and will be out in a minute."

Boone pulled out a chair for Dana, and she settled on the hand-woven cushion. She'd sat at a loom and helped Jane make them when she was fifteen. This warm kitchen with its cheery blue-and-white decor and wide windows felt like coming home. She'd cried on Jane's shoulder many times over the years.

Shuffling footsteps came from behind her, and Dana twisted in her seat to see Owen entering the kitchen. Without his coat, she could tell he'd lost some weight.

He smiled at her and reached past to snag a cookie. "Ya, it's about time you got here. Jane hasn't even let me have a cookie crumb since I got back from the doctor's."

"Only one cookie." Jane walked toward them with cups of coffee. "The doctor says your sugar is too high, and you've got to watch your diet."

Owen sighed. "Woman, I'm eighty-five. I hope my Maker doesn't make me hang out on this old earth until I'm a hundred. Might as well enjoy the time I have left. I've made a particular request to the good Lord that I get a never-ending supply of snicker-doodles in heaven."

Jane sniffed and rolled her eyes. "He can't take you until I go, so I plan to keep you as healthy as possible."

Dana wrapped her fingers around the cup and let it warm her

fingers. The thought of anyone believing this sweet couple could have had anything to do with the accident was ridiculous.

Boone took a sip of his coffee. "Thanks for seeing us. We had a couple of questions and wanted to see if you remembered."

Jane glanced at her husband, and a slight frown creased her forehead. "Owen is having a little trouble in that department, but we'll do what we can."

"Jane." Owen's voice held a thread of warning.

She waved her hand. "Oh posh, Owen. You think people don't notice when you forget what day it is? You know what the doctor said. No sense in trying to hide it."

Alzheimer's? Dana hated the thought of her friends going through that. Maybe they shouldn't have come.

Boone shot her a warning look and his hand clamped onto her wrist when she made a move to rise. "If you can't remember, it's fine. I noticed a round hole in the boat's hull, and we saw mention of it in the official report too. Do you remember where you got that boat and if you'd had to make any repairs on it?"

Owen stared back at them. "I bought that boat brand new and had it for years. The only thing I ever had to do to the body was paint it. I'd done some repairs, but it was only to the engine. The hull was in fine shape when it went out. Chris had taken it out fishing just the week before. I know it looked strange that the hole was so round, but it was just a fluke. Believe me, I hid nothing from the sheriff." He glanced at his wife.

Jane nodded too. "That was my favorite boat. It was small enough for me to handle easily, and I often took it fishing myself. Because it was mine, Owen babied it." She nudged the plate toward Dana. "Have another cookie."

"Do you think there was anything suspicious about the

accident?" A tingle went up Boone's spine when the Corks looked at each other. "What is it?"

"Owen . . ." Jane's voice held a warning note.

"She might as well hear it, hon."

Jane pressed her lips together and got up to get the coffeepot. "Oh go on, you old coot."

Owen stared at Dana. "There was talk in town that your dad scuttled the boat. He'd lost his job and was despondent, or so the rumor mill went."

Dana gasped and stared at the old man. "That's not true. We were moving to a new place where he'd gotten a different job. He was happy that week. All I remember is laughter and fun."

Owen reached for his cup. "There was likely nothing to the story then, but that's what everyone was saying. Even Chris mentioned he'd wondered about it."

"I'll talk to Chris." Dana couldn't believe this was the first time she was hearing this rumor. But it wasn't true. She was sure of it.

CHAPTER 29

The sun shone weakly through the thin clouds, and the wind tried to tear Boone's knit cap from his head. He tugged his hat back over his ears and went to the mailbox to see what had been left for him yesterday. The door, thick with rust, squealed as he opened it. He pulled out a handful of junk mail and a small padded envelope.

He hadn't ordered anything. He frowned at the return address, somewhere in Washington, but it wasn't his sister's address. Her apartment had been cleared long ago. Tires crunched on gravel and snow, and he looked up. Dana's blue Prius slowed in front of the cabin. She'd worked overtime yesterday so he hadn't seen her since Thursday when they'd talked to the Corks. She must have the day off. Something he was hoping for.

She got out and patted Spirit who was sniffing noses with Phantom. "Anything new in Allyson's file?"

"Nothing yet. I'm still going through the notes. A lot of them are handwritten, and she wasn't the world's best writer." He unlocked the workout building and let them in. The lights hummed as he flipped them on. "You're off all day, right?"

She took off her coat and hung it on a hook. Her navy stretch pants and sleeveless tank showed off her slim figure. "Yes, why?"

"Just wondering how long I've got you for." His gaze lingered on her small feet tipped in red nail polish. She was so darned cute with her hair up and her face devoid of makeup. "You ready to get started?"

"Sure."

They sparred for an hour, and he was breathing heavily and dripping with sweat by the time they finished. "You're getting pretty good. I think you can hold your own if you're attacked."

She grabbed a towel from her bag and dabbed her forehead. "I think so too. I feel confident."

"Have you heard anything more from Garret since he called?"

She shook her head. "Nothing. I hope it stays that way. Maybe he really is gone."

His gaze landed on the padded shipping bag he'd forgotten, and he picked it up. After he ripped open the top, a USB drive fell into his hands. "What the heck?"

"What's wrong?" Dana came to stand beside him.

He spied a paper inside and pulled it out. "It's from Detective Morgan. This is all the data off Renee's phone. They have to keep her phone for the investigation, but he was hoping I could look at the data and see if anything rings a bell with me."

"That's generous of him."

"He's a good guy. He really wants to find the killer." He tossed the envelope and junk mail in the trash. "You have time to look at this with me? I've got leftover pizza for lunch."

"Sounds good to me. I've got to get Chris at the airport in an hour and a half, but I have time now."

He carried the drive to the desktop computer in the corner and plugged it into a port. The screen came up, and he scanned the list of files. "Looks like her pictures, files, and e-mails are all here." He dragged the files to his desktop. "I want to see the pictures first. I'm hoping to see a picture of her fiancé."

Dana pulled up a chair beside him. "I'm not sure how much help I can be."

He didn't say that her presence alone calmed him. She'd think he had lost his mind. "You might see something in the background I miss."

He took his time scrolling through the pictures, pausing long enough to absorb the entire scene. Renee having Mexican with two girlfriends, mugging it up poolside with Allyson, on an ATV in the desert with a giant saguaro in the background, hiking on Mount Ranier, and cooking at someone's house.

"I think these are older." He called up the information on one. "They're from two years ago. Let's keep looking."

He scrolled past six months' worth of pictures, then stopped at a birthday party. "This was her twenty-fifth birthday. I wish I'd been there. I think she met Tyler there though. Keep an eye out for anyone who seems to be looking at her too. Maybe he is with another group at this party."

His eyes were going bleary from looking so hard at the screen, and he blinked. His finger was on the button to go forward when Dana stopped him.

"Can you enlarge this one?"

"I think so." He enlarged it and leaned forward. "What are we looking at?"

"That guy half hidden behind the woman in the white dress. He looks a little familiar, but it's too blurry to see his face since he's half turned away."

"I'll see if I can enhance it later with another program." He started moving through the pictures again, but an hour later they were no closer to seeing Tyler Dixon, at least as far as he could tell. The last picture was of Renee's engagement ring on her hand. It looked vaguely familiar though he didn't consciously remember seeing it.

Dana rose and reached for her coat. "It's nearly five so I'd better go get Chris. Let me know if you see anything." She moved closer to him and lifted her face for a kiss.

It was beginning to feel so natural to hold her and imagine she was his. And maybe that dream would come true.

———

United Airlines serviced the Houghton airport. Dana sat in the parking lot with the heater pumping out warmth until she saw Chris, roller bag in tow, stride from the terminal. She tooted the horn and waved as she pulled the car up beside him and popped the trunk.

He slung his bag into the trunk, then climbed into the passenger seat. "Thanks for picking me up." His cologne filled the Prius's small space.

She sent a smile his direction as she pulled into traffic. "It's good to see you even if you make me jealous with your tan."

He grinned. "They don't call it sunny California for nothing. Everything okay at home?"

She hesitated, then decided now was as good as any other time to question him about the accident that killed her parents and brother. "I ran into the Corks on Thursday. They haven't changed a bit, just gotten a little older."

Foot traffic from shoppers and college students was thick as she drove through town. She had to concentrate to avoid running down careless students. "Have you seen them?"

He shifted in his seat and shook his head. "I haven't seen them in ages. Not since I moved away. I'm here so rarely there's not much time to socialize. How are they doing?"

"Still spry. Listen, I've been thinking about the day my family drowned. I wanted to see the boat and just try to make sense of it for myself."

"What the heck? Why would you want to relive all that, Dana? It's painful so leave it in the past."

"I know, but I can't. Owen mentioned there was a rumor going around after the accident. People said my dad was despondent after losing his job and killed himself, Mom, and Aaron. Do you remember hearing a rumor like that?"

He pulled off his sock hat, and his blond hair stuck up. "Yeah, I heard it. I thought there might even have been some truth in it."

She shook her head as she accelerated out of town on the windswept road. "It's not true. Dad had a new job, and we were heading for a new place after our vacation. He wasn't despondent at all. We had a great time when they got here. He took me fishing and pushed me in the swing. Mom laughed a lot. I remember." Why was she so desperate to prove the theory wrong? She was just a kid and could have done nothing to alter things. And the laughing man she remembered could never have killed his entire family. "Besides, if it were true, why didn't he make sure I was in the boat with him? They took you instead."

"Are you sure you're remembering that week and not something when you were younger? You were only eight, Dana. Most people don't remember all that much from their childhood. I don't."

Was she wrong? A memory of her dad and mom on the ferry to Isle Royale National Park flashed into her mind. "I remember lots from that time, Chris. We went to Isle Royale and up to Copper Harbor. We ate lots of ice cream and went swimming in Superior. I remember it all."

He fell silent a moment, then turned his face toward her. "I didn't want to say anything, but I heard your parents fighting one night. The night before the accident. Your dad yelled something about he was good for nothing and all he had facing him was a low-paying job and humiliation. That your mom would be better off without him. So yeah, when that rumor started, I thought it might be possible."

"But why scuttle it with you in the boat too? Why not make sure I was in there?"

"I don't know. He made sure I had on a life jacket, but he said nothing to anyone else. After the accident I began to wonder about that."

She gripped the steering wheel so tightly her fingers ached. What did she do with all this? It turned everything she'd thought about her life upside down. But even if it was true, why did Allyson write that cryptic note about it?

CHAPTER 30

Rock Harbor's early December weather was as far from Hawaii as it was possible to be. The ferocious wind blew snow across the road in front of Lauri's car as she fought to keep the wheels on the road. She was still reeling from her conversation with Peter in Indy. Did she really even know him?

The coming sunset limned the barren trees in yellow and red and highlighted the buildings in town with vibrant color. It was hard to summon a smile to wave at Anu who was locking up her shop for the night. Lauri could just hear the hullabaloo when she announced she was breaking her engagement. It would be more proof that she was immature and impetuous. And maybe she was. She'd gotten engaged after only five days. Who did that? Only a stupid kid with her head in the clouds who didn't stop to realize she didn't know the man who was asking.

The crux of the matter was that she still loved Peter. At least she thought that's what this pain in her chest signified. She'd had such rosy dreams of the future, a future that seemed almost too good to be true. And clearly it was.

Or was she overreacting? She'd sprung her ideas on him after a long flight, and maybe he'd just been tired. They had time to figure all this out. She shouldn't have pushed him like that.

Stopping at a light, she rubbed her forehead. Maybe Bree could shed some light on this, though Lauri hated to admit that her fairy-tale romance was already in trouble. She glanced to her right and froze. A black SUV accelerated through the green light with its driver clearly visible.

Peter Lovett.

He didn't see her as he turned off Jack Pine Lane onto Quincy Street. Lauri closed her dangling mouth. What was he doing in Rock Harbor? Her pulse roared in her ears, and she tried to think through what he was doing here. She'd told him where she lived, so maybe he'd come to see her. But why wouldn't he call to meet her or at least ask for her address? Could he be here to scope out buying a house? Maybe he wanted to surprise her with a home.

That was it. Her heart rate settled, and she smiled. That would be just like Peter. When the light changed, she turned onto Quincy as well and watched for that black SUV. There it was, parked in front of what used to be the Copper Junction Hotel. Someone had bought it and turned it into a three-story mansion with mullioned windows and a new front door. She hadn't heard who had bought it, someone from out of town maybe? Maybe the owner was a friend of Peter's.

She slowed her car and nearly pulled in behind the SUV. What would he do if she showed up and knocked on the door? She shook her head. The last thing she wanted to do was cause another argument. She wasn't ready to say the relationship was over.

She turned around at the end of the road by the church and drove back past. Lights were on inside now too, but she didn't see anyone through the windows. She drove back to the light and turned left onto Houghton and followed the curve onto Negaunee Street. Bree and Kade's lighthouse home was just ahead on the right, and the lights twinkled out over Superior.

Home. More and more she was coming to realize how blessed she was to have her brother and Bree. She hadn't been the easiest teenager, and Kade had always loved her. Bree too.

They would understand her dilemma now. They always did. She pulled into the drive and parked behind Bree's green Jeep. That thing should have been retired long ago, but Bree loved it so Kade had kept it in top working condition. Lauri's boots crunched through the snow, and she felt a surge of joy as she pushed open the front door and heard the children laughing as they played tag with Samson.

She'd always taken this place for granted. How wrong she'd been. She shed her coat and hung it up in the closet in the foyer, then stepped into the living room. Zorro leapt up with a happy bark and raced to put his cold nose against her hand. "Good boy, did you miss me?"

Kade's face lit in a smile when he saw her. "I didn't expect you until tomorrow." He rose and moved toward her.

She stepped into his hug and burrowed against his broad chest. "I missed you, big brother."

He dropped a kiss on her hair, then took her by the shoulders and pulled her away enough to look into her face. "Whoa, what's wrong?"

"Does something have to be wrong for me to miss you?" She knelt and hugged the twins who had rushed over to greet her. Hannah had Bree's pointed chin and hairline and was crazy about dogs. Hunter was stocky like his handsome father and loved helping his daddy with orphaned wildlife. They both had Kade's soft, dark hair.

Davy hung back a bit, but she pulled him into an embrace too. He didn't protest but threw his arms around her waist.

Bree got up also, and her gaze studied Lauri's face. "I'll make some coffee. There's vegetable soup cooking, and I'm sure it's ready if you're hungry."

"Starving." Lauri followed her into the kitchen and left Kade with the kids. Zorro stayed on her heels.

Her brother always knew when to lag behind and let Bree counsel her. Smart man. Lauri went to the coffeepot. "I'll make the coffee." She opened the canister and put beans in the grinder. "Hey, that remodel of the old hotel downtown looks pretty good. Who owns it?"

Bree stirred the soup, then began to ladle it into bowls. "Chris Newell, Dana's brother. He'd been gone from the county for about ten years, then moved back and bought it two years ago. He's done a great job. Dana lives there with him for now."

Lauri tried to remember what Chris looked like. "I'm not sure I've ever met him."

"Probably not. You don't really run in the same circles. You would have been like thirteen when he left the area. Nice guy. I'm sure you'll run into him at some point." She carried bowls of soup to the table. "You going to tell me what's wrong?"

Lauri made a face. "Just wondering if I've made a mistake about Peter. Everything moved so fast. I'll look like a fool if I give him his ring back though."

Bree set down the bowls and turned to face her. "It's not foolish to be careful of a lifetime commitment. You don't really know Peter yet, not really. If you have even a hint of trepidation, it's smart to put on the brakes. This is your whole future, Lauri. You're only twenty-three. If he's the one, going slower won't hurt anything."

Just the advice Lauri needed. Bree always saw things with a clear gaze. "I love you, you know. You've always been there for me, Bree, and I haven't always appreciated it."

Bree's green eyes filled with moisture, and she hugged Lauri. "We're always here for you, Lauri, always."

And Lauri intended to count that blessing more often.

———

After church on Sunday, Boone opened a photo-editing program and pulled up the half-hidden figure they'd seen earlier. He played with the settings a few minutes until the man's face came into focus a bit more.

Frowning, he studied the enhanced photo. The guy looked a bit like Chris. His gut clenched, but Boone couldn't ignore the similarity either. Was it possible? Chris traveled a lot. He went back to the picture of the ring and looked at it again. Where had he seen it? His jaw tight, he studied it until it clicked. It looked a lot like Lauri's ring.

He flipped over to Lauri's social media page and scrolled through her pictures until he found one of the ring. Surely it was the same ring. He couldn't be sure unless he looked at it more closely, but he was 99 percent sure. But what about Faith Rogerson's ring? He found her social media profile as well, and it had open settings so he was able to look at the pictures. There it was. The ring looked the same.

He struggled to catch his breath. Reaching for the phone, he called Detective Morgan's office and asked an employee to scan and e-mail the police drawing they'd made of Tyler. A few minutes later the attachment came through. It also looked a lot like Chris.

Boone wasn't sure what to make of it all. He would have to talk to Dana about it privately as soon as he could. Boone called up the college Chris worked for and looked at the recruiters listed.

Boone's gut clenched as he thought about telling Dana his suspicions. Maybe this could be resolved by talking to Chris. They'd been friends for a while. Boone couldn't wrap his head around his own suspicions. He glanced at the clock: only one thirty. If he could catch Chris before Dana got home from work, maybe he'd get some answers.

Chris picked up on the first ring. "Hey, Boone, good to hear from you."

"Hey, buddy, you alone?"

"Yeah, just downtown at the café for lunch. Dana had to work today. What's up?" His voice held a touch of wariness.

This wasn't going to be easy. Boone stood and paced the floor. "Did you ever meet my sister, Renee?"

"Nope. She never visited when I was in town. You doing okay, Boone? You sound stressed."

Something in his tone made Boone doubt he cared about his stress or anything else. "So you never attended a party in Washington or Arizona and met her there?"

"Not to my knowledge. What's this all about?"

Boone looked at the picture on his computer screen, then flipped to the police composite. It had to be Chris or his doppelgänger. But how could Lauri's ring be the same? Nothing made sense. "I got a copy of the files on Renee's phone. There's a picture of you at a party she attended." The silence on Chris's end of the conversation grew so long Boone wasn't sure Chris was going to answer. "Chris?"

"I'm not sure what your accusation is all about, Boone." Chris's voice was as cold as the wind outside.

"You travel to Washington as well, and there's a police sketch of Tyler Dixon that looks a lot like you."

"Who's Tyler Dixon? You know what, scratch that question. I don't care who he is, but I don't like your tone. I'm hanging up now. You can call our friendship over."

The phone went dead, and Boone ended the call. Had his own friend killed his sister and his cousin? His chest squeezed as he struggled to control his grief. He'd been blind. He had to tell Dana. She might be living with a maniac.

Boone tried to call her, but it went to voice mail so he hung up and called Detective Morgan's number. He had to leave a message for the detective so he just asked him to call. He prayed he was wrong. But he couldn't risk Dana's life by leaving it. Once he talked to Morgan, he'd tell her.

CHAPTER 31

The beeping from low fuel caught Dana's attention as she pulled away from the curb after work on Monday to head home. She turned around and drove toward the city limits. Konkola Service Station was the only place in town to get gas, and it was on the corner of Whisper Pike and Houghton Street. Only one other vehicle was at the pumps when she pulled in. She'd have to pay inside, so she started the flow of gas and went inside.

A man behind the counter looked up with a smile when she entered. His mechanic's clothing threw her for a minute, then she placed his face. "Kory? Kory Gibbons?"

His smile faltered, then came flooding back. "Dana Newell, as I live and breathe. I'd heard you were in town, and I figured you'd eventually make an appearance here. Everyone in town does sooner or later."

He hadn't changed much, and her smile froze as her shoulders tightened. His grin endeared him to most people, and his copper coloring and freckles put her in mind of Rupert Grint who played Ron Weasley in the *Harry Potter* movies. One change was that she caught the glint of a wedding ring on his left hand.

She'd once daydreamed about marrying him herself.

"My Prius doesn't need gas very often, but here I am." She glanced at the clock on the wall above his head. There was a little time to chat, though everything in her wanted to run. "How have you been?"

"Fine, just fine." He wet his lips and took a step forward, then paused when she flinched and stepped back. "I had a speech all prepared, and now that you're here I can't remember what I wanted to say." He ran his hand through his longish red hair. "I'm sorry. That's about all I can remember of that speech. Really sorry I scared you like that."

She fingered the tiny scar, a visible reminder of that night, by her right eye. "I forgave you long ago, Kory. Why'd you do it though? That's what I've always wondered."

"I hero-worshiped Chris, and I would have hijacked a car if he'd told me to. I didn't stop to think how it would scare you."

She frowned. "Chris. What's he have to do with it?"

Confusion clouded Kory's eyes. "He told me he confessed. You didn't know?"

She clenched her fists together. "Confessed what?"

"It was all his idea to have you come with us to the abandoned boat, then leave you. I didn't want to do it, and he talked me into it."

Was this some kind of joke? Chris would never do that. He was the one who had found her the next morning huddled in a corner after having cried out every tear in her eyes. He soothed her and comforted her. And since she'd gotten back to town, he'd even said something about punishing Kory back then for what he'd done.

She finally found her voice. "I don't believe you."

He blinked and held out his hand, the fingers stained with grease. "It's true. Ask Chris."

"Why would he do that? It doesn't even make sense."

"He never told me." Kory hesitated. "Chris could be a little different, and I went along with him. You ever see his trophy box?"

"Trophy box?"

"Yeah, all the people he's gotten even with. He keeps a tally."

Her hand shook as she fumbled for her debit card. "I have to go. I got gas on pump two."

"It's on me. That's the least I can do. I'm really sorry, Dana."

She didn't stop to argue with him but dashed outside into the wind. Though Kory had urged her to ask Chris about it, she wasn't sure how she could even bring it up, not without sounding like she believed Kory. And she didn't.

She got in the car and slammed the door with more force than necessary. The sound of the door closing took her back to the hatch snapping shut over her head.

She sat on the back porch steps and swiped tears off her cheeks. Chris had said she couldn't come with them to the old boat lying on its side on a deserted Lake Superior beach. They were going to have a campfire and roast marshmallows, and while that sounded like fun, the real reason for her low spirits was she'd hoped to sit by Kory. Though he was five years older than her, he was everything she wanted in a boyfriend. She had two whole notebooks filled with his name.

Not that her dad would think she was old enough for a boyfriend. At twelve she knew Chris and his friends considered her a kid. But she wasn't! She rose and walked into the yard, then picked up a rock and threw it as hard and as far as she could. It made a satisfying thunk against a tree. She might as well call a friend and see if she could go over there for the night. It would get her mind off all she was missing.

She checked with her mom and was told it was okay to call her best friend, Betsy, then picked up the wall phone in the kitchen. Before she dialed the number, Kory poked his head in the back doorway.

"There you are." He came inside and let the screen door slam behind him. "I was looking for you."

Her mouth dried. "You were?" She loved the way his hair fell over his forehead. Her fingers itched to stroke it.

He nodded. "Want to go with us? Chris said it was okay. You can ride with me. Let's bounce."

"Sure." Her heart pounding and her face hot, she followed him out the door to his pickup.

He didn't say much on the way to the boat, but he glanced at her from the corner of his eye a couple of times. Did that mean anything? Maybe he liked her but thought he shouldn't because she was too young.

Chris and two friends were already there when they got to the beach. They'd collected a big stack of firewood, and Chris's girlfriend, Chloe, had brought out the Hershey's bars, marshmallows, and graham crackers. No one said a word to her most of the evening and she sat on the outside edge of the group. Why had she bothered to come? Kory hadn't paid her any attention.

"Let's play hide-and-seek," Chloe said. "I need to move."

Chris groaned. "I'd rather go swimming."

She ignored him and turned her back to a tree. "One, two, three."

Dana leaped to her feet and rushed away to hide. Kory held his finger to his lips and pointed at the old sailboat on the beach. The thirty-five-foot sailboat's wooden hull had holes in multiple spots. It hadn't been on the water in years and sat decaying in the Michigan sun. They were going to explore it, but no one had made a move to look inside. She climbed onto the slanting deck and looked for a place to hide. The door to the inside was open, so she climbed down the ladder into the interior. A bit of light came through the many small holes in the side. No one would think to look for her here.

The fabric covering the bench sofa was still in relatively good condition so she settled onto it and waited to be found. She couldn't hear a thing but her own breathing. She focused her attention on the light shining from the open hatch above her. Just a few more minutes and she could climb back out. They'd never find her here so she just had to give it enough time.

The minutes seemed to tick by so slowly. She rose and stretched. Surely it had been long enough. Before she could move toward the ladder, she heard quick steps above her, and she leaped back into the shadows. A jagged piece of metal sliced the skin by her eyes, and she bit back a screech. Her fingers came back wet. She must be bleeding.

Then the hatch slammed shut above her, and the space plunged into darkness. Only the small amount of light from the holes in the hull allowed her to see a bit.

"Hey! I'm down here." She rushed to the ladder and climbed to the top, then pushed against the door. It didn't budge. She pounded on it. "Let me out! Hey!"

She paused to listen but heard nothing. She climbed back down and looked for something to use to bang on the side, but everything was firmly attached. She went to the hull and pounded on it. "Someone let me out!"

She scrabbled along the side to peer out a small hole. She could just make out everyone heading to their vehicles. "Hey, don't leave me!"

The air squeezed from her lungs at the thought of being left here. Surely they knew she wasn't with them. But then why would they notice when no one had looked her way all evening? She'd sat on the edge of the group and hadn't said a word for hours. When the vehicles left, she looked around. There had to be a way to escape. Maybe she could break one of the holes bigger. But she had no tools, no way of figuring it out.

When the sun finally sank and the space went pitch dark, she crawled along the dirty floor to the sofa, then curled up on its filthy surface and prayed for deliverance. But it was morning before Chris came for her. He said Kory had played a trick on her, but that he would "take care" of Kory.

She took a deep breath as she shook off the memory and started the car. Had it all been a lie? She didn't believe it, couldn't believe it. It was more of Kory's mean streak. She started her car and drove for the house. She'd love to talk this over with Boone. It felt like forever since she'd seen him on Saturday.

He was going stir crazy since he got back in town. Maybe a hike through the woods would blow off some steam. Garret parked along the road by Copper Lake and got out. The temperature hovered at ten degrees, a bone-chilling cold that stung his face when he slipped on snowshoes. The bracing air perked him up though, and he was ready to do something other than plan what he was going to do to Dana.

The snow, hard and crunchy from the cold, squeaked against his snowshoes. His breath steamed the air as he trudged toward the iced-over lake. He paused on a small hill a few feet from the lake and watched an iceboat skim past in the center of the lake. The sound of scraping of the runners against the ice carried clearly in the cold air. He didn't want to be seen though, so he retraced his steps back toward his truck.

He'd only taken a few steps when his cell phone rang. With his teeth, Garret yanked off his gloves and swiped at his phone. "Chris, I've been waiting for your call."

"Good afternoon. I hope I'm not disturbing you." Chris's voice held an edge.

"Nope. How's it going in your neck of the woods?"

"Could be better. I need to get Dana settled before I can't really help her anymore. Any chance you could hop a plane and get here by evening? Tomorrow at the latest."

Garret grinned and did a fist pump with his left hand. "I wasn't exactly honest when we spoke last. I'm not far away. Not in Rock Harbor but within an hour. Where do you want to meet?"

Chris's displeasure was evident in the long pause before he spoke again. "You didn't think you could trust me?"

"Do you blame me? You haven't tried to hide the fact you didn't think I was good enough for your sister."

"That's all past now. I have to make sure Dana is safe."

"What's going on? You sound upset."

"Life is about to become a challenge, but it's too much to go into on the phone. I'll tell you more about it when I see you. Since you're so close, just wait for my call and I'll tell you where to come. Where are you now?"

Should Garret tell him? He didn't fully trust Chris. What if it was all a trap to get him in custody? And what was all that "make sure Dana is safe" business? It was a little wonky.

"Garret, did I lose you?"

He marshaled his thoughts. "I'm here. Near Copper Lake." That would tell Chris the general direction without giving away too much information.

"The place where I plan to have you meet us is between here and there so just stay put. I'll call with more directions later this afternoon or tonight. Don't try to contact me or Dana until I call. I have to handle this carefully."

"You got it, buddy." Why was Chris being so vague? Something smelled off, but he couldn't put his finger on it. Still, he had Chris's approval now, or so it seemed.

The phone rang so long Lauri didn't think Peter was going to pick up.

"Lauri? Everything okay?" He sounded perfectly normal, not at all stressed. There was some background noise as if he was in a store.

Lauri paced the floor of her bedroom and wished she was as calm as he seemed. She'd feel better once this was over. "I saw you a little while ago, Peter. Did you follow me here?"

"What are you talking about?"

"You, here in Rock Harbor. I saw you go into a house on Quincy Street. Who lives there and what are you doing here?"

The pause lengthened before he finally cleared his throat. "I, ah, a friend lives there. I was going to call you and let you know I was in town. Want to get some dinner tonight?"

For a second she was tempted to let him soothe her fears, but she needed to be a grown-up now. "I'd like to meet you, but not for dinner. I want to give you back your ring. We went into this way too quickly, Peter. Neither of us knows each other very well. I think it's best if we start over and just date until we are better acquainted."

"Give back my ring? You can't be serious. I thought you were the one, different from all the rest."

All the rest? She didn't like the sound of that. "You've been engaged before?"

He seemed not to hear her as he spewed out curses so fast she had a hard time following where his rage led him. She managed to break into his tirade. "You can't be surprised, not after our argument. We want different things in life."

"Is this about having a house? If it's that important to you, we'll buy a house."

"It's not just that. I let myself get caught up in the romance of Hawaii. You're handsome and sophisticated, and I forgot that I didn't really know you. There's more to a marriage than physical attraction. We might be suited, but we need more time to know that."

"You said you'd die before you hurt me. Now look what you're doing. I'm disappointed in you, Lauri. You're not the person I thought you were." His tight, clipped voice vibrated with anger.

She perched on the edge of the bed beside Zorro who laid

his head in her lap. Something in Peter's tone scared her. He had held back so much of himself from her. She didn't know if he had siblings or where he'd grown up. He deflected every personal question she'd asked him.

She rose and walked to the window, then looked out onto Lake Superior, icing over with the extreme cold weather. It symbolized how the feelings she thought she had were icing over as well. "Look, let's not get upset with each other. I'm not saying we're breaking up. Just that I want us to move at a slower pace and not rush things. We'll both be in Phoenix next week, and we can go out like usual. I won't wear your ring until we know it's right, okay?"

"No, it's not all right. I don't take well to being treated like an afterthought, Lauri. I thought you loved me."

She watched a big ship move past on the water. "I did—I do. But marriage is for a lifetime, and I want to make sure we're doing the right thing."

He didn't answer right away, and she pulled the phone away from her ear to make sure the call was still connected. "Peter? Are you still there?"

"I'm here. Let's meet so I can get the ring back." His voice was terse.

She suppressed a sigh. Lauri was pretty sure she could forget about seeing him in Phoenix or anywhere else. He was done with her. "Okay, where do you want to meet?"

"I need to check on my cabin by Chassell, but I'll be back in a few hours. I'll catch up with you later and get the ring. Oh and Lauri? You're going to be very sorry you did this. Very sorry."

The connection went dead, and she put down her phone. That hadn't gone well. She pulled off the ring and stared at it. That beautiful ring. She was mourning its loss more than Peter's, and that was a sad situation for sure. She slipped it in the pocket of her jeans and went to find Bree and Kade in the living room.

The kids were playing a board game with Samson in their midst, and she plopped between Bree and Kade on the sofa. "I called Peter and told him I was breaking the engagement."

Kade's arm came around her in a comforting squeeze. "I'm sure that wasn't easy. How'd he take it?"

Lauri leaned into him, taking in the reassuring scent of his cologne. "Not well. But I'm relieved, you know. It was the right thing to do. He's going to catch up with me later tonight to get the ring back. Then it will be over. He made it clear we won't be dating when this is over." His "fair warning" about her hurting him floated back, but she pushed away the misgivings. It was just a silly thing he said.

"It's a little strange," Bree said. "And how is he going to catch up with you to get the ring back? He's not in Rock Harbor, is he?"

Lauri thought back and realized she hadn't told Bree she'd seen Peter. "He is. I saw him going into the Newell house. That's why I asked you who owned it. I wondered who he was here to see."

"I'll have to ask Dana about her impressions of him." Bree took Lauri's hand. "Sure you're okay?"

"Better than okay. I can focus on my job and building a future. I let Peter distract me. I wanted the perfect life all at once, you know?"

Bree squeezed her fingers. "God's got a plan for your life. Don't run ahead of him."

"I'll try not to." Lauri rose and yawned. "I'm in the mood for some pulla. I think I'll run to the café. Want some?"

"I never turn down pulla," her brother said.

Smiling, Lauri headed for the door feeling lighter than she had in weeks.

CHAPTER 32

This almost looks like a sleigh!" The little boy bounced on the soles of his feet as if he could hardly stand still. "But it's got sails."

Boone grinned at the eight-year-old. "You ready to be a sailor, Tyce? I'm going to show you and your parents how to get across the lake fast."

His small ice-sailing boat only held four, so this family of three was the perfect size. It would be a fun excursion with the kid's enthusiasm. His parents, Amber and Kyle, were an attractive couple in their late twenties. They held hands and focused on each other and their son.

And it would get his mind off his investigation. His thoughts went round and round like a tiger in a cage all night long. Could Chris really have killed Renee and the other women? Lots of people had similar looks. Maybe he was jumping to conclusions. Morgan still hadn't called him back, but it was early on the West Coast. He had to be patient.

Boone helped the family climb into the boat, then stood next to the vessel, released the brake, and grabbed the hold of the tiller.

He pushed into the wind then at an angle before jumping in and trimming the sails. He showed the family how to tack the sails to take advantage of the breeze. Tyce picked it up quickly and was grinning from ear to ear as the boat picked up speed across the frozen lake. The runners scraped across the ice, and the sails flapped above their heads, creating the perfect sound backdrop to the feel of the stinging wind. The ice was a little rough and bounced them as they hit the bumps.

A few hardy leaves clung to the bare branches of the trees that rimmed the lake. The sky was a beautiful blue bowl overhead, and Boone's sense of well-being rose a couple of notches. He should have been doing this before now. Staying hunched over a computer was not conducive to a happy attitude.

He needed to bring Dana out here sometime. She claimed to hate boats, but there was no risk of drowning today. He'd checked the ice before bringing this family out here, and their puny weight wouldn't come close to breaking through the thick ice.

The vulnerability in Dana's eyes drew him in ways he hadn't felt in years, maybe never. Seeing Esther again had made him realize his feelings for her had been pretty juvenile, based on looks and not character. He didn't plan to ever make that mistake again.

He pointed out a remote boathouse restaurant on the other side of the lake. "We're heading there for lunch. Anyone hungry?"

"Me!" Tyce shouted. "I want a pasty."

The family was from New York, but they'd quickly fallen in love with the local cuisine. Kyle was even talking about buying a place here and opening a restaurant. The boat sped over the top of the ice toward the boathouse. Boone's cheeks stung from the wind as his gaze swept the ice for any protrusions like rocks or tree branches. As they neared the other shore, he spotted a figure moving from the ice toward a truck parked along the road in the trees.

An old blue truck. His pulse kicked, and he reached for his binoculars. Once he focused them in on the truck, he looked at the license plate. Garret's truck. Obviously, he hadn't left the area.

Boone changed directions and headed toward the truck. The man had reversed course and was moving back toward the water. Boone wanted to see his face, though he was sure it was Garret. The wind was too tricky in this direction to let his customers steer, so he couldn't use the binoculars. The man stepped out of the cover of trees, and his face came into the sunlight.

Bingo.

Boone wanted to run the boat aground and grab him, but he didn't have any authority to arrest him. He couldn't even call Dana because there was no cell service out on Copper Lake. All he could do was grit his teeth and make for the boathouse again. As soon as he could get a signal, he'd let Dana know to be on her guard.

Dana breathed a sigh of relief when she realized Chris was gone. She wasn't ready to talk to him about what Kory had said. She went to her room with Phantom on her heels, but before she stepped into the shower enclosure, she remembered she'd forgotten to get more shampoo. Chris wouldn't mind if she borrowed his. A message came in on her cell phone as she reached for her robe. The office wanted her to come back and work a double shift. *Great, just great.*

Dressed in a fluffy terry robe, she went barefoot down the steps to her brother's room and into his bathroom where she scooped up his shampoo and cream rinse. She hadn't been in his bathroom so she took a moment to look around. He'd had it finished in real marble tile in the shower that complemented the travertine floors. An antique dresser had been retrofitted into a sink cabinet, and she touched its beautiful surface. *Nice job in here.*

She went to his bedroom again and paused. It felt odd to be invading her brother's sanctuary, but Kory's comment about Chris's trophy box wouldn't leave her alone. Was it possible she didn't really know her brother?

Her gaze swept the space. It was a big room with an expensive aqua Persian rug atop gleaming hardwood floors and furnished with heavy wooden furniture that had to cost the earth too. The walls were a pale aqua color that complemented the white duvet cover and blended with the accent pillows.

She should leave. What if Chris caught her poking around? But she couldn't force her feet to the door. This would be a great opportunity to poke around, put her doubts to rest. She went to the large walk-in closet and flipped on the light. The illumination revealed neat rows of suits and dress shirts as well as casual shirts and jeans folded on shelves. His shoes lined one wall, and she hadn't realized he owned so many pairs of shoes. He had more than she did.

She walked the length of the closet looking for anything that might hold his so-called trophies. There was a chest at the back of the closet, and she opened every drawer. The bottom one held a battered metal box that looked out of place in the pristine closet. About a foot square, its gray surface was chipped and dented. She lifted it out, but it wouldn't open. Maybe the key was here somewhere too.

A further examination of the closet didn't reveal any keys, so still carrying the box, she went back to the bedroom and set it on the bed so she could rummage through the bedside table. In the back of the top drawer, she found a small ring that held one key. It fit into the lock.

She stared at the unlocked box and tried to tell herself not to open it, but resisting the impulse was as impossible as telling Pandora not to open her box. Dana had to know. Lifting the box, she blinked. She didn't know what she'd expected—maybe severed fingers or ears—but she hadn't thought to find the yellowed pages from various newspapers. What on earth? She perched on the edge of the bed and lifted the first article out to unfold it.

It was an article about Renee's death.

Her chest compressed and she stared at the picture. Why would he have this? Could it just be articles he'd found interesting? She wanted to believe it, but deep inside she knew it was more than that. She folded the newspaper clippings and returned it to the box, then started to sort through the other papers.

The front door slammed. Her heart banged against her ribs, and she rushed to put the box back before she scooped up the hair products and ran for the door. She nearly collided with Chris in the hall. Only then did she realize she still had the key in her palm.

She stuck her hand in the pocket of her bathrobe and smiled at him. "You scared me."

His fists were clenched, and he was red faced. He blinked when he saw her. "Dana? What are you doing in my room?"

She forced a smile and held up the shampoo and cream rinse. "Raiding your bathroom. I ran out and forgot to get more. I just got home, but they're swamped at work and wanted me to come back for a few hours. I didn't think you'd mind."

"No, no, of course not." His smile was a little wobbly when it came, and he relaxed his fists. "There's more in the guest bath though. For next time."

It was a warning to stay out of his room. "You okay? You look a little upset."

"Fine." He drew a deep breath. "Just going to take a nap for now."

He never took naps. She stepped out of the way. "Sounds like a great plan. You're a little pale. Get some rest."

Chris hesitated, then grabbed her arm. "I've been a good brother to you, haven't I?"

She stared into his blue eyes. Something was clearly wrong. "The best." She kept seeing Renee's face in her head. What did Chris know about all this?

"I always knew we'd be together forever. Your face is the last one I want to see before I die."

She mustered a laugh. "You're not counting on making that anytime soon, are you? I have plans to keep you around for a long time."

His brows drew together, and his grip on her arm tightened. "You would never hurt me, would you, Dana? You're not like other women. You're the type who sticks around no matter what."

She stepped closer and palmed his cheek with her other hand. "You're my brother, Chris. I'll always be here for you. What's this all about?"

He shook his head and released her. "Go get your shower. It's nothing. I'm being maudlin for no good reason."

She didn't want to leave him like this. "Want to watch a movie after I get back? I could call Boone to join us."

His expression turned even darker. "Let's just keep it the two of us."

The door closed with a soft *click*, and she stood staring at it a moment. She breathed a thanks to God that Chris hadn't caught her going through his box. But what did it all mean?

Acid churned in her stomach, and she didn't want to examine it all.

CHAPTER 33

The dispatch office already felt like home. Dana hung up her coat and greeted her coworkers on the way to her station. Karen and Tracie were already at their desks, though none of them were on the phone. The place held the scent of fresh floor polish, and the vinyl tiles gleamed.

Karen glanced over at her. "Thanks for coming back. The place went nuts, and Mark had an accident on his way in. He's okay, but the other guy isn't." The traces of gray at the temples of her hair were gone, and her hair was a little darker today. "I brought in brownies. They're by the coffeepot."

"Thanks. Are we celebrating something?" It wasn't uncommon for dispatchers to bring in food for birthdays.

"Nope, just trying out a new recipe. This one is made with black beans. It's pretty good, so I thought I'd share."

"Sounds yummy." Dana glanced at her monitors, which were calm. She went to the refreshment area and grabbed a brownie and a cup of coffee, then carried it back to her station. Karen was a great cook.

She pulled out her chair and settled into it. "What's been

happening since I left? Any excitement? Things look calm at the moment." In fact, they were so calm she had to wonder why they'd called her back in. The two of them should have been able to handle it.

Tracie swiveled in her chair to face her. "I've had all the excitement I can stand for months, thank you very much. I'm still looking over my shoulder for your Garret. Are you sure he's gone?"

"He's not *my* Garret. And it's impossible to be sure of anything with him. He hasn't called, and I haven't seen his truck anywhere. Has he contacted you?"

Tracie shuddered and hugged herself. "No, and I want to keep it that way. The guy is downright scary. No wonder you were terrified of him."

Terrified. That's what she'd been her whole life. Dana stared at her monitors, still silent. No more. Nothing could keep her in this paralyzing place but her own actions. Moving back home wasn't enough to change her life. No one could do that but her. She'd already found it was impossible to please others. Every time she'd tried to do that, she'd failed.

Time to focus on pleasing the only one who mattered.

Today was going to be a new start for her.

A call came in on her monitor, and her pulse kicked as she answered it. "Nine-one-one, what is your emergency?"

"He's not breathing!" The young woman's voice held a note of hysteria.

Dana glanced at the location monitor and rattled off the address only a few blocks from the firehouse. "Is that your location?"

"Yes, yes! Please, I don't know what to do. He can't breathe!" Her voice grew fainter as she spoke out of the mic. "Oh, baby, Mommy's right here."

Dana pitched her voice to an even calmer timbre. "Tell me what's happening. Who is the patient?"

"It's my little boy. He's only two. I think he has something stuck in his throat and he can't breathe! His face is turning red."

"Do you know the Heimlich maneuver?"

"No. I mean, I've seen it but I don't know how to do it. Please, you have to do something!"

There was no time for the ambulance to get there and save the little guy. "I'm going to tell you what to do. Listen carefully." While she was speaking, she shot a message to the paramedics with the location. "Stand behind your little boy." She gave the mother instructions on how to perform the maneuver. "I'll wait while you do that." The terrible sounds of the child choking were painful to hear.

"Okay, I'll try. Pray for me."

"Of course." Dana launched into a fervent prayer for the little boy to breathe. She ended the prayer but continued to pray silently until she heard the sweetest sound on earth—the child crying. "You did it!"

"Oh, thank you, Lord." The woman was sobbing almost too hard to be understood. "He almost died!" She broke out in even harder sobbing.

"The paramedics are on their way, and they'll make sure he's okay. They may need to transport him to the hospital. Watch for them. You'll need to open the door."

"Can you stay on the phone with me until they get here? You were an angel today, sent straight from the Lord." The woman's voice sounded raw.

"Of course. I'm proud of you. You stayed so calm." Dana heard the little guy's cries taper off, then his small voice asked for a drink.

"Sounds like he's doing fine. You can give him a sip of water. His throat is probably sore."

"Okay."

Dana heard footsteps, then the *whoosh* of the fridge opening. A thin wail built in the background. "Is that the ambulance coming?"

"Yes, yes, it is! Thank you for staying with me. He seems to be fine. I'm going to hang up now. What's your name?"

"Dana. You're Brylee?"

"Yes. Thank you so much, Dana. I'll never forget what you did."

Smiling, Dana ended the call. "Shew, thank the Lord."

Karen rose and went to get some coffee. "Let's hope all our calls go that well today."

Dana's personal cell phone vibrated on the desk, and she looked at the screen before answering it. "Chris, is everything okay? You never call me at work." And he'd seemed so strange when she left.

"Sorry, I hope I'm not interrupting."

"No, you're fine. No calls at the moment."

"What time do you get off? I need to talk to you about something, and I'll stay up if I need to."

"I just have to stay until Mark gets here, maybe another couple of hours. You're scaring me. Is it serious?"

"Just a little bump in the road. It's not worth getting upset about. I just wanted to talk it out with you."

Her pulse didn't believe him. He was way too somber. She glanced at her watch. Only four.

Karen motioned to her and mouthed, *"Go ahead and leave."*

"My coworkers have it handled okay. I can come back and we can talk. Where are you?"

"That's great! I'm still at the house."

"I'll grab some food from the Suomi and bring it there. That way you don't have to starve to death just to talk to me." She drummed her fingers on the desk. "I'll be right home."

———

The sun went down early up here in the winter, and the streetlights were on as Dana sped down Houghton Street in her Prius. What could be wrong? Chris had been so mysterious and subdued. She turned onto Quincy at the light and headed for their house with as much restraint as she could summon. The radio announcer was making dire predictions of a massive blizzard headed this way.

The house was unlocked when she let herself in. "Chris?"

"In here."

Sounded like he was in the kitchen. She hurried through the foyer to the door into the kitchen and found her brother sitting at the granite island with a glass of wine in his hand. And she'd rarely seen him drink. This must be serious.

She took off her coat and tossed it over the back of a chair at the dining table. "What's going on?"

He looked up at her with red-rimmed eyes. "Sorry to call you home this way."

She stepped to his side and hugged him, her fear intensifying when he gave a sob into her shoulder and clutched her. Patting his back, she tried to instill as much confidence as she could dredge up. "Whatever it is, we'll figure it out together. We'll fix it."

He shook his head. "It can't be fixed, Dana. I'm dying."

Her hands gripped his sweater, and she shook her head. "No, Chris, that can't be true."

He released her and drew a shuddering breath. His mouth worked soundlessly in his pale face before he managed to grate out

any words. "It's true. It's pancreatic cancer. There's no good treat-
ment, and I'm not about to let them dump all that chemo into my
body in a fruitless attempt to stop it."

Pancreatic cancer.

The diagnosis burned into her brain, and her knees went weak.
She grabbed the edge of the granite and lowered herself onto the
stool next to him. "Oh no."

He nodded and ran a shaky hand through his hair. "I'm
stunned. I need you right now, Dana."

"Of course. You know I'll be right here with you." What could
she do? She knew a great naturopath in Colorado. Shauna Young
might be able to help him. Dana would call her as soon as possible.
Maybe she could talk Chris into flying out to Durango.

"I want to be alone, just the two of us. Maybe at my cabin in
the woods so I don't have to deal with people asking me how I'm
doing. I want to be in nature and not be thinking about anything
else. Will you come with me?"

How would they live? They both had jobs and bills. In spite of
her questions, she just nodded. "I'll do whatever you want."

He smiled then. "You always have. I know you think I'm crazy
and are wondering where the money will come from. I have some
put back. But I'm not talking about forever. Maybe just a few weeks
until I can get my head wrapped around this and make my peace
with death."

She hoped that meant his peace with God. She intended to do
all she could to help him. "When do you want to go?"

His dark-blue eyes burned with turmoil. "Tonight, right now."

"T-Tonight? What about my job?"

"Call the sheriff and tell him you've had a family emergency
and have to leave for a couple of weeks. I'm sure he'll understand."

She managed a nod. "He would. Mason's a good man. Okay, I'll pack some things and call my friends."

He shook his head. "Please don't. I'm not ready for the whole town to know what's happening. Maybe in a day or two."

"But I'm supposed to do some SAR training with Bree tomorrow. She'll worry when I don't show up and will probably come by the house. Plus, Mason will tell her about my call. And Boone will be looking for me. We, um, we're dating."

Anger flashed across his face. "I don't want Boone or anyone else to know right now. We'll worry about that tomorrow." He clutched his head in his hands and groaned. "I just have to get away before I go crazy!"

She patted his shoulder. "Okay, okay, whatever you want. I didn't even know you had a cabin. Where is it?"

"I've had it about five years. I often go there in the summer when I'm off for a few days. I like to feed the porcupines and chipmunks. It centers me." He rose and headed for the bedroom. "I'm going to pack. How long will it take you?"

"No longer than an hour."

"Let's make it half an hour. I've got to get out of here."

She caught the hysterical edge to his voice and rose. "I can do it."

After taking the stairs to the second floor two at a time, she rushed to her room and pulled out her largest suitcase. There was no telling if there was a washer and dryer in the cabin, so she'd better pack enough for two weeks. And what about food? There was no way she could be ready to go in half an hour. In a frenzy, she threw in jeans and sweatshirts atop a jumble of underwear and pajamas. No sense in taking makeup. He might not even have a mirror there. Soap and shampoo were a must though.

She grabbed her Bible and her Kindle, then packed her computer as well. There probably wasn't Internet, but she could turn on the hotspot on her phone. Was that it? She glanced around the large bedroom she'd come to love and suffered a pang of homesickness already.

But Chris needed her. She couldn't let him down.

Lugging the heavy suitcase, she descended the stairs and left it in the foyer before heading back to the kitchen. She found Chris at the open refrigerator throwing items into a cooler.

"I'll get stuff from the pantry," she told him.

He pointed to a blue plastic tub. "You can pack the food in that."

She grabbed it and took the tub to the pantry. With both of them moving fast, the clock showed it had taken them just an hour and five minutes to pack. She helped Chris carry it all to his black SUV and loaded Phantom and his food in too. Tears pricked her eyes as they pulled away. The future without Chris wasn't something she wanted to face.

CHAPTER 34

Frustration had nipped on Boone's heels all afternoon. There hadn't been cell service at the boathouse, and then he'd had trouble with the rudder, which had to be fixed before he could take his customers back across Copper Lake to his home base.

Garret had gotten into his truck and left, and Boone was frantic to warn Dana. The boathouse phone had been out, and it was after six and dark by the time they got back across the lake. Two messages from Morgan were on his phone too.

Kyle had complained about the delay in getting home, but Amber had reminded him it wasn't Boone's fault. The family thanked him and hurried to their van as soon as they docked. Boone secured the boat, then whipped out his cell phone and called Dana. After four rings, he was dumped into voice mail. He left a message asking her to call him, then carried the gear into the office. She was probably at work and couldn't answer her phone.

He locked the office, then went over to his cabin. Spirit greeted him at the door. His dog usually came with him, but Amber had been frightened of his wolflike looks so Boone left Spirit at home. The dog paused long enough for a scratch on the ears, then rushed out the door. Boone heated up some soup and made himself a pea-nut butter sandwich, then let Spirit back in. He carried his dinner into the living room to watch the news while he ate.

An hour later, Dana still hadn't returned his call. He tried again and still got only voice mail. There was no choice. He'd have to try the dispatch office directly. There was an alternate number so he didn't tie up 911 so he punched it in.

"Dispatch, this is Tracie."

He'd met Tracie Pitt a few times. "Tracie, this is Boone Carter. Is Dana busy?"

"Her brother called her home even though we needed her here." She sounded miffed. "The phones are crazy tonight. Probably because it's a full moon."

His stomach clenched. Chris knew Boone was suspicious. Surely he wouldn't hurt his sister though. Boone shook his head. If Dana was missing, Garret was the mostly likely culprit. Chris loved Dana. "Has anyone tried to call her or gone by her place?"

"I don't think so. Why would we? Her brother called her around four and asked her to come home. Dana was worried it was some-thing serious."

"I'm going to run over there. I'll let Mason know if I find out anything." He ended the connection, then called Bree. "Hey, Bree, you heard from Dana?"

"No, not tonight. Why?"

Boone told her what he'd found out about Garret still being around, but he didn't mention his suspicions about Chris. "I guess I'd better head over there. I'm worried. What if Garret grabbed her on her way back to the dispatch office?"

"You sure you're not overreacting just because she isn't answer-ing her phone?"

"I don't trust Garret."

"Me neither. I'll come too. We'll see if Samson noses out any-thing. I don't have a key to Chris's house though, do you?"

"No, but that won't stop me." He promised to meet Bree at the house in fifteen minutes. Grabbing his coat, he called Spirit and took him along. If Garret had Dana, Boone would need all the help he could get.

The roads were slick as he rounded the curves into town. Bree's Jeep already sat at the curb behind Dana's Prius, and she stood on the stoop with Samson. If Dana's car was here, why hadn't she answered the phone? Boone got out and waited for Spirit to leap out behind him.

Tail wagging, Samson came to sniff noses with Spirit. "You try knocking?" he asked Bree who was huddled in an army-green coat.

She nodded. "No answer so I pounded on the door and shouted her name. I also looked in the windows, but the place appears to be empty."

"And her car is here."

Bree nodded. "Doesn't look good. I'm scared Garret has grabbed her."

"I'm going to call Mason." Boone pulled his phone from his pocket and punched in the sheriff's number. "He's on his way," he said when he ended the call. "Let me try calling Chris." But the call went straight to voice mail.

Boone went to the front door and jiggled the handle. With Mason on his way here, he knew breaking in the door was out of the question. "I'm going to go around back and look in the kitchen. Maybe the door's unlocked."

She nodded. "I'll wait here for Mason."

The three-story brick building sat on the corner, so he skirted the side of the house and tromped through the snow in the minuscule backyard. There was a small deck back here with a gas grill and a tiny table with two chairs. He tried the door, but it was locked. The kitchen light was still on though, so he moved to the window and cupped his hands around his eyes to peer in.

The pantry door stood open, and dinner plates still sat on the granite counters. Several boxes of macaroni and cheese sat on the counter closest to the pantry. It almost looked as if Dana had left in too much of a hurry to clean up. Something about the scene made his gut clench.

He retraced his steps and found Bree starting for the side of the house. He told her about the kitchen scene.

He turned at the sweep of lights along the dark street and saw the sheriff pulling to a stop behind his truck. "Maybe Mason will have an idea."

He trusted Chris like a mouse trusted a hawk. Garret's initial burst of elation ebbed as he stared out over the water from the back deck and watched the sun plunge into Lake Superior. There was more to this situation than it appeared. Chris had no reason to reunite Garret and Dana. There was no logic to it, and Chris was one of the most logical men Garret knew. His chess moves were legendary with their unit, and he had understood more about ambushes and how to avoid them than most generals.

What was Chris's endgame?

Garret had thought to abandon his initial plan about Dana and see if they could build a future together, but a dark rage swelled up in his chest. He'd always prided himself on being a realist. No amount of wishing would change what Dana had done. She'd tossed his love back into his teeth. She deserved punishment.

He'd be saving any future boyfriend from being taken in by her beauty and sweet manner. It was all a facade hiding her true nature. She didn't care for anyone but herself. She never had. Any love he'd thought he'd seen in her eyes was all a sham.

She'd proven that when she tricked him into meeting her with her new man.

He shook his head and went back inside. Time to put his plan into action.

Garret took off his coat and tossed it onto the table, then went to the garage and found the two ropes he'd bought two days ago. He slung them around his shoulder, then grabbed the ladder hanging on the garage wall. He carried it inside and stood it under the great beam in the massive living room. Tying a bowline knot came back to him easily, and he secured the first rope on the beam, then did the same with the second, placing it about three feet from the first.

He climbed down the ladder and looked at his handiwork. The rope ends touched the floor, giving him plenty of room to tie the slipknots on this end.

But how did he get her here? Chris's involvement had messed up Garret's plans. There was no time to grab her after work, so how would he snatch her from Chris? He didn't dare just go along with Chris's plan. Garret would show up and Chris would likely blow his head off.

What if he headed to Rock Harbor now and staked out the Newell house? He could follow Chris and Dana from a distance and figure out where they were heading.

He couldn't use the old pickup though. The owners of this

place would never know he'd taken their Lexus for a little spin. Surely spare keys were around somewhere. He went to the kitchen and rummaged in the drawers. No keys. Half an hour later he was ready to admit defeat until he got to the garage. Maybe, just maybe, they were in the car.

Bingo. He found a key ring under the mat on the driver's side. Now to gather some tools he might need. He made sure his pistol was fully loaded, then grabbed a hammer and an ax from the array of tools along the wall. He might need one of them to break a window.

He took a roll of duct tape from the workbench as well. Dana might object to going with him, and duct tape was perfect for securing her hands. And her mouth. His last piece of equipment was a ski mask. It was a cold night and no one would think it strange to see a driver in a ski mask.

With everything stowed on the floor in the back, he opened the garage door and looked at the dash to orient himself. His gaze lit on a radio. Was that a police radio? Maybe the house owner was in law enforcement. He flipped it on and listened to the reports of a break-in at a local café. Grinning, he did a fist pump. Nothing about him on the frequency. For now, he turned off the radio and thought through his strategy.

The stars weren't out yet as he drove along the narrow highway to Rock Harbor. Traffic was light as he drove down Houghton Street toward Quincy. He slowed as he turned at the light, then braked. Several cars, including the sheriff's, were parked outside the house. What the—?

He gawked at several people with dogs standing around outside. The sheriff talked to them, and he wore a serious expression. Had something happened to Dana? Garret leaned forward and flipped on the police scanner. He winced at the squawk and turned it down.

The broadcast was filled with small incidents—nothing that referred to Dana. How would he find out what was going on? Garret slammed his palms against the steering wheel. He couldn't wait around for the law to lead him to Dana.

He grabbed his phone and called a friend who worked for the police department in Chicago. In five minutes he knew where Chris's cabin was located.

And he had a very strong suspicion Chris and Dana were both there. Once the sheriff and his minions were inside the house, Garret pulled away and headed toward Chassell. It was only an hour drive, but the storm was due to start in about an hour. He accelerated once he reached the highway and sped north.

CHAPTER 35

M-26 was a familiar highway to her, but with the dark night and empty road it somehow felt alien. Dana glanced several times at her brother, but his flexed jaw and tight lips warned her against starting a conversation. She had to fight tears and still couldn't wrap her head around his diagnosis.

She bit her lip and realized she'd never called Mason. She fumbled for her phone in the pocket of her coat but came up empty-handed. Where was it? She was sure she'd left it there. "Have you seen my phone?"

"I took it out of your coat and left it on the table. I don't want us to be disturbed."

Anger burned up her neck, but she fought to control her response. She didn't want the tension to escalate. "I didn't let Mason know where I was. The office will be worried when I don't show up tomorrow."

Chris didn't answer, and he whipped the SUV to the left. Her head slammed into the window. Stars exploded in her vision and pain burst in her forehead.

"Sorry."

There wasn't any true remorse in his tone. She inhaled and

pressed her throbbing head against the cold glass. What was his problem? She was beginning to be frightened at the way he was acting.

She wasn't ready to admit defeat. They'd fight this cancer. She'd talk him into seeing someone who could try an alternative method, maybe in Mexico or Europe. This couldn't be the death sentence it seemed.

They'd been driving through the darkness for nearly an hour, and she needed a break. The lights of what she thought was Houghton lay ahead. "You mind if we stop at the next gas station? I want to get something to drink and visit the restroom."

He glanced at her, then shook his head. "No need. We're nearly there."

The SUV slowed, and he whipped the wheel to turn the vehicle right onto a dirt road. The potholes caused him to slow the vehicle to a crawl, but the SUV still bottomed out several times as it crept along the icy track of road.

"Where does this lead?" She'd never been in this area before.

"I have a cabin on Keweenaw Bay. It's nice and quiet where I can think." He pounded the steering wheel with both hands. "I have to think! My life is unraveling all at once, and I can't stop it. Boone will pay for this."

"Boone? What's he got to do with anything?" She curled her fingers into her palms and forced back a gulp. "It's okay, Chris. We'll figure it out together. Don't think about it right now."

The headlights punched holes in the darkness, but it wasn't enough to make the area seem familiar in any way. The evergreen trees loomed in weird, leering ways. She clutched the door handle. "Look, Chris, let's just go back, okay? I want to talk to your doctor and see what can be done. It can't be as bad as you think."

"It's worse, Dana, much worse."

At least he'd calmed down, but his voice was flat and wooden, and something about it raised the hair on the back of her neck. Had he had some kind of breakdown at the news?

The thick trees began to thin, and she caught a glimmer of water. A tiny cabin sat at the end of the lane. He parked beside the cabin and shut off the engine.

Dana opened her door and stepped out into the wind blowing off the bay. She let Phantom out of the back and headed to the cabin. The snowpack crunched under her feet, and her breath steamed the air. This was probably beautiful in the daylight, but tonight with the way Chris was behaving she felt only trepidation as she looked out at the black water.

"Is it unlocked?"

"Nope." He tossed her a key ring, then grabbed a lantern and turned it on. "You can unlock the door while I grab the cooler of food."

She nodded and went toward the cabin. The key turned easily in the lock, and she opened the door and stepped inside. It was cold, not much warmer than the outside. She looked around for a thermostat but there was none.

Chris stomped the snow from his boots, and she moved out of the way. "The heat isn't on."

"I'll build a fire in a minute."

"Running water?"

He shook his head. "An outhouse on the other side of the cabin."

She shuddered. "Mom and Dad used to come for a weekend away to the Hamar House in Chassell. We could see if they have room. We can't stay here with no running water. It's one thing in the summer, but traipsing to the outhouse in minus-twenty degrees doesn't sound like much fun."

"We aren't going anywhere." His gaze, flat yet somehow menacing, lingered on her. He stepped to the small counter on the other end of the room and set the cooler on it. "You can put things away in the ice chest, and I'll get the box of dry goods."

Fear was a hard ball in her stomach. Dana moved to the cooler and began to unload it. She'd have to get ice for the ice chest, and where on earth could she put the other things he was bringing in? Only two floor cabinets were in the space as well as a tiny dry sink. And there was only one cot plus a lumpy sofa by the fireplace. She had to talk Chris out of staying here. She couldn't imagine sleeping here for one night let alone the couple of weeks he'd mentioned before they left.

———

The wind howled through the buildings with as much frustration as Bree felt. She stood on the front stoop and rattled the doorknob with all her strength. "We have to get inside."

Mason wore a knit cap with the word SHERIFF emblazoned across the front of it. "I have no authority to bust down the door."

"But what if she's injured inside and can't get to the door?" Boone slammed his fist against the side of the building.

"He's right. We've got to get in there." Sensing Bree's agitation, Samson whined low in his throat, and she touched the top of his head. "You saw the way the kitchen looked. Maybe an intruder broke in and he hurt her."

Mason glanced at the door, then back at her. "I could probably make a case for that." He sighed and motioned to one of his detectives. "Get the door open."

Bree stepped out of the way to let the man do his job. "If we don't find her right away inside, I'll have Samson search for Dana. That will tell us quickly what's going on."

His gaze on his deputy, Boone nodded. "It could have been a family emergency."

"Or Garret could have taken her," she pointed out.

Boone didn't answer, and she knew he realized the seriousness of the situation too. Dana wasn't the kind to blow off work and ignore Bree's call. Something sinister was taking place.

"Got it." The deputy opened the door and stepped inside. Mason and the deputies fanned out calling for Dana.

Bree crowded in behind them. The lights were still on. No Phantom, no Dana. Opening the hall closet, she located Dana's favorite Michigan Tech sweatshirt. She snapped her fingers and called Samson to her side, then thrust the article of clothing under his nose. His tail wagged as he sniffed it.

She waited until the men came back. Mason shook his head. "She's not here."

"But her car's outside. Something's happened to her." She put the sweatshirt under Samson's nose again. "Search, Samson. Find Dana."

He barked and ran off with his curly tail high over his rump. Boone followed as Bree tracked her dog to the kitchen.

Boone picked up a phone on the counter. "Isn't this Dana's?" He swiped it on. "Seven missed calls, probably most of them from us."

"She wouldn't leave her phone voluntarily." Bree watched Samson as he nosed through the pantry, then he reversed and she followed him down the hall to a closed door and barked.

Dana's rooms were on the second floor so why was Samson interested in this room? She opened the door for the dog. It was a masculine room, and it had to belong to Chris. Samson raced to the bed where he sniffed around before going to the closet door.

Bree's pulse pounded, and as she opened the closet she fully expected to find Dana's body on the floor, but only clothing hung neatly from the racks. Samson went straight to a built-in set of drawers at the back of the closet and sniffed around, spending the most time on the bottom one. Frowning, Bree followed him inside and opened the bottom drawer first.

An old metal box was inside, and she pulled it out. "Samson seems very interested in this." She turned and showed it to Boone. The dog was sniffing it all over and wagging his tail. She opened the lid and found newspaper articles.

Mason looked over Boone's shoulder. "That hardly seems important enough to explain the way you're poking into Chris's private belongings without a warrant."

Her face went hot at the rebuke. "Humor me for a minute. It might be a clue to where they are. Samson zeroed in on this for some reason." When he shrugged, she carried the box to the bed and pulled out the clippings.

The first one was of Allyson's murder. When Bree gasped, Mason took it from her and looked it over. "He was probably interested in the case."

"Maybe." She lifted another clipping, this one about Faith Rogerson. A smiley face had been drawn on the margin. Her stomach plunged, and she passed it to Mason. "This was the engaged woman killed in Portland."

His eyes widened. "He'd never heard the case mentioned, did he?"

"Not to my knowledge. Only Allyson did." She knew what the next article would be and she was right—it detailed what had happened to Renee. She looked at Boone whose face went white as he saw the heading.

She inhaled as her knees went weak. "Chris is the Groom Reaper. He's taken Dana."

"And he killed my sister." Boone spoke through gritted teeth. "I was suspicious yesterday when I found a picture of Renee's with Chris in it. I asked him about it, and he denied that he knew her. It ticked him off and he hung up."

"And you're just now telling us?" Mason demanded.

"I had no proof, not really. I got this from Detective Morgan." He pulled out his phone and showed them a police sketch. "The police in Washington say this sketch looks like Justin Leyland too."

"So Chris knows you're on to him." Bree felt the blood drain from her head. "What if he plans to kill her?"

"She's his sister. I don't think he'd hurt her," Mason said.

"Stepcousin, really," Boone said. "And he's a little weird with her, possessive. I thought it odd."

"Where could he have taken her?" Bree tried to remember any other place Dana might have mentioned. Nothing came to mind.

Her cell phone vibrated in her pocket, and she pulled it out. "Hey, honey, what's up?"

"There's a new development here with Lauri." Kade's deep voice was somber.

Lauri was the last thing she needed to worry about now, but before she could tell him what was happening here, he put Lauri on the phone.

"Bree, Peter isn't really Peter at all. He's Chris Newell." Lauri sounded breathless. "I was looking around online at the house where I saw him. I happened to click on an article about Chris, and there was his picture. It's my Peter. Well, not really mine, especially now."

Chills ran up Bree's neck. "Listen very carefully, Lauri. You are to stay in the house. If he tries to call you, don't answer. If he tries to see you, call for Kade. And have Kade make sure he's armed."

"Bree, you're scaring me."

"He's a serial killer, Lauri. He's the Groom Reaper."

"The one who kills the women before the wedding?" Lauri's voice shook.

"I think you were next. Did he say anything about another place he might go while he's here? Anything at all?"

"Well, he mentioned a cabin near Chassell, but he didn't say where it was."

"We'll find out. Remember what I said. I'll let you know what we find." Bree ended the call and told Mason and Boone what Lauri had discovered. "Let's get toward Chassell."

CHAPTER 36

Garret peered up at the sky, the dark night already beginning to spit snow. He parked in a pull off by the track back to Chris's cabin, then grabbed his gun and knife.

This should be a piece of cake if he didn't get cocky. Chris wouldn't be expecting him, and certainly not on foot in an incoming blizzard. The storm was churning now, dropping thick, fat drops that stuck to everything.

Garret took a chance on using his flashlight and flipped it on, then increased his pace to a jog. His breath fogged in the cold air, but he ignored the deep bite of the wind. He'd be there soon, and Dana would be his. Forever.

He reached a stand of pine and paused to catch his breath. He caught a glimmer of light through the trees and quickly extinguished his flashlight. There it was. He drew his Glock from the holster at his waist and crept toward the cabin. Dinky thing. He'd have thought Chris would have a lavish place. He spotted the outline of an outhouse and grinned. Dana was probably appalled when she arrived. He didn't take her for the camping sort.

In less than an hour the storm had dumped four inches of snow. He crept forward, moving toward a window where he could peer inside. The distinctive scent of smoke wafted to him, and when he looked inside, he saw Chris building a fire in a wood-burning stove. Dana was putting things into the few cabinets in the room. Tight quarters. What was Chris doing out here with her?

Could his offer to reunite Garret and Dana be genuine? Maybe he'd driven her out here to talk sense into her. Maybe Garret had been overly cautious.

He ducked down when Chris rose and headed for the back door. Garret looked around for a place to hide. Maybe Chris wouldn't notice the tracks he'd left in the snow since it was dark. He darted around the corner of the cabin and stood listening while he held his breath. The back door banged, and Chris muttered as he went to a woodpile by the outhouse.

There were several *clunks*, and he peeked around the cabin's edge to see Chris loading his arms with firewood. Good. Even if Chris saw him, he'd be hampered by the wood, and Garret could shoot him. He ducked his head back as Chris started to turn, then listened as his heavy treads went up the steps.

The door banged again. Garret waited a full five minutes in the cold darkness before deciding Chris wasn't coming back out for more wood. He took a step toward the back door.

"Hello, Garret. You're more resourceful than I'd thought." Chris's voice held the edge of steel.

Garret turned slowly. There was just enough light coming from the window to make out Chris pointing a Glock casually his way. He didn't have a coat on, and his blond hair held a thick coating of snow. "I thought I wouldn't wait for the invitation to join you."

"Just as well. This storm is about to undo all my prepara-tions." He motioned with the gun. "Let's go inside where it's more comfortable. Toss your gun onto the ground."

Garret did as directed. Chris wouldn't know about the knife in its sheath under his jeans. There would be an opportunity to get to it. He shuffled through the snow, six inches deep now, to mount the back steps and move onto the deck. As he neared the back door, he saw Dana working over a propane one-burner stove. She wore slim-fitting jeans and a red sweatshirt. Steam rose from the pot on it, and he caught a whiff of pasta as he opened the door.

She turned, and her mouth went open. Her gaze darted past his shoulder to Chris and relief lit her eyes. She looked back at Garret. "Can't you just let go, Garret? You're going to go to jail now."

He thrust out his chin and glared at her. "Chris invited me. He's going to help us mend things between us."

Dana's eyes widened, and her gaze shot back to her brother. She shook her head. "That's not true."

Chris paused at the back door. "Actually, it is true. Well, partially anyway. I did tell him the two of you would get back together, but it's not what he thinks. Or you either, Dana."

Chris swung the Glock around toward Garret, and Garret saw the intent before he pressed the trigger. "No!" Time slowed as the gun recoiled and an agonizing pain spread through his chest. His vision went dark, and he pitched sideways into the snow.

Heavy, fat snowflakes came down fast and furious driven by ferocious winds that blew out of the north. Boone stepped out onto the stoop and looked out on Quincy Hill. In the hour they'd been inside Chris's house, the storm had already dumped four inches, and it wasn't letting up anytime soon.

Head tucked against the wind, Bree stepped out beside him.

"Let's take my Jeep. No sense in having more vehicles on the road than we need, and I've got a backseat for Samson."

"Mind if I drive? I've got a thing about control." He grinned across the snow-covered hood of his car at her.

She tossed him the keys. "I'm all too happy to let you." Samson hopped into the backseat and settled down with his head on his paws. She climbed into the passenger seat and shut the door against the wind, then buckled her seat belt. They would be lucky to make it to Chassell with this storm.

Boone got in and buckled up, then engaged the four-wheel drive and started the car. "Mason will be right behind us. He's making a call to see if he can find a property record up there for Chris. Keep your cell phone where you can hear it. He's going to call you."

She held it up in her gloved hand. "All ready."

The windshield wipers were having trouble keeping up with the snow by the time they reached the outskirts of town. Boone pulled out onto M-26, and the Jeep slewed toward the ditch until he managed to get it going in a straight line. He gripped the steering wheel with all his might and leaned forward to see through the driving snow. Piles of snow six inches high were on either side of the tire tracks in his lane.

The speedometer barely topped fifteen miles an hour. It would take several hours to get there at this speed. It was going to be a long, miserable drive.

Bree's cell phone played Elvis singing "Love Me Tender," and she snatched it up. "Kade, we're on our way to Chassell. Is everything okay there? Chris hasn't tried to contact Lauri, has he?"

She went quiet as she listened to her husband. Boone concentrated on the road. Luckily, there weren't many foolish enough to be out here. He was beginning to regret they hadn't taken his truck.

He had new studded tires on it and chains in the back in case of bad weather. Food and water and blankets were also in the back behind the seat. He had no idea what kind of emergency equipment Bree usually carried.

She ended the call. "Kade was just checking on me, but he said Chris tried to call Lauri. She didn't answer, so he left a message saying the weather was too bad to go out tonight. So I think she's safe."

"That's good. Hey, what kind of emergency equipment do you have onboard?"

"Chains, blankets, food, and water. You need something?"

"No, just making sure we're prepared. This storm is supposed to dump up to three feet overnight, and it may take us that long to get there."

"My middle name is prepared." She leaned forward and stared out the window. "I still can't believe what's happened."

Her phone played again, this time "Jailhouse Rock."

"That has to be Mason."

She grinned as she answered the phone. "Hey, Mason, got anything?" She grabbed for a paper and pen from her purse. "Uh-huh. Got it. We aren't even to Donken yet. It's going to take hours. Okay, I'll keep you posted."

"He found an address?"

She nodded. "And he's just a few minutes behind us. He's contacted the Houghton County sheriff's department to see if they can meet us out there, but they're dealing with a multicar pileup at the moment and can't spare anyone. Maybe not until morning."

"So it's up to us to find her." He gripped the steering wheel tighter.

"Exactly."

The snowflakes were so thick and large and the road was so

bad that he was having trouble figuring out whether he was even on the road or not. The only thing that helped was the occasional fence post and road sign. His sense of foreboding kept rising, and he kept swallowing it back down.

Bree glanced at him. "You really care about her, don't you?"

His defensive movement on the wheel made the Jeep head for the ditch until he righted it. "Am I that obvious?"

She smiled. "You look like you're about to crawl out on the hood to help the Jeep go faster."

"I've never met anyone like her. She's always thinking of other people." He touched the ridged flesh of his cheek with one hand. "She never seems to notice my scars."

"She sees people and not what's on the outside. We've got to find her before Chris hurts her. We can't lose her."

He managed to increase the speed a bit without spinning out. "We won't."

CHAPTER 37

Dana caught the smell of gunpowder and felt sick to her stomach. Chris had shot Garret down as if he'd been playing a video game. She stared at her brother and struggled to catch her breath. "C-Chris?" Phantom came to her and whined. She entwined her fingers in his fur and struggled to regain her composure.

He lowered the gun and smiled at her, a perfectly normal happy-to-see-you smile. He stepped inside and shut the door against the wind and snow. "I hope that didn't upset you too much. I always exact justice, and he deserved to die. I didn't want to leave my revenge undone." He covered his mouth with his hand and chuckled.

Her blood went as cold as the wind outside at the sound of that chuckle. She swallowed down the tightness in her throat. "Hey, dinner is about ready. You hungry?" What a crazy thing to say with a dead man on the back deck. Still, she had to do something to erase that maniacal grin on her brother's face.

She stood frozen by the stove trying to think what to do. She had no phone. A blizzard was bearing down on them, and there was no way to get out for help. She could shut and lock the door the next time he went out for wood, but he had a gun and could shoot out the lock. The best thing was to try to act normally until she could get help. Somehow.

He washed his hands at the dry sink with water in the bucket from melted snow. He turned back toward her with that crazy grin still splitting his face. She tried to wet her lips but couldn't dredge up the moisture to do it.

Quickly turning back to the pasta, she stirred in some cheese. "It's just macaroni and cheese, but I made it your favorite way with a little paprika and red pepper flakes."

"Dana, let's not play games. You know why I brought you here."

She looked up and stared into the face she'd loved most of her life. The man who'd protected her and stood by her no matter what. And yet fear shuddered along her back. How could she fear him? This was *Chris.*

She swallowed. "I'm not sure what you mean. You said you needed time to think. Isn't that why we're here?"

He ran his hand through his hair and swore. "You're as obtuse as a post stump, Dana. You'd swallow anything, wouldn't you? You always made it too easy." He took the gun casually out of his waistband and pointed to the sofa. "Sit."

"What about dinner?"

"I don't care about dinner!" His face flushed and spittle flew from his mouth. "Now sit down!"

Shaking, she turned off the pot and went to sit on the sofa. She clasped her hands together in her lap. "You don't need to scream at me, Chris. I'm your sister."

"Only because I decided you'd be. It was what I wanted so I made it happen." He shook his head. "You're so stupid. I really thought you'd figure it out once you started looking at the boat."

The accident. "My parents?" Her voice trembled. "Are you saying you had something to do with it because you wanted me to be your sister?" She half rose to her feet to scream at him. "You were only fourteen!"

He shrugged. "I was an early learner. My parents told me they weren't going to have any more kids, and I'd always loved you so it seemed the right thing to do."

There wasn't a hint of remorse in his expression or voice. He was a sociopath.

"I'd like to have had a brother too, but he insisted on going on the boat with your parents." Chris sat on the edge of the cot and his creepy smile faded. "It was only because I loved you, you know. For years I've tried to find a good replacement for you, but they have all been inferior. They say the right words, but they soon show their true colors, and I have to eliminate them and move on."

The cold that shivered down her spine had nothing to do with the temperature. The metal box flashed into her memory, the article about Renee. Chris traveled a lot. He wasn't a pharmaceutical rep, but he was obviously a good liar.

"Renee? Faith? Who else have you had to eliminate?"

"You wouldn't know them."

"How many?" Her voice wobbled, and tears blurred her vision. She had to get hold of herself or she was going to be next. He'd brought her here to kill her.

"Six others. It would have been seven, but I'm about to be found out so I might not get to her. I'd planned to, but this storm blew in and I ran out of time. Boone figured it out. He found a picture on Renee's phone, and he looked at a police composite. I'm sure the FBI will be descending any moment." He gave that weird chuckle again. "That's not counting family, of course."

She felt light-headed. "The fire? You surely didn't set the fire."

He shrugged. "Mom started putting things together. She wanted me to check myself into a hospital, if you can imagine that."

She closed her eyes to hide the smirk on his face. If she looked at him any longer, she'd vomit. Tears trailed down her cheeks until his other boast penetrated. He'd been targeting someone else.

She opened her eyes and sprang to her feet, then dropped back down when he waved the gun in her direction. "Please don't hurt Lauri. I'll do whatever you want." *Think, Dana, think!* "S-So there's no pancreatic cancer?"

He laughed. "No, you dork. I'm perfectly healthy. This is all cleanup."

"Chris, y-you're not well emotionally. Let me call and get you some help. You won't go to jail. You just need some help."

His face went red, then white and he stood. "Tonight I'm going to chain you to the bed frame. Tomorrow you'll drown beneath Copper Falls just like the rest of your family." He raised the gun. "I'll join you in death. I'm not going to jail. No one understands me, not even you." Tears filled his eyes.

Her vision wavered as he came toward her and reached for the chains. Before she could react, he snapped a leg iron around her ankle. Phantom whined again and pressed his nose against her, but she couldn't reassure him. She was trapped.

———

The snow was nearly up to the Jeep's grille by the time they neared Chassell. Boone's shoulders hurt from the tension of driving in the horrific storm. "How much farther?"

Bree consulted the GPS on her phone. "We're still about two miles from the turnoff to the property."

Two miles, then what? The drifts along the side of the road were six feet tall in some places. There would be no traffic along the drive back to the cabin, and that drive was half a mile long by itself. They had to get there though. *Had to.* No telling what Chris intended to do with Dana. He prayed they'd bust into that cabin and find them cozied up to the fire. That they'd find Dana safe.

And it was all up to them. The sheriff's car was already in the ditch about fifteen miles back.

The Jeep shuddered from the force of the wind striking it as they hit an area of road unprotected by trees on the north side. The wheel twisted in his hand as the vehicle slewed to one side. The Jeep tilted as one wheel hit the ditch, then the entire front end slid into the snowbank. Snow flew up over the windshield as the vehicle finished its trajectory off the road and came to a stop.

"No!" Boone slammed his palms onto the steering wheel, then forced open his door to survey the damage. The wind blew with such power that he had trouble standing upright.

"My door won't budge." Bree slid across the seat with the dog and stepped out beside him. "We're going to need a wrecker."

"And I bet we won't get that until sometime tomorrow." He relived that moment when he began to lose control of the Jeep. If only he'd managed to keep it on the road. He whipped out his phone and looked up the closest tow truck service, then called the number. A recorded message told him the weather was too bad to answer any calls for assistance.

He ended the call and told Bree. The snow was still coming down heavily, and it was hard to see more than a few feet in front of them. "I think we need to follow the road and see if we can find a house or something. Maybe we can find a wrecker willing to come out."

"We sure can't stay in the Jeep in this weather." Bree called Samson to her, and he leaped down from the backseat. The snow was over the top of his back even on the road.

Bree reached behind the second seat. "I've got snowshoes in the back. That should help." She handed him a set, then sat on the edge of the seat and put on a pair herself.

Boone did the same. The storm howled around them, and he was already shivering from the cold in spite of his coat. "Let's go."

She slipped her phone into her pocket and put her glove back on. "I texted Mason to let him know what we're doing."

It was going to take a miracle to even see a house unless the place had a light on. The wind was driving the heavy snow sideways creating a whiteout. They were in trouble, and it was all his fault. "I should have let you drive."

She shook her head and raised her voice over the wind. "I'd have put us in the ditch miles back. This isn't your fault."

He pulled out his phone and called up the GPS. "Hey, there's a bed-and-breakfast just a few feet away. Hamar House."

"Oh I know it! Kade and I have stayed there a couple of times. Let's try to get there."

"It's this way." He set off in the thick snow.

The dot signifying their location quit working after a few feet, and he frowned. "We've lost the signal." The best they could do was to try to continue on the path the map had shown and hope they didn't get disoriented in the storm. He called up the compass app. "We need to stay in a slightly northeasterly direction. It should only be about three hundred yards this way."

He trudged on and wished he could carry the poor dog who was having trouble bounding through the snow. It had to have been hours since a car came this way, and even the tracks in the road held a foot of snow. The snow was suffocating and disorienting.

He peered through the swirls. "I think I see a light."

"Me too!" Bree's breath was labored.

They both headed toward the welcome beacon. He passed a sign. "It's Hamar House." The snow-covered steps loomed in the faint light penetrating the snowstorm.

He mounted the steps with Bree at his side and rang the door-bell to the stately red Victorian building. He glanced at his watch. It was nearly midnight, so he was surprised a light was still on.

"I'm coming, I'm coming." The breathless female voice accom-panied footsteps across a hard surface, then the door opened and a woman dressed in pajamas and a fluffy red robe appeared. Her gaze flickered from Boone to Bree. "Bree Matthews, what are you doing out on a night like this? And Samson." She slapped her leg, and the dog, tail wagging, went to her. "Come in."

"You're a lifesaver, Barbara. My Jeep went off the road a little ways from here. We couldn't get a wrecker to pull us out."

"One of my rooms is free, and I can put your friend here up on the sofa in the parlor." Barbara shut the door behind them.

The welcome warmth touched Boone's face, but he stayed near the door. "I've got to go out and try to find Dana."

"I want to find her too, but it's hopeless tonight, Boone. You have to know that. There's no signal to follow the GPS, and you can't see well enough to navigate by yourself. We have to wait until the storm breaks."

Barbara nodded in agreement. "Let me fix some hot cocoa and sandwiches, then we'll get you settled."

Boone rubbed his forehead, still tempted to go back out. He hadn't been able to get to Allyson in time, and the thought of failing Dana was too painful to contemplate.

CHAPTER 38

The howling wind would have kept her awake even if her thoughts hadn't. The skin on Dana's ankle was raw from her efforts to free herself through the night, but the chain still kept her within three feet of the cot. Chris hadn't seemed to stir all night, and he still lay on the sofa with his back turned to her as the thin light began to poke through the windows.

She sat up and yanked on the chain once again. Maybe he'd be himself this morning, not that cold-eyed stranger who had shot Garret without compunction right in front of her. There had to be a way to get through to him. Scenes of her childhood had run through her mind all night long, and she understood so much of what had happened now. Kory had been right about Chris, but she hadn't wanted to see it. She loved Chris so she'd only seen what she wanted to see, what fit with her image of a loving brother.

She'd been so blind, so deluded.

And her parents and brother were dead because of some sick fascination Chris had with having her for a sister. And he'd killed his own parents as well when his mother realized he was a sociopath. She'd be dead by evening herself if she didn't think of some way out of this.

The springs on the sofa creaked as Chris rolled to his back and sat up. His blond hair was in disarray, and his blue eyes were sleepy. "Good morning. Did you sleep well?"

She lowered her feet to the ground. "What do you think? I need to use the outhouse. Can you unchain me?"

"I'll take you." He rose and fished a key from his pocket, then unlocked the leg iron.

If only she had some kind of weapon to smash into his head. She'd steal his keys and get to the truck. But as he marched her to the back door, she realized she'd never be able to drive out of here. The blizzard had left a foot of snow behind, and the drifts were six feet high in many places. The track from the road was snowed in.

The wind nearly took her breath away, and she rushed through the knee-deep snow to the outhouse. Phantom loped off into the woods to do his business. The chill inside the outhouse was as bad as outside, and she could see Chris standing in front of the door after she closed it. She looked around for a way out the back, but there was no other exit. She quickly finished, then shoved the door open and hurried as fast as she could for the cabin's back door.

She called to her dog, but he didn't come. Maybe it was just as well. Chris might shoot him.

Did he have his gun? Maybe she could lock him out, then use his phone to call for help. But who could get here even if she knew where to tell a would-be rescuer to come? She reached the back door and yanked it open, but Chris was right on her heels. She'd be unable to shut the door before he could stick his foot inside.

Her face felt numb when he closed the door behind them. She went to the tiny kitchen. "I'm famished. You want an omelet?"

"Sounds good." He measured coffee into the stovetop coffee-pot, then carried it to the wood stove and put it on top before he threw more wood on the fire.

She found an iron skillet and put it on the propane burner. Could she use the skillet as a weapon? It was heavy and soon it would be hot as well. Keeping her options open for the moment, she cooked the omelets and put them on paper plates. A knife was somewhere here too, but she wasn't sure she could bring herself to thrust it into Chris. She handed him a plate of eggs, then sat beside him on the sofa.

They ate in a silence that deepened as the wind quit howling around the eaves. Surely he'd have to wait for the weather to break to carry out his plan.

He wiped his mouth with the back of his hand. "Storm's over."

"The road is still impassable."

He shrugged and rose to check the coffee. "I've got a snow machine in the shed out back. I can't wait until the road clears because they'll come for me. If you love me, you know I can't live in jail, Dana. I have to do this."

"Why punish me? I don't understand."

He stood with his back to her and poked at the fire. "I've always protected you. You're not a good judge of character. Look how you let Garret manhandle you. I love you too much to leave you alone to face men like that. You're too weak to handle life. And I sure can't let you end up with Boone when this is all his fault."

Her face went hot at his mention of her poor judgment about men. Maybe there was some truth to what he'd said. "I let Garret manipulate me too easily, but I'm stronger now. I figured out that I cared too much about what other people thought when all I really needed was to pay attention to what God wanted."

He turned and his mouth twisted. "Religion never did anyone

any good." When she opened her mouth to argue with him, he held up his hand. "Enough. I don't want to hear it. Get your coat and boots on. There are scarves and hats in that chest too." He pointed toward an old battered metal chest that served as a coffee table. "Bundle up well for the trip."

She lifted her chin and stared deep into his eyes. "And if I don't?"

He plucked his gun from his waistband. "Then I'll have to shoot you too."

Where there was life, there was hope. She might be able to jump off the snow machine and escape in the woods on the trip to the falls. Pressing her lips together, she went to get her coat and boots. There was still no sign of Phantom, and she prayed he was off chasing squirrels where he'd be safe.

The scrape of the snow plows outside shot Boone into high gear. He'd just finished a crazy-good muffin still warm from the oven and gulped down coffee. "I'm going to get out there and see if I can find the cabin."

Bree looked dubious. "I'm sure the lane back to the cabin isn't plowed. It will take hours to try to walk it in the snow even with snowshoes. I talked to Mason this morning, and he's mobilizing some help. It will be an hour before he gets out there though."

"I have a snow machine you can borrow," Barbara said. "I just had it serviced."

Boone caught her in a hug and lifted her feet off the ground. "Thanks for saving us last night and again today. I'll get it back to you as soon as I can." He set her feet back on the ground.

Her cheeks pink, Barbara snagged a key ring from a hook by the door to the garage. "Keep it as long as you need it." She picked up a basket on the end of the beautifully set dining room table. "I fixed you some sandwiches, and there's hot coffee in a thermos as well." She led them to the back door. "The garage is unlocked. I'll pray for you."

He and Bree pressed through the snow with Samson. The air was cold and crisp, but at least the wind had died down. Two minutes later they were sailing over the tops of the massive snowdrifts. The machine would be a tremendous boon getting out to the cabin. Bree held Samson on her lap with one arm and clung to Boone with the other.

It only took fifteen minutes to reach the cabin on the machine. Boone cut the engine down the trail a bit, then dismounted. "I don't want them to hear us coming."

Bree let Samson jump down. "I see smoke spiraling from the chimney. They must still be here."

Boone nodded, and he pulled off his right glove with his teeth, then pulled out his gun and made sure the safety was off before putting his glove back on. "Stay here until I call for you. I'm going to take a peek inside."

She grabbed Samson's collar when he started after Boone. "Signal me when you want us to join you."

Boone waded through the thigh-high snowdrifts. A Lexus partially hidden in the scrub caught his attention. Someone else was here. He stopped and glanced back to where Bree stood with Samson. He motioned to her, and she headed toward him with Samson laboring to keep up.

He pointed to the Lexus. "We've got double trouble."

Her expression mirrored his dismay. "It looks like it's been here overnight too."

"Maybe Garret is behind this. He might have taken Dana and Chris." That didn't explain the box of newspaper clippings though or the pictures. Chris was clearly the Groom Reaper. Boone held his finger to his lips and moved toward the rear of the cabin. An outhouse and old shed with its door hanging open occupied the small yard before the forest began.

His stomach plunged and he stopped and stared at the snow machine tracks. "They're gone." He pointed to two sets of footprints.

"Only two," Bree said softly. "Where's the third?"

"Let's find out."

The drifts back here were enormous, and he struggled to keep his balance. He followed the tracks to the back door and stopped when he saw a hand sticking out from under a snowdrift on the back deck. Brushing away the snow, he flinched when he saw Garret's white, lifeless face.

Behind him, Bree gasped. "What happened to him?"

Boone brushed away more of the snow and saw the red stain on the snow. "Looks like he was shot."

He straightened and went to the back door, but the morning's muffin congealed in his stomach at the thought of what he might find inside. The knob turned easily in his hand, and the door opened. The scent of burning wood curled out the door. He nearly sagged against the door in relief when he found the space empty.

Bree shut the door behind them. "At least he didn't kill her too. She must be with him on the snow machine." She looked around. "Where's Phantom? I don't think they would have taken him with them." She called to the dog, but he wasn't in the small cabin.

"Tell Mason we'll text him coordinates along the way as we track them. The FBI will have the equipment to get the job done."

He glanced at her dog. "You think it would be faster to let Samson track them instead of following the trail?"

She shook her head. "He's going to follow the skin rafts so he'll be taking the same path they took. The snow is too deep for him to move very fast. We'll be better off to have him on the machine with us." She pulled out her phone and shot off a text to Mason, then read an answering chime a few seconds later. "He's about half an hour behind us."

Boone yanked open the door and rushed for the snow machine. He lifted Samson onto Bree's lap. "Any idea where he might be taking her?"

She tied the hood on her bright-red parka more tightly and shook her head. "The property is the only one Mason found in his name."

Some memory danced just out of his reach. What was it? "We know his favorite method of meting out death is by drowning." Then it struck him. "Her parents and brother died in a boating accident. Drowning again."

Bree's green eyes grew troubled. "What about their boat, Boone? That perfectly round hole that popped free. Dana said the Corks told her Chris often borrowed the boat. What if he meddled with it? Maybe her parents were his first victims."

His gut clenched. "Copper Falls is where they died, and it's that direction. Call Mason and have him meet us there." He leaped on the snow machine and started it, then raced for the falls.

CHAPTER 39

The edges of the lake were frozen and snow-covered, but the interior reflected the sunlight with an eye-piercing brilliance. Copper Falls, beautiful in its iced-over condition, rose twenty feet in the air. Dana hadn't been here since her family's bodies had been pulled from the water, and the memory of that day brought acid surging up her throat.

Chris had chained her to the snow machine, so she'd been unable to leap off and make a break for freedom and safety. He cut the engine on the machine, then dismounted and unfastened her shackles. "Beautiful, isn't it? A fitting place to end everything for us both." His voice held a feverish intensity.

She dismounted and rubbed at her sore ankle a moment. "Chris, this is wrong. You say you love me, but if you do, you won't go through with this."

She vaguely remembered the path they'd taken here after her family's bodies were found, but she had no idea how to get back to the road. A bright cardinal, its red feathers brilliant against the snow, seemed to look at her in commiseration.

Chris grabbed her arm and dragged her toward a snowdrift.

He kicked at the snow, and it slid off the hull of a rowboat. "Turn it over."

She knelt and pushed more snow off of it until it was light enough to flip over. The paddles were attached to the inside with Velcro strips. There were no life jackets, but the boat looked sound enough.

"Put it in the water and get inside."

What were her choices? Her gaze went to the icy lake and the barely trickling waterfall beyond it. If she darted for the forest, he'd shoot her in the back. She was a strong swimmer. Even if he threw her overboard, she might make it to shore. She bent over and shoved the boat toward the water. Her boots broke through the thin ice and freezing water soaked her leg and ran down into her boot. She waded farther out and climbed in.

He put his gun back into his waistband, and she took that second when his attention was diverted to yank an oar from its home and whack him upside the head with it. He went down, and she dug the oar into the ground, shoving the boat farther out into the water. If she hurried, she could get out into the water and paddle for the other shore. A burst of elation fueled her strength, and she grabbed the other oar and began to row.

She spared a look back at Chris. He got to his feet and shook his head as if to clear it. He started for the water, then paused as he took in the distance to reach her. He'd have to swim and the water was glacial. She was going to make it! She paddled harder.

A gunshot rang through the trees, and something zinged off the aluminum hull. She glanced back and saw him taking aim for another shot. It thunked into the side of the boat.

He wasn't trying to hit her. He was trying to sink the boat.

She put her back into rowing, thrusting the oars deep into the water for the most movement. It took several seconds before she realized the sound she heard was water running into the boat. He'd damaged it.

She paused and looked around for something to plug the hole, but there was nothing. Another shot rang out, and a hole spewing water sprouted at the bow. Then another. Water poured into the boat through three holes, and it quickly held three inches.

"It's better this way," he called across the water. "I was never really sure if I had the courage to throw you overboard. And I wasn't sure if you might take me with you, which might have been a better option anyway. You'll join your parents right where they died."

He was right. This was the spot where their capsized and damaged boat had been found. She struggled with the oars, but the boat was heavy in the water and sluggish. It wanted to go in circles rather than head for the opposite shore. Water was already halfway up the sides. It was going to sink.

She paused and evaluated her options. If she could get even a little closer to the other side it would help her, but she might be trapped in the boat with her coat weighing her down. If she went in now, she could shuck her coat and boots so they didn't weigh her down and swim for all her might for the shore.

Chris watched avidly from shore with that eerie grin. "I wish I were closer. I'd like to watch the life go out of your eyes. It's a powerful feeling."

She shivered and looked away. The water beckoned and seemed her safest choice. She quickly shed her coat and boots. Everything in her shuddered at the thought of getting in that water, but she had no choice. With a deep breath, she stood and dove over the side.

The hum of the snow machine engine echoed off the pine tops and bounced off the snow. The falls weren't far ahead, but were they in time? Boone hunched over the bars of the machine and urged it faster. They crested a hill, and he spied the blue of the lake below.

Was that a gunshot? He tensed and headed the machine toward the sound. A flash of movement caught his eye, a bright-blue parka. Bree shouted into his ear, "It's Chris, but I don't see Dana."

Boone didn't see her either. Chris turned toward them as the snow machine roared his direction. His mouth dropped open when his gaze met Boone's, and he shouted something. Maybe "no" or "not yet." Boone couldn't hear over the noise of the engine.

Chris ran for his own snow machine, parked at the edge of the water, but Boone drove his machine in front of it and blocked him in just as Chris reached it.

Chris reversed direction away from Boone and ran toward the hill, but Bree yelled, "Samson, attack!" The dog leaped from her lap and sank his teeth into the back of Chris's parka. The man jerked backward into the snow, and the dog leaped on top of his chest.

Boone shut off the snow machine and leaped off. He spared a glance toward the water as Bree ran toward Samson and Chris, who was struggling to stand. Boone turned and squinted toward the lake. Wait, was that a boat out there? It rode low in the water, the top of it barely visible above the waves.

"Secure Chris! I'm going to look for Dana." He rushed to the water. "Dana!" The light was so bright off the water it was hard to see. He heard a splash and saw a figure about ten feet from the opposite shore.

A boat! He needed a boat. But there was nothing. He'd have to go in by himself. Shucking his coat and boots, he waded out into the water and plunged in. Every cold water swim he'd taken had built up some stamina. Was it enough to reach her?

The cold numbed every inch of his skin as he swam. He reached the boat in the middle and grabbed an oar that was floating nearby. He might need it to save Dana. She hadn't made much progress since he'd jumped in and was still eight feet from shore. She was floating on her back, and her eyes were rolling back in her head. She would drown if he didn't get there in time. He kicked with new determination and ignored the way the cold pulled at his muscles and slowed his thoughts. He had to reach her.

"Dana, fight!"

She rallied a bit at his call, and her face turned toward him. Her lips moved but no sound came out. Nearly there. He smacked the paddle down in front of her face. "Grab hold!"

Her eyes fluttered again, and she flopped one arm toward the paddle. There was no strength in her movement though. She'd never be able to hang on. He cast away the oar and grabbed at her arm. At least she wore no parka to drag her under.

"I've got you. Relax," he said in her ear.

He flipped her to her back and began to tow her inert body toward the shore. His movements were slow and awkward, and he needed to get out of the water too. Then what? They had to find a way to get warm over here. Bree was clear on the other side of the lake, and even if she brought the snow machine around, that would take a while. The cold air would chill them even more.

He couldn't let himself dwell on it. *Just get out of the water.* His bare foot hit a rock, and he reached for a better purchase. Both feet touched mud, and he pulled her to his chest. "We made it. Dana, we made it."

Her eyes opened, then closed again. He waded into shallower

water, but his arms were too weak to carry her. He half dragged her into a snowbank and collapsed with her against his chest. The snow felt almost warm and oh-so soft as they plunged into it.

His eyes started to drift shut, then popped back open again. They could burrow into the snow and create a haven with their body temperatures. It might not be enough to save them for long, but Bree would figure out a way to get to them. It was all they had.

Using the last of his strength, he hollowed out a hole in the biggest snowbank, then dragged Dana into it. He got into a sitting position in the darkness of the shelter and pulled her onto his lap. Skin to skin would be best. He shucked his wet shirt and jeans, leaving his underwear, then did the same to her before pulling her cold, wet body against his.

The difference was immediate, and a bit of heat began to generate between them, though they both still shuddered. He blew warm breath against her upper chest and neck.

It was better maybe, but was it enough? He tucked her face into his shoulder and lowered his head protectively over her. His eyelids began to lower, then he snapped them open. *Stay awake!*

Warmth stole into his limbs, but as he drifted off to sleep he feared it was the warmth of freezing to death. If he was going to die, he couldn't think of anyone he'd rather have in his arms.

Samson had Chris pinned to the ground and stood over him with his teeth bared. Bree snatched up Chris's gun that had flown from his hand when Samson attacked. "Samson, release!"

Her dog gave a final snarl, then stepped off Chris's chest. Chris sat up slowly and eyed the gun in Bree's hand. "You won't use that."

She kept the weapon aimed at his chest. "I doubt I'd have to. Samson can take you down again. Stay where you are." In the distance she heard the choppers heading their way. Help would be here shortly.

Chris tipped his head to one side, and the color drained from his face, leaving his eyes starkly blue against his white skin. "I can't live in prison."

"After all you've done, you don't deserve to live at all. You killed Allyson and Renee. Others too." Sudden tears blurred her vision. "Allyson figured it out, didn't she? She realized you were the Groom Reaper. How did she know?"

He smiled but the lack of warmth in the gesture left it as more of a grimace. "She saw pictures of the engagement ring." When he got up and took a step toward her, Samson bared his teeth and growled. Chris held up his hands. "Lay off, Samson."

The dog snarled again and didn't back up. Bree put her gloved hand on his head, but his ruff stayed raised. Chris had something in his hand, and she only recognized it when he raised his arm and threw it in an arc over her head.

The stick flying by distracted Samson for a moment, and in that brief pause, Chris leaped forward and wrested the gun from her hand.

Samson lunged at him and tried to sink his teeth into his leg, but Chris kicked him away. "Call off your dog, or I'll shoot him!"

And he would. Bree grabbed Samson's collar and dragged him back against her. "Easy, boy." She'd trained her dog to recognize an "easy" command as one to stay on the alert for a chance to strike.

She eyed Chris warily. The noise of the choppers grew louder, and he was going to be caught. Did he plan to commit suicide by cop? Some people thought sociopaths never committed suicide, but as part of her training, she'd learned differently. Many couldn't take the contempt they received about their actions.

She or Samson could be in the line of fire. Easing her grip on her dog's collar a bit, she took a step closer to him.

His eyes narrowed. "Stay where you are."

"How did Allyson know the ring was yours?"

"She asked to see me, said she needed me to help her in her investigation." He tapped his nose with a gloved hand. "I can always smell a lie. Her dad owns the jewelry store in town. The ring belonged to my mom. Dad was going to give it to her the night of the fire, on their anniversary. I thought no one had ever seen it, but Allyson was working in the shop the day my dad bought it. She recognized the picture, though it took her a few days."

She cast a glance to the sky but still didn't see the helicopter, though the sound was getting closer. "She shouldn't have gone alone."

"She didn't. I followed her and grabbed her in the parking lot by the hiking trail."

Bree wanted to close her eyes and wipe out the image of his smirk. Had Allyson realized what was happening? Had she fought for her life? *Oh dear friend, how I miss you.*

"She put up a better fight than you, but there wasn't anyone out here but me." His blue eyes went even colder. The bore of the gun moved to her head.

He was going to shoot her. She didn't dare tell Samson to attack because he'd shoot her dog first. A dark shadow moved behind him. She struggled to show no expression as Phantom crept into view. In spite of his size, he wasn't much more than a puppy, and she didn't think he could help. Unless she used him as a distraction maybe? She squinted and forced surprise into her face.

Chris half turned, and she released her dog, then leaped toward him. A silent snarl lifting his muzzle, Samson moved with her. His teeth clamped down on Chris's arm, and the gun went flying. Phantom barked and ran for the melee as well. Both dogs jumped on Chris, and he went sprawling onto his back. Samson put both of his front paws on the man's chest and held him down.

Bree grabbed a length of rope from her pack and trussed him up. He was going to jail after all. She turned toward the lake and prayed Boone had been able to save Dana.

CHAPTER 40

Delicious warmth crept into Dana's limbs. The soft bed enfolded her. Wait, she shouldn't feel warm. Her eyes popped open, and she blinked as she focused on the room. Monitors beeped at her head, and she looked down to see an IV in her hand. She smelled antiseptic and floor wax and tasted something acrid from whatever was in her IV. She was in the hospital.

She struggled to a seated position. "Boone!"

A figure rose from a chair. "I'm here." His thick black hair was unkempt and heavy whiskers darkened his jaw. His eyes were tired but alert. "You're awake."

She shuddered as her full memory returned. Chris had tried to kill her. It was almost impossible to believe. "I was in the water. You came for me."

Bree stepped forward from the shadows too. "This is where you say I'll always come for you. Just like Westley told Buttercup."

Boone's grin broke out. "Corny." His grin faded, and his gaze searched Dana's. "If I could sing, I'd break into 'All I Ask of You,' from *Phantom of the Opera*, but that would probably be even cornier."

"I think I like corny right about now." Dana reached for his hand. "What about Chris?"

Boone raised the head of her bed and nudged her back against it. "In custody. Bree and Samson took him down and kept him in custody until Mason arrived with the FBI."

"It was more Samson than me. And Phantom showed up to help."

"You've got Phantom? He ran off, and I couldn't find him."

"He trailed you and showed up in time to distract Chris so Samson could take him down. He's home with a nice, juicy bone as a reward." Bree went toward the door. "I'm going to get coffee. I'll be right back."

Dana wanted to enjoy this moment of complete comfort and safety. The sheets were soft and clean, and she wasn't soaking wet and freezing to death. "I don't remember much past when you had me try to grab the oar." She touched his arm, covered with a red-and-black flannel shirt that felt deliciously warm and soft.

"We got to shore, then I dug us out an igloo sort of hole in the snow until an FBI chopper arrived. The paramedics warmed us both up, but you were severely hypothermic and had to be admitted. That was yesterday. Everyone has been calling to check on you."

"Chris told me he killed a total of six women, not counting our family. Lauri was going to be number seven. He'd planned to kill her before he killed me, but the storm messed up his plans." Her vision blurred, and he handed her a tissue. How could a man she'd loved all her life turn out to be a monster? His handsome looks had masked such ugliness and evil.

"I know. Bree figured it out too. Lauri was lucky." He touched the blanket on her feet. "Need another blanket?"

She shook her head. "I'll have to see Chris, won't I?"

His expression turned fierce. "Not if you don't want to."

"I don't want to, but I know I should be Jesus with skin on for him." She went quiet a moment. "I'm not quite sure how to even face him. He's done so many evil things."

Chair legs scraped on the tile floor as he pulled his seat closer to the bed. "One of the many reasons why you're so special." He picked up her hand and interlaced his fingers with hers. "I was terrified when I thought I'd lost you, that Chris had already killed you. Bree and I were trapped at a bed-and-breakfast by the storm, and it was the longest night of my life. I don't plan to let you get away."

"I don't plan to leave." There was no hurry either. They had all the time in the world to figure out where their relationship was going.

Scars and all, his face was so handsome, so beloved. Her experience had taught her the truth of how the soul was the true repository of beauty. Unlike the Phantom who was as ugly on the inside as he was on the outside, Boone's scars hid an astoundingly beautiful soul. She'd spent too much of her life worrying about the face she presented to the world and much too little on the character she needed to be developing every day.

Life was short, and she intended to seize every day with both hands and live it to its fullest.

"Kiss me," she whispered.

His lazy grin came along with a light in his hazel eyes. He stood and leaned over her until his breath touched her face. "That's what I've been wanting to do ever since I found you."

His lips came down on hers, and she wrapped her arms around his neck like a drowning woman. In a world totally crazy they'd found the stuff of fairy tales. No, not fairy tales but life in all its complexities and beauty. Real life was much better than a fairy tale because they would continue to shape and mold each other. And that's what a meaningful relationship was all about, growing together and sharing light into the world.

Together they burned brighter. It was a wonderful reality she intended to savor as they explored the future together.

A NOTE FROM THE AUTHOR

Dear Reader,

What fun it is to be back in Rock Harbor! I hear from readers *daily* about this series so I decided to revisit the perennial favorite. I hope you're as excited to be back as I am!

Many of us focus on our outward appearance and what other people think of us, but the inward character we are developing is infinitely more important. And that is the hardest thing to work on when we're constantly bombarded with things that seem to need our urgent attention.

I'm going to work on that, and I hope Dana's story encourages you to do the same. Let me know what you think. I love to hear from you so e-mail me anytime!

Hugs!

Colleen

colleen@colleencoble.com

DISCUSSION QUESTIONS

1. We all have things we don't like about ourselves. How do you deal with yours?
2. Have you ever known someone who had to deal with a stalker? What would you do if you were faced with something like that?
3. There's something special about our home town. What do you love about yours?
4. Dana wanted to make a difference. How do you try to make a difference in the lives of other people?
5. Dana was so hungry for acceptance she let Garret manipulate her. Some people are good at manipulation. How do you recognize it?
6. Lauri wasn't a good judge of men. Why do you think she was so blind to Peter's true nature?
7. Do you believe true evil exists? Why or why not?
8. Have you read any Rock Harbor novels before?

ACKNOWLEDGMENTS

I'm so blessed to belong to the terrific HarperCollins Christian Publishing dream team! I've been with my great fiction team for fourteen years, and they are like family to me. I learn something new with every book, which makes writing so much fun!

Our fiction publisher, Daisy Hutton, is a gale-force wind of fresh air. She thinks outside the box, and I love the way she empowers me and my team. The last three books have been with my terrific editor, Amanda Bostic, who really gets suspense and has been my friend from the moment I met her all those years ago. Fabulous cover guru Kristen Ingebretson works hard to create the perfect cover—and does. I have a terrific marketing team in Paul Fisher, Kristen Golden, Allison Carter, and Meghan O'Brien. My amazing fiction team also includes Becky Monds, Karli Jackson, Kim Carlton, Jodi Hughes, and Kayleigh Hines. You are all such a big part of my life. I wish I could name all the great folks at HCCP who work on selling my books through different venues. I'm truly blessed!

Julee Schwarzburg is a dream editor to work with. She totally gets romantic suspense, and our partnership is pure joy. She brought some terrific ideas to the table with this book—as always!

My agent, Karen Solem, has helped shape my career in many ways, and that includes kicking an idea to the curb when necessary. We just celebrated fifteen years together! And my critique partner of seventeen years, Denise Hunter, is the best sounding board ever. Thanks, friends!

I'm so grateful for my husband, Dave, who carts me around from city to city, washes towels, and chases down dinner without complaint. My kids—Dave, Kara (and now Donna and Mark)—love and support me in every way possible, and my little granddaughter Alexa makes every day a joy. She's talking like a grown-up now, and having her spend the night is more fun than I can tell you. And as I write this, my little grandson, Elijah, was born five weeks ago. I'm totally obsessed with his cuteness. ☺ Exciting times!

Most important, I give my thanks to God, who has opened such amazing doors for me and makes the journey a golden one.

THE
ROCK HARBOR
series

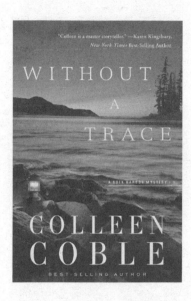

"Colleen is a master storyteller." —Karen Kingsbury,
New York Times Best-Selling Author

WITHOUT
A
TRACE

A ROCK HARBOR MYSTERY · 1

COLLEEN
COBLE

BEST-SELLING AUTHOR

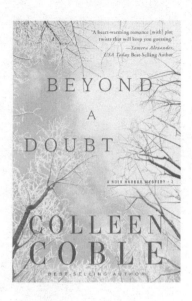

"A heart-warming romance [with] plot
twists that will keep you guessing."
—*Tamera Alexander*,
USA Today Best-Selling Author

BEYOND
A
DOUBT

A ROCK HARBOR MYSTERY · 2

COLLEEN
COBLE

BEST-SELLING AUTHOR

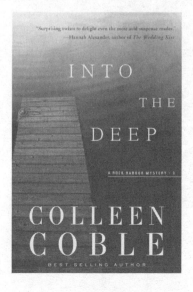

"Surprising twists to delight even the most avid suspense reader."
—Hannah Alexander, author of *The Wedding Kiss*

INTO
THE
DEEP

A ROCK HARBOR MYSTERY · 3

COLLEEN
COBLE

BEST-SELLING AUTHOR

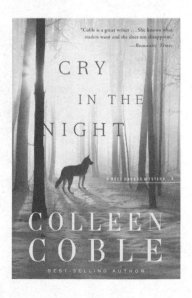

"Coble is a great writer . . . She knows what
readers want and she does not disappoint."
—*Romantic Times*

CRY
IN THE
NIGHT

A ROCK HARBOR MYSTERY · 4

COLLEEN
COBLE

BEST-SELLING AUTHOR

Available in print, audio, and e-book

THE
SUNSET COVE
series

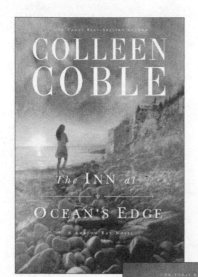

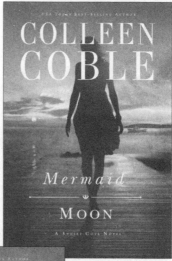

AVAILABLE IN PRINT,
E-BOOK, AND AUDIO

AVAILABLE IN PRINT,
E-BOOK, AND AUDIO

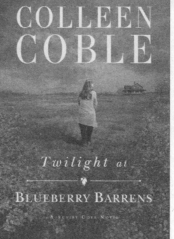

AVAILABLE IN PRINT,
E-BOOK, AND AUDIO

From USA TODAY bestselling author

COLLEEN COBLE

comes a news series set amid the gorgeous lavender fields
of Washington state—but the beauty masks deadly secrets.

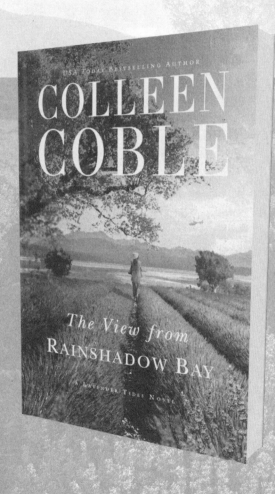

AVAILABLE JANUARY 2018

Don't miss this exciting story from
COLLEEN COBLE!

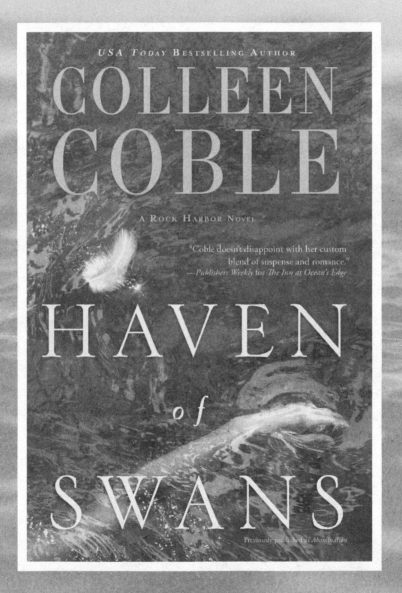

Available in print and e-book

9781401690328-A

GET SWEPT UP IN THIS EXCERPT
FROM *HAVEN OF SWANS!*

Night crept over the hills, smothering the landscape in a cocoon of darkness that would hide him in a few minutes. He'd abandoned his real name for one more fitting of his strength and intellect. Gideon was what he called himself when clouds hid the moon and the shadows gathered. Gideon, the Destroyer of Evil.

Before the moonlight could fade completely, he flipped down the sun visor and stared into the face of his wife, Miranda—a photo of her as she had once been.

As she would be again.

The blare of a horn startled him, and he slapped the visor back into place as a gray SUV careened past where his car sat on the narrow shoulder. The vehicle splashed water from a mud puddle over his car. He bit back an expletive, knowing such words ill befit a man of his intellect. He twisted the key and heard the car engine purr to life. Easing onto the road, he hunched over the wheel and stared into the fog. The turnoff to the lake was just ahead. No car lights illuminated the road ahead or behind. He turned the vehicle onto the muddy track and rolled down the window to let in the fresh scent of the water. The lane was meant for tractors, and visitors rarely trespassed. The owners would never even know he'd been here.

The lake reflected the golden orb of the moon. He parked and turned off the car. The cacophony of crickets and tree frogs paused, then started up again as he stepped into the mud and went around to the trunk. The lid sprang open at his touch, and he looked down into the woman's face. As with the others, preludes to the grand finale, he'd stripped her of beauty. This one would never lash a man with her tongue again.

Securing the gray wool blanket around the body, he hauled it out and dumped it on the ground. He tucked a partial peanut butter sandwich under the sinner's blouse. He took hold of the end of the blanket and pulled the bundle down to the water.

Reaching the small pier, he paused and listened, then stepped onto the rickety boards. The body slid easily across the worn wood. Once he reached the end of the dock, he dropped the end of the blanket and settled onto the weather-scoured boards to wait. He pulled his GPS from his pocket and noted the coordinates. Close enough. He didn't plan to go far from shore.

A hint of pine mingled on the night air with the scent of water. The chilly night began to creep into his bones. Loons called, and he straightened and stood to stamp his feet.

Then the angels came.

Gideon held his breath as they glided into the shaft of moonlight. Silent and beautiful, they moved as one along the placid surface of the water. He counted one, two, ten. The largest one's wings spanned at least eight feet.

He shoved the body into the bottom of a small boat, where it lay amid the flotsam of tackle boxes, tarps, and fishing poles. Gideon hurried to the shore, where he gathered rocks in a bucket. Carrying his burden, he went back to the boat and set the bucket into the boat as well. The boat tipped when he stepped in, but he was quick on his feet and moved to the center, where he settled onto the seat.

Years of use had worn the oars smooth, and they fit into his palms as if they'd been carved for his hands. His muscles flexed, and he dipped the oars into the water. The boat moved smoothly through the ripples. They barely noticed his approach. Their voices raised the hair on his arms and back.

About five feet from them, he laid the oars back against the sides of the boat, then crouched beside the body. Opening the blanket, he piled rocks from the bucket inside, then tied the ends with the rope he'd brought.

They moved around him. One bent her neck and looked at him. Some-thing about the way she held her head made him catch his breath. She glided nearer. They would wait with him, patient, long-suffering, until he secured the ultimate prize. Then one rose into the air. The others soared heavenward as well, and he was left alone with a single feather wafting toward him on the shifting fog. He caught it in his hand and brought it to his face. He brushed it over his lips like a kiss. A benediction.

His gaze lit on the body. Frowning, he put the feather in his pocket. He balled his fists, then stooped and heaved the bundle over the side. The water rippled, then closed over the space. He turned around and began to row back to shore.

The house was quiet when he got home. He peeked in on his daughter, Odette. Seventeen years old with a soul as old as Moses, she slept with one hand on her cheek. So innocent the sight made his heart swell in his chest.

What would happen to her if he were caught?

His lip curled. They weren't smart enough to find him. Besides, he was surrounded by a mantle of protection. He was invincible as long as his angels stayed with him. Pressing a kiss on his daughter's hair, he went down the hall to his office and entered, shutting the door. The computer screen lit as soon as he lifted the laptop's lid. He launched the browser and went to the geocaching site.

After he put in the GPS coordinates, he typed:

ABOMINATIONS WILL FIND YOU.

The adventure continues in *Haven of Swans!*

ABOUT THE AUTHOR

C olleen Coble is a *USA Today* bestselling author and RITA
finalist best known for her romantic suspense novels, including *Tidewater Inn*, *Rosemary Cottage*, and the Mercy Falls, Lonestar,
and Rock Harbor series.

Visit her website at www.colleencoble.com.
Twitter: @colleencoble
Facebook: colleencoblebooks